Beach Hut

Catherine Lawless

Sarah

GRACE

PUBLISHING

Dedication

For my beautiful, funny daughter Hannah, my kind husband
Carl & Alka Cashyap, my very own Dr Bhakta.

'A beautifully crafted and heartwarming read.'
–Sarah West, director

In Memory Of

Philip Fielder & Michael Hare

First published 2019 by Sarah Grace Publishing, an imprint of Malcolm Down Publishing Ltd.

www.sarahgracepublishing.co.uk

British Library Cataloguing in Publication Data
A catalogue record for this book is available from the British Library.

ISBN 978-1-912863-14-3

Cover illustration by Barry Diaper
Cover design by Esther Kotecha
Art direction by Sarah Grace

Printed in the UK

Chapter 1

'You're joking.'

'No, I'm not.'

'No way.'

'Way, and can you believe it – she had three of them turn up last night. Sheila said that one of them had so many tattoos and facial piercings that it frightened the children.'

'Three?' chorused the other mothers standing at the school gates, desperate to be fed another crumb of Sue's gossip.

'Yes! Apparently they stayed for several hours and then past midnight, she brazenly walked them out to their car and gave them all a hug, as if it was the most natural thing in the world.'

Sue paused long enough for her words to sink in, and only when she was suitably satisfied with her audience's reaction did she continue her tale.

'Three nights ago, Sheila heard a car pull up really late. A man got out of a limo, left his driver outside in the car and then went inside for what must have been less than an hour. Then he came out, and the new woman came out in what looked like pyjamas. The man handed her an envelope – Sheila said it looked like money – and pulled her into his arms for the world to see, apparently. Sheila said that the woman stood and waved the limo off then turned around smiling, looking most pleased with herself, and went back indoors.'

'No!' the chorus cried.

'Yes! Anyway, I had a long chat with Sheila this morning and she thinks that it's about time something is done about it. Do you know, she's got a little girl?'

'I thought she had two, and one boy.'

'I'm talking about the new woman who's moved into Wisteria Cottage, not Sheila, you ninny,' Sue snapped impatiently.

'She hasn't,' said one woman pulling a long face.

'How disgraceful!' another cried.

'Sheila said she is going to speak to Reverend Gibson straight away, because we really don't want women like that in the village. Apparently, according to Sheila, this could affect the house prices, you know.'

'What, how come?!' they shouted in unison.

'Well, think about it,' said Sue, warming to the task. 'Sheila said that that sort of behaviour can spread. She said before we know it, more of her type could move in, trailing their illegitimate children behind them, cluttering up our lovely school, then word will get out and we will no longer live in a sought-after village. More importantly, nobody will want to buy our property. Sheila said it's happened to other places, you know.'

'Oh no, Sue, that's awful!' one hanger on cried. 'Our house is on the market at the moment.'

'Sheila told me that the night this one moved in, there was another woman hanging around, too. There was a right downpour, and this other woman stripped off down to her t-shirt and knickers and spun round and round, laughing and dancing in just her undies and bracelets all up her arms.'

Sue paused a moment to let the damning evidence sink in.

'Luckily Martin wasn't in, because you know what he's like! Apparently, by all accounts, Sheila said this other woman was most striking, although Sheila said she looked possessed, like some kind of witch. Anyway, it's worried me, because Sheila said that in Cornwall witchcraft is rife.'

Sue folded her arms and paused again for effect.

'Is that where she's from, then?' A mum from the edge of the gathering asked.

'Oh, for goodness sake, Emily, Sheila was born here.'

'I don't mean Sheila, I'm talking about the other woman, the witch woman,' Emily pressed on.

'Good heavens, Emily, how on earth would I know? I was just saying that Sheila said it happened in Cornwall, that's all.' Sue shook her head at poor Emily.

Sam, who'd been listening to the whole sordid tale, had heard enough. Part of her wanted to stay quiet and slip away, leaving these awful gossipers to their sad drama and speculation. Problem was, her daughter Lucy was starting in Reception class today, and she realised there was a strong chance that one of these women may have a child in the same class. Sam knew Lucy didn't need any extra stress or worry at the moment. She'd already survived the move to a new home, away from London and all that was familiar, and without her daddy. So, with a heavy heart, Sam took a huge breath, walked up to the ringleader and held out her hand.

'Hi, I'm Sam, and you are?'

'Er, I'm Sue,' the chief gossip said, looking irritated to be cut off mid-flow.

'Hello, Sue. Look, I couldn't help overhearing, and I thought I should introduce myself before you get the entire village round to burn me at the stake.'

'I beg your pardon?' Sue snapped.

'Oh, sorry, I'm not making much sense, am I? You see, I am the "one" who has moved into Wisteria Cottage. Next door to your friend Sheila, I think you said?'

'Oh. Gosh. I…' Sue was stuttering now, and scarlet in the face. Suddenly all the hangers on were looking elsewhere. Sam continued, growing in confidence.

'My daughter Lucy is starting in Reception this morning, and bless her little heart, she's so nervous. Anyway, I couldn't help overhearing your conversation and felt I should reassure you all about my lifestyle before I'm driven out of the village and my daughter's school life is ruined by malicious gossip and innuendo.'

Sue looked so embarrassed, and tried mouthing an apology.

'I'm afraid that the reality is far less exciting than all this speculation. I am a writer, a songwriter in fact, and not a debauched sex fiend who preys on young men. Neither am I charging money for sexual favours.'

'I never said you were,' Sue said somewhat defensively.

'No, you didn't, but you implied that I was, which could have a devastating effect on my daughter and I if this carries on…'

Sue was really trying to back pedal now. 'It was Sheila, not me. I…'

'Look,' interrupted Sam. 'Like I said, I write songs, and the three young men Sheila spied at my house last night are part of a band I'm working with which, to make it crystal clear, means I am writing a couple of songs for them. If Sheila had only asked me, I could have put her out of her misery.'

Sam could feel one of her headaches coming on, but decided she really wanted this nonsense sorted out here and now.

'The gentleman who turned up the other evening is my manager, who is also a very good friend. He had been out and needed to drop off some information for one of his artists that I am writing for. The envelope he handed me contained nothing more than a CD and a few photographs. Oh, and on Saturday night, for Sheila's information, I have a nineteen-year-old singer coming to my door. Don't worry, though. If memory serves me right, she only has her ears pierced and maybe one little stud through her nose. Perhaps I should ask her to come around to the back door... I wouldn't want her to frighten Sheila's children. What do you think, Sue?'

Sue and her chorus line were speechless. Sam, who had never talked for so long uninterrupted, continued, actually feeling most proud of herself now that she was on a roll.

'However, I must apologise to Sheila for my friend's behaviour the night we moved in. I can see that perhaps it was a little daunting. I'm afraid Suzy had one glass of wine too many, and she can get a little carried away. I think the combination of the wine and the country air all got a bit too much. I shall try to get around to Sheila's to explain, but at least you can fill her in in the meantime.'

Sue realised that she had been made to look a complete idiot in front of all of the parents. Those mums who just a few moments ago had been only too pleased to join in the gossip with their chorus of mock horror were now sloping off, and the parents who did have the guts to stick around seemed to be taking an unusual interest in their shoes. She shook her head and vowed never to listen to Sheila's gossip again. Oh yes, she was going to march round there and give Sheila a piece of her mind.

Sam, on the other hand, felt relieved, but decided to leave before her anger reared its ugly head and she said something she really regretted. She was glad she had walked Lucy into the classroom this morning, or else she may not have caught the gossip at the gates. She held her head up high, walked out of the school grounds and headed for home.

Liz, who had heard the whole twisted tale unwind in the playground, hadn't enjoyed herself so much in years. Sue had had this coming to her for months. She was fond of her and Sue could be a lot of fun, but gossip hurts, and ever since Sue had got close with Sheila, she had become quite sharp with her opinions. Liz had tried several times to urge Sue to be careful with what she did or didn't repeat from Sheila, but alas, it seemed to have bitten her on the backside today.

Liz decided that Sam from Wisteria Cottage must be a brave woman to stand her ground like that, and well worthy of getting to know. She watched her leave the school grounds, her wonderful shaggy red-blonde hair swinging in time with her beautiful floor-length white gypsy skirt.

How exciting, a new mate, pondered Liz.

She turned to walk home, passing Sue, who was now attempting to justify herself to the few worshippers who remained. Liz knew there was no time like the present and, realising the confrontation at the school gates must have hurt Sam, decided to call round to see her this morning.

Sam was still upset an hour later when the doorbell rang. She was tempted not to answer it, but was waiting for a delivery so thought better of it. As she pulled open the front door, she was pleasantly surprised to see a pretty woman standing on her doorstep with a bunch of flowers and a bottle of Prosecco.

'Sam, hi. A little house warming gift.' Liz grinned as she handed Sam the wine and flowers. 'I'm Liz. I think you were wonderful and wanted to tell you so, as well as welcoming you and your daughter to the village.'

'Thank you, um, Liz,' replied Sam, a little taken aback.

'Oh no, the pleasure's all mine! That scene this morning will keep me laughing for weeks.'

Sam's mother had warned her that life in the village could be a whirlwind. 'Be prepared,' she had said. 'You could have anyone or anything turn up at your door at any time.'

'Um, I was just warming some, um… would you like to come in and have a cup of coffee?' Sam suggested.

Without missing a beat, Liz stepped forward saying, 'Love one, thanks! White, no sugar.'

Whilst Sam put the kettle on and searched the cupboards for flower vases, Liz gazed around the kitchen in awe and chatted nonstop about the cottage. Sam found Liz and her chatter very comforting to be around considering they had only just met. Liz told Sam how she had longed to look inside Wisteria Cottage for years.

Wisteria Cottage was old and very beautiful. The kitchen had a mellow aged flagstone floor and contemporary styled light oak units, with a matching island and beautiful baby pink Aga. Photos of Lucy were pinned carefully onto a notice board.

Liz wandered through to the huge open plan lounge and orangery, which was tastefully decorated with the palest shades of cream and ochre. Minimal furniture, consisting of one enormous gold L shaped sofa and a low light oak table, created a tranquil yet comfortable atmosphere. There was an enormous matching oak framed mirror above an inglenook fireplace, which was fitted with a log burner and a store of neatly stacked logs ready for the first frosts of winter. Liz smiled. Her fantasy of Wisteria Cottage had not disappointed. In fact, the reality was even lovelier than she had imagined.

Sam appeared, placed a tray holding a powder pink coffee pot with matching mugs, milk jug and sugar bowl on the table and returned to the kitchen. She removed two pain au chocolat from the oven and carried them back to the lounge. For Liz, the aroma of coffee and warm chocolate made the scene complete.

'I'm glad you popped in, I would have eaten them both otherwise,' joked Sam.

Liz studied her new friend's face as she busied herself with the coffee and pastries. As Sam offered Liz a pastry, she noticed that Sam had the palest blue eyes she had ever seen. They were beautiful, but they looked troubled and sad.

'Please don't take any notice of that lot, Sam. Especially Sue, she really can be lovely. Her husband is away a lot on business – he's hilarious, by the way. Anyway, to relieve the boredom she tends to create all sorts of nonsense to keep herself amused. Sadly she's kind of got hooked up with your neighbour who, by all accounts, is an absolute menace with bells on. You were fantastic, by the way. You should have heard Sue trying to justify herself after you left.'

Sam smiled and shrugged her shoulders. She liked Liz and appreciated her support and understanding.

'I hate having to tell anybody what I do. I like to keep myself pretty private, but I thought that under the circumstances I should nip it in the bud. Anyway, I guess I should have listened to my mother. She warned me about village gossip.' Trying to change the subject, Sam asked Liz how she filled her days.

'Nothing much to say. My days are taken over by playing mum and housewife. All dead boring I'm afraid, unlike you.'

'Oh, I think that takes a considerable amount of work and energy, being a good mum. Don't you? Shall we take these outside? It's a shame to waste this beautiful weather.' Sam gathered their mugs and plates and picked up the tray. They headed to the open patio doors, carrying everything outside which, noted Liz, feeling a little envious, was as perfect as the inside of the cottage.

Birds serenaded them from the trees and the seclusion and lushness of the garden made Liz gasp with delight. Roses and clematis weaved in and around several arches, which framed a long garden. A quaint cobbled path invited the visitor to wander a while. Gorgeous blooms offered their colour and scent to all who walked there.

'Wow, this place is perfect,' Liz breathed.

'I must admit I'm still pinching myself,' Sam replied, before placing the tray down on the ornate table. It was positioned perfectly in the little courtyard area, a pergola providing them with shade from the morning sun. Sitting in silence and enjoying the fresh air, Liz was amazed at how comfortable she felt in Sam's company and decided at that moment she was going to get to know her a whole lot better.

'Ooh, so where does that lead?' Liz said, nodding to the locked gate attached to the side of the summer house. She could make out a little cobbled footpath beyond the gate.

'It leads to my retreat, but I'm waiting to get it fenced in as it sits directly next to the stream. I know it's shallow and gentle, but I just don't feel comfortable with Lucy getting up there,' Sam said.

'Ooh, sounds intriguing. What is it?' Liz was hellbent on finding out.

'It's kind of a secret garden.' Sam smiled.

'Can I take a peek?' Liz asked.

Sam smiled and got up. She unlocked the combination lock and led the way. A little cobbled footpath weaved in and out, around and around, tantalising Liz. It seemed to go on for miles and finally Liz's heart flipped, for in front of her was the most beautiful sight she had ever seen. The large open space took her breath away. Grass so green and perfect that it looked unreal, almost. The grassy bank led to the cool stream. Ducks swam past, paying little attention to the two women watching them. And there was what could only be described as something out of a children's fairytale. A beach hut! Pale baby pink and white stripes. A little veranda was built around it, with a comfy garden chair and a blanket draped over it. In front of the veranda was a beautiful stretch of sand. For the first time that day, Liz was speechless. Sam smiled.

Chapter 2

'It's so peaceful. It's where I am going to write.'

'Can I look inside?' Liz asked.

Sam took a key from under the little flower pot and opened the door. This, too, took Liz's breath away. There was a little pink sofa, a tiny little kitchen area with a mini fridge, powder pink kettle and accessories, and a guitar was hanging on the wall. There was a bookshelf with an assortment of books, and fairy lights seemed to cover every available space. Reading her mind, Sam switched the lights on and Liz's face lit up like a child's.

'Wow, Sam. I thought the house was perfect enough. Did you do this?' she asked.

'I guess you could say I added my own twist. I furnished the interior and chose the pink and white stripes as it was blue before, but the previous owner bought it for his wife. She had always dreamt of having a beach hut, but couldn't travel far, and so he built one here and gave her her own little bit of a seaside. It really is the most relaxing space to write. He even ran armoured cable up, so it has electricity and gets quite warm and cosy.'

'I bet your daughter loves playing on the beach,' Liz said, nodding to the sand and the bucket and spade.

'She does! Sadly it's too cold for her to paddle right now, but I can't wait for the summer. She is so cute, she goes fishing with her little rod and red wellies.' She nodded at them, resting near the beach hut.

They gazed at the ducks swimming gracefully past them and the sheep grazing in the water meadows beyond. Sam eventually turned off the fairy lights and locked up.

'This has to be the most perfect view,' Liz announced.

'I know, isn't it stunning?' Sam replied, smiling.

'So, what made you choose to move to Willow Green? I heard you were living in London before,' Liz asked as they made their way back to their coffees and pastries.

'My parents live opposite, at Lavender Cottage. They retired here about seven years ago. Mum was born in the village and her parents had lived here all their lives.'

'Ah, so Mary's your mum?' Liz said, smiling.

'She is,' Sam smiled back.

'I like her, she's lovely,' Liz said, beaming.

'Thank you. Mum grew up here, then met and married my dad and moved to London. He lived there back then, but she always wanted to come back here. Can't say I blame her, this place is something special.'

'Do you miss London?' Liz asked.

'I grew to hate London to be honest. Matt and I – that's Lucy's father – we're not together anymore.'

'Yeah, I guessed that much… I'm sorry.'

'To be honest, it's fine. I've wanted out of London for some time now and Matt couldn't bear to live anywhere else,' Sam said.

'So is that why you split up? Sorry, tell me to mind my own business!' Liz said.

'No. Well, partly for that reason, but mainly because of a beautiful twenty-two-year-old singer called Jasmine.' Sam reached for her coffee.

'No! You poor thing,' Liz exclaimed, flopping back in her chair. Sam held up her hands and started laughing.

'Please don't feel sorry for me, Liz, it's fine. We tried to make it work for Lucy's sake, but… Anyway, Matt's a good dad,' said Sam, suddenly brightening.

'Must be hard for you all, though.'

'To be honest, Lucy will probably get more quality time with Matt now, as he will have to make time for her. He's a sound engineer and he's always been away a lot and works antisocial hours.'

'What about the new woman-child, how does Lucy get on with her?' Liz asked. Sam giggled.

'Jasmine is nice. Lucy likes her. She's known her a while, only Matt works with her.'

'Oh no, you poor thing,' interrupted Liz. 'How can you be so nice and generous? Are you prozac'd up to the eyeballs or something?'

Sam just shook her head and laughed. She liked this outspoken woman.

'Corny as it sounds, life really is too short to hold grudges, and besides which, I can't spare the time to get bogged down with doom and gloom. Of course, it does make for fabulous writing material, you know.' Sam decided that was enough talk about her sorry love life, so she quickly asked, 'Have you always lived in the village, Liz?'

'Oh no, I grew up in Cornwall. Then I studied in London for a bit and that's where I met Paul. Willow Green is not exactly the Cornish Rivera, but it's been the perfect compromise for us once we had kids. Paul grew up here.'

'Oh, I know what you mean. I love Cornwall. Looe and Polperro are my idea of perfect,' Sam announced.

'Ooh, I love Polperro too,' sighed Liz. The two women sat in silence for a while, contemplating their shared passion.

'So how come you're not part of Sue and Sheila's pack?' Sam asked, genuinely interested.

'Oh, I'm a lone wolf and I like to hunt alone.' Both women laughed. 'I actually feel sorry for people like that,' said Liz.

'I do too, but they are dangerous. They don't realise the effect their gossip can have. Lucy has a lot on her tiny shoulders already. She's having to adapt to country life, away from all her friends and knowing that her daddy doesn't live with us anymore. She was reluctant to go to school today, and she really doesn't need to be singled out because of her mother's allegedly corrupt lifestyle,' Sam said.

'Oh, bless her little heart. Listen, don't worry about all that nonsense. My Faye started today as well, and Lucy will be in good hands. Faye tends to be a bit of a mother hen and takes people under her wing.'

A bit like you, it seems, Sam thought but didn't mention. Liz continued.

'My son Marcus is in year two. He's in the same class as Daniel – he's Sue's son – and he can be as mischievous as his mother, but like his mother he can be charming too, and you can't help but like him… then he does something stupid and you're back to hating him again. My Marcus loves him, though.'

Sam pulled a face that made Liz laugh.

'Yeah, I know what you're thinking, how can a grown woman

dislike a small child? Trust me, Damien in the Omen has nothing on this little guy. I hope Sue's learnt a valuable lesson today, because she's been spouting Sheila's gossip for ages now and it's gotten out of hand. I'm not blaming it all on Sheila, Sue's an adult and has her own mind, but she was lovely before those two became close. Do you know that I don't think anyone has stood up to Sue or Sheila before today? So high five to you, our new village mascot.'

Sam found Liz's conversation very refreshing, and quite funny too.

'I doubt my outburst will make much of a difference. I don't know about you, but I often find that people like that never really change. It's as though conflict and drama keep the world turning for them.'

The two women sipped their coffee and contemplated Sam's last comment.

'I think it most definitely will have an impact on her. It's a shame you met Sue at her worst, as she can be fun when she isn't being such a gossip. She never used to be like that, only since Sheila befriended her. Oh, and I love her husband, wait 'til you meet him.'

'Okay, I shall keep an open mind, I promise. She just hit a couple of raw nerves today, that's all. Lucy's my achilles, so I tend to kick out when it comes to protecting her.'

'Quite right, too. You had every right to respond the way you did. Sue was out of order and you made that crystal clear to everyone today. I think you've done her a big favour.'

'So, you were saying Faye has started reception and Marcus is in year two. How do you cope? I struggle juggling around one!' Sam asked.

'It will be easier now they're both at school. I don't go out to work but I guess it takes its toll sometimes. Luckily my in-laws live close by and my husband Paul is pretty good, so…'

'What does he do?' Sam asked, leaning forward.

'He designs websites and does computer stuff.'

'Oh, that could be useful. Is he busy?' asked Sam.

'Fabulously, it couldn't be better. He's also managed to get a few good retainers from businesses in the surrounding towns which help a lot, too.' Liz thought her life sounded so dull in comparison to Sam's, so she switched the subject back to her. 'Do you mind my asking how old you are, Sam?'

'No, not at all. I'm thirty-five.'

'Wow, so am I. We're virtually twins. I don't want to give you the creeps, but I'm so pleased that you moved here. We get people arriving from London all the time, but they are real city folk who commute and don't seem to want to join in with village life at all.'

Sam felt a little panicky. She didn't want to be pinned down so quickly, and thought she better make it clear that she too might be one of "those folk".

'Oh gosh, Liz, I'm afraid I'm not so sure how involved in village life I intend to become. I'm not exactly a social butterfly, and I've been pretty flat out what with the move and work and everything.' Sam ran out of excuses and saw the disappointment on Liz's face, so she offered a quick tour of the cottage instead.

'Ooh, yes please,' Liz chuckled. 'I thought you'd never ask. I mean, have you noticed I've been hinting at that since I got here?'

'Well, don't get too excited. It really will take just a couple of minutes.'

Sam led Liz back through the orangery and into the lounge. Climbing the old cottage stairs, Liz discovered the three bedrooms. Sam's room, the master bedroom, was huge and was also the most beautiful, peaceful bedroom that Liz had ever seen. It had four huge sash windows, two framing a perfect view of the village green and the other two overlooking the beach hut, stream and the water meadows. The bedroom had a thick cream carpet, light oak furniture and pale cream blinds. Liz spied a large ensuite bathroom just a few steps away with a huge corner, copper jacuzzi bath. Enviously she pictured Sam soaking there with candles and a glass of bubbly.

Lucy's bedroom was along the landing. Liz peered around the door and noted the familiar colours and accessories popular with most young girls of Lucy's age, but it was a lot tidier than Faye's. It was fit for a princess.

The third bedroom overlooked the rear. Sam had a lot of musical equipment in the room. It seemed to resemble an air traffic control room to Liz, and she was terrified in case she leant on something or switched something off. The family bathroom was stunning; lights seemed to twinkle and reflect from the tiny, mirrored tiles covering the entire surfaces of the walls. The tour had come to an end, so Sam guided Liz back downstairs to the kitchen. Liz kept on gushing over and over.

'I am afraid I cannot take much credit. The previous owners had the most amazing taste. The one thing I treated myself to was the Aga, only I've always wanted one, and now all that's really left for me to do is to convert the attic. It's a lovely big space up there and they've done a really good job so far by having a staircase fitted and dormer windows put in. I'm going to get it soundproofed and converted into a studio.'

'But what about the studio you already have in the spare room, what would you use that one for?' Liz wondered.

'I'm storing the equipment in there, I just needed somewhere safe to put it, besides, I need a spare bedroom in case Suzy – she's my best friend,' she added, 'stays over, and to be honest the attic will make the most incredible studio.'

Liz had noticed a few framed gold disks leaning up against the wall of the spare room. They featured artists familiar even to Liz, but they were also adorned with the words 'written by Sam Tate'. It was only now that Liz realised what Sam truly meant by 'songwriter'.

'Sorry, Sam. I had no idea. I think I'm starting to feel a little star struck, you'll probably think me a weirdo.'

Sam laughed. 'Not at all, but it really isn't as exciting as people believe.'

'Leave Me Gently is one of my all-time favourite songs. I can't believe you wrote that, it's beautiful.'

Sam was laughing, embarrassed.

'Thanks, but I think there are so many better songs out there.'

'But don't you ever wish you were performing them yourself?' Liz asked.

'Oh, I always perform each and every song I write,' Sam replied wistfully. 'They are my own private creations before anybody else gets to hear of them.'

'But why do you give them away, does your voice suck or something?' Liz's mouth was full and she sprayed a few crumbs.

Sam giggled. She really did like Liz and found her most refreshing.

'I've been told my voice is pretty strong, and I've been offered recording contracts over the years, but to be honest I like my life the way it is. I get to have the best of both worlds. I write and sing on my own terms, I get to keep my privacy and the copyright of each song.'

'But don't you resent them all, making so much money out of your hard work? I'd be so twisted.' Liz said, piling more pastry in her mouth.

Sam shuffled uncomfortably and felt a little awkward with the line of questioning.

'Oops, have I said the wrong thing?' Liz asked.

'No, not at all. Truth is, in this industry the songwriter gets to make most of the money, not the artists. You know, some of them end up working for next to nothing just to pay back the enormous advances they've been given by the record companies, whereas I get to earn a living and stay at home with my little poppet. Talking of which, I wonder how they're getting on. Do you think they'll hit it off?'

'I'm sure of it. Faye's very sociable, and if Lucy is anything like her mother then Faye will love her. Their class is very boy heavy this year, and considering there are only fifteen in the class I bet the girls have hooked up already.'

'Oh I hope so, Liz. Poor little Luce really didn't want to go to school today, you know.'

Liz noticed how troubled Sam looked.

'Don't worry, Sam. It's a wonderful school and the teachers are amazing, you'll soon see. I don't think you can go too far wrong with only ninety odd children in the school. Ofsted gave it top marks as well.'

'I know. I suppose I'm just panicking a little. I must admit I was having serious doubts about this whole 'move to the village' until you showed up on my door. Thanks, Liz.'

Liz nodded and reluctantly turned to leave.

'Well, I really do hope I have restored your faith in village life. Sheila is just a tiny blip, an irritating rash that flares up occasionally. Most of the locals are warm and friendly and they all pretty much respect one another's privacy.'

'She's very glamorous, Sheila, isn't she?' Sam said.

'Hmm, I guess! Mind you, she does invest an awful lot of time and money on her appearance. Sorry, you probably think I'm being a terrible bitch now.'

'Not at all. I've never been good at that glam thing, I'm no yummy mummy. Always leaving everything to the last minute, that's me,' Sam smiled.

'Well I think you've got that perfect English rose thing going on which no amount of grooming can touch,' Liz said wistfully.

'Yeah right, and one that got tangled in the hawthorn bush,' joked Sam.

'You shouldn't deny how attractive you are,' Liz said, staring Sam straight in the eye and making her blush.

'I know I scrub up okay, but to be honest I'd far rather have your dark, smouldering look myself. I've always envied people with olive skin who don't burn easily,' Sam said, deferring the attention from herself.

'Now you be careful, Sam, if Sheila is listening it will be all round the village by the morning. She'll have us indulging in an affair, then we'll both need to move. "Sheila said!"' Liz mimicked Sue. The two women laughed.

'Oh gosh, yes, and then the Reverend… Gibbons, was it she called him? He will need to visit,' Sam added, laughing.

'Gibson. She'd have no joy there – he is so wonderful in every way, he doesn't put up with any gossip. To be honest, he has done wonders for the village. Wait till you meet him, he is so handsome,' Liz added mischievously.

'Yes, so I heard. My mum said he is most dashing,' Sam said, mimicking her mother's description of the Reverend.

'I know. Faye asked him if he was a proper vicar and when he said he was, she told him that he wasn't like a proper vicar. Honestly, I was so embarrassed,' Liz said, squirming at the memory.

'Oh, that's hilarious. What did he say?' Sam asked, laughing her head off.

'He asked, 'What are proper vicars meant to be like?' and she said, 'Well, Mummy told Daddy that you are too handsome to be a vicar, and Daddy said he likes to drink beer with you and God never drank beer did he?"

'Oh wow, that's hilarious! What did he say to that?' Sam asked.

'He said, 'Well I can't speak for God, however, I do believe that Jesus was partial to the odd glass of wine or two.' Honestly Sam, I was mortified. Fortunately, he found it amusing.' Liz was scarlet in the face, and Sam realised that her new friend was perhaps a little smitten with the Reverend, too.

'Perhaps we could fix a date in our diary for tea this week so that the girls can play?' Liz said, still blushing.

'That sounds like a good idea. I like to keep three to seven free each day to be with Lucy, so tea time would be perfect,' Sam explained.

'Oh, wow! So when do you actually get down to work?'

'I tend to work evenings, and I plan to get in a few hours through the day now Lucy is in school.'

'Oh, sorry. I guess I scuppered your plans this morning, didn't I?'

'No, it's fine. To be honest, I was feeling a little flat after the episode at school, so you did me a favour, you've cheered me up. So, thanks! Anyway, I find it difficult to write when I'm wound up.'

Chapter 3

After Liz had gone, Sam made another cup of coffee. She knew she should be trying to finish some lyrics, but Liz had been such lovely company that she felt too relaxed to move from her secret spot.

Sam sighed. She thought of Suzy. She missed her so, so much.

She thought back now to the first time she had sat and played 'Cut Raw' to Suzy. She had written it for her when they were both seventeen. It had been a life-changing moment for the two of them. The song allowed Suzy to witness first hand the love, yet devastation, she had caused her friend. It was only now, when Suzy was safe in the confines of Sam's home or presence, that she would strip off to reveal the physical scars from her troubled past.

Sam felt sad that Suzy felt the need to disguise her scars, hiding herself in long sleeves even in the summer.

Sam shuddered now as she remembered being called into hospital late one evening by Suzy's adoptive father. The girls had been fourteen. Three girls had written horrible messages about Suzy on the toilet doors at school. This, combined with her adoptive mother being taken in for an emergency operation, had pushed Suzy over the edge.

Sam had been greeted that night by a very concerned doctor and led into a room and there, her best friend was quite literally fighting for her life. Wires seemed to be coming out of every part of her body. Her beautiful eyes were sunken and had black shadows beneath them. The doctor on duty announced that they had had to stitch her stomach, arms and breasts. Suzy had attacked herself with a razor. He announced that they would need to section Suzy in a psychiatric unit for her own safety. Suzy had been absolutely furious, and Sam and Suzy's father had to convince her that it was for her own safety.

Suzy's visiting hours were limited, but Sam kept her a diary and each day would fill in all she was thinking and feeling about Suzy and all that she loved and missed about her. Suzy had been angry for weeks, refusing any therapy. Sam found it hard to reach her, especially with the short amount of time she was allowed to spend with her friend.

She would take in the diary to show Suzy. She also took in paints and colouring pens and a lot of the time the two girls would sit and colour. It was during those times that Suzy chose to reach out and tell Sam how she was feeling.

It would be eight months until Suzy was well enough to come home and once she did, Sam kept a close eye on her friend. Suzy grew stronger and kept up her therapy sessions.

Suzy had been adopted by Reverend Fellows and his wife Kathleen at the age of seven. She had been taken from her birth mother who had been addicted to heroin and had overdosed. Poor Suzy had had to run screaming for help, and had travelled in the ambulance with her mother, begging her not to die or leave her. Her mother recovered. However, social services were so horrified by the neglect of Suzy that she had not been allowed to go home. The little girl was absolutely filthy, grossly underweight and had a suspicious urine infection.

Reverend Fellows and Kathleen had been desperate for a child of their own, but sadly it had not happened. They were delighted when Suzy had been placed in their foster care. It wasn't long before they had applied to adopt the little girl.

Suzy adored her adoptive parents, who couldn't have loved her more. She could not believe her luck. Finally she had her very own bedroom, and was able to sleep through the night without being woken by shouting or her mother crying. Reverend Fellows and Kathleen were the kindest of parents, they had tried their best to make sure that Suzy kept in touch with her birth mother. However, each time they arranged to meet, Suzy was left disillusioned and rejected all over again. Her birth mother never showed up.

The rejection that Suzy had carried around with her had started taking its toll when she was very young. Being adopted made her feel different from the other children and being mixed race had made her feel different, too. Her early experience in life, combined with the self-loathing caused by her being severely bullied in school, had pushed her too far. Sam had always tried her best to protect Suzy, but when Suzy's grades started slipping, her parents moved her to a private girls' school where the bullying grew worse. Suzy swore Sam to secrecy; she said she could handle it, but unknown to Sam, she'd turned it around on herself and started self-harming.

Once when she was seventeen, she plucked up the courage to have a relationship, which sadly went wrong.

Sam had wanted to kill Tim Harper, Suzy's one and only boyfriend. Tim had seemed genuine. He had dated Suzy for a year and finally managed to win her over and persuaded her to go on holiday with him and his folks to their villa in the South of France. On his return he had announced to his friends that Suzy's body resembled the map of the London Underground, it had so many scars.

After that, Suzy decided to remain single and kept herself safe inside her own little happy bubble. Sam had feared that after Tim, Suzy would self-harm again, but fortunately she managed to keep herself safe.

One of Sam's most treasured possessions was her snow globe. It sat on her dressing table and each night before going to bed, Sam would hold it in her hands and say a silent prayer to her beautiful friend. Inside the snow globe was a tiny doll. The doll was striking a beautiful and elegant pose and she had a smile on her face. She had black hair and olive skin; Sam had found it in a shop in Brighton and had had to have it. The doll looked just like Suzy and the snow globe depicted perfectly the isolation which seeped from the soul of her friend who lived within the confines of her apartment.

On the rare occasion she went anywhere, Suzy turned heads. People saw the elegant, stunning woman, unaware that the body underneath bared the true soul of a tortured past. Suzy was crippled by Post Traumatic Stress Disorder, linked to her childhood. The only people who got to share the secret with her was Sam and her parents. The two of them cocooned themselves together, resulting in the closest of friendships.

Sam had understood and sympathised with her best friend because like Suzy, Sam was renowned too for being a recluse; sadly, this had built barriers between herself and Matt who, on the other hand, was a first-class party animal.

Sam still found it remarkable that Matt had made such a play for her. He had known all about Sam and her little quirks. In fact, he had said it was what had attracted him to her – her shyness, her privacy – and yet no sooner had they been together than he had been hellbent on trying to change her. She often wondered why people did that. Why not just choose someone they want in the first place?

Sam made it clear to Matt that socialising was not an easy task for her, and that parties were her idea of hell. She had always tried to be professional in her working life, turning up for the after-show get-togethers, however, as soon as it was polite, she would make her excuses and leave…

She got up and went in. She didn't want to waste the afternoon dwelling on Matt, she had far too much to do.

At three fifteen she stood nervously at the gate. She was dreading seeing Lucy, just in case she looked upset. Sam looked up and felt her shoulders ease a little as she saw her mother's smiling face coming into view.

'Darling, I hope you don't mind, but I wanted to come and see how you were doing. I know how worried you were yesterday. I'd have popped across earlier, but your father and I went to the garden centre.'

Sam gave her mum a hug. 'Oh Mum, thanks for coming. I've been so worried, but I'm sure she will be fine.'

Mary smiled at her daughter just as Sue appeared at their side.

'Sue, hello, nice to see you. Have you met my daughter Sam?' Sue looked so uncomfortable that Sam actually felt sorry for her.

'Yes, Sue and I met this morning,' Sam said, smiling encouragingly at Sue, who instantly looked relieved as her anxiety faded.

'Sue has recently joined my flower arranging classes, haven't you dear?' Mary said. Sue tried to engage Sam in a conversation about her mother's marvellous classes, but the words didn't sink in. She was too anxious to collect Lucy to talk to anyone other than her mother.

At last, the sound of laughter and squeals of delight echoed around the playground as the children started filtering out, and Sam could see Lucy's dear little face amongst the others, looking all rosy-cheeked and giggly. She was holding hands with a pretty little girl who had long dark hair and beautiful olive skin.

'Mummy, this is Faye. She's my new best friend. Hello Grandma, can Faye come and see Sooty?'

'Yes, I'm sure we can arrange that, my dear,' answered Grandma with a chuckle.

Sam bent down, kissed Lucy and smiled at Faye. 'Hello Faye, how nice to meet you! Have you two had a lovely day at school?'

Liz appeared at Sam's side and gave her shoulder a squeeze as she lifted her daughter into her arms. She covered her with kisses before turning and bending down to kiss her son.

Faye and Marcus were very beautiful, like their mother, and whereas Faye was full of confidence and oozing mischief, Marcus was very shy and quiet.

Mary and Liz chatted like old friends whilst Lucy and Faye ran over to the play area to burn off yet more energy. Sam took the chance to have a quick word with Lucy's teacher.

Sam was pleased to hear how well her daughter had fitted in on her first day at school. Apparently she had got in a bit of a pickle at lunchtime when she had been given orange squash, but Mrs Holland had managed to establish that Lucy liked to drink water and only water.

Oh gosh, I had put that down on her form because I'm not keen on her having sweet drinks, although she loves hot chocolate, um...' Poor Sam was embarrassed. She needn't have been, Mrs Holland understood and nodded her approval.

'Yes, Lucy did inform the fellow diners on her table that too much sugar is very bad for them, not only for their teeth but their bodies too,' Mrs Holland said. Sam cringed a little.

'Oh no, I'm sorry,' Sam said.

'Well, I think it's good to start as you mean to go on. We encourage the children to have an opinion, and to be honest I think she may have converted half the table to drinking water. Lucy is a very bright little girl, I must say.'

'Thank you, Mrs Holland.' Sam returned to her mother and Liz, and the three of them watched whilst the children played.

At four o'clock, when most of the other parents had taken their children home, Sam, Liz and Mary finally managed to persuade the girls it was also time to go. When Faye hugged Lucy and refused to let her go, it was only by the promise of tea at Liz's the next day that prized them apart.

As they walked home down the lane, Mary invited Sam and Lucy to join them for tea. She had made a chicken and ham pie, which was presently cooling on her kitchen table, and it would be lovely to have them join them. They both jumped at the offer.

Sam adored her parents' home and her mother was a fantastic cook.

Sam and Lucy quickly got changed and then set off to Lavender Cottage. Lucy raced off across the wide-open space of the village green. Sam attempted to keep up with her young daughter, but it was no use. Sam slowed down and looked around. She loved this village; it really was so beautiful.

The green was divided in two by a wonderfully restored cricket pavilion, where the local cricket team played throughout the long summer and early autumn months. The post-match teas and get-togethers were popular events in the village and many pleasant evenings were spent under the fairy lights strung from the pavilion. They would twinkle and cast their friendly light amongst the friends who gathered there drinking and chatting by the ornate tables and chairs placed outside.

The Fox and Hounds Public House stood by the green and all around it were grand houses, cottages great and small, and ancient alms houses, each with their own character and eccentric architectural detail providing the setting for the perfect English village.

Stretching the entire length of the river on the north side was a magnificent backdrop of mature willow trees, the pride of the village. They had provided welcome shade for generations of families to picnic under during the lazy summer months.

Sam remembered the article Mary had sent her last year about Willow Green, which had boasted of its many awards and attributes. It regularly won the prize for best 'Village in Bloom' and for its 'Care of the Elderly'.

Sam gazed fondly at her parents' home which, as usual, was bursting with cottage garden colour. She remembered a similar day last summer, when she had been in her mother's kitchen staring across at Wisteria Cottage, its namesake in full glory, and Sam had been smitten. She smiled now as she remembered her thoughts that day. John had described in fine detail all about the little beach and its hut at the end of the garden. Sam had wondered, if only she could live somewhere as perfect as that, then life couldn't fail to be good?

I hope I wasn't wrong, she thought.

Mary had excitedly called her daughter a few months ago with the news that the current owners had decided to sell up and downsize; their son was getting married and they wanted to help him get on the property ladder. John, Sam's father, played bridge with the couple and he had managed to persuade them to consider giving his daughter first refusal on the property. Sam hadn't needed any persuasion, saying yes there and then. Of course, panic had set in as she realised the enormity of her decision. She would need to tell Matt, and then there was the move from London, which was bound to be a nightmare…

Sam turned back and glanced at Wisteria Cottage.

'Yep, still perfect,' she said out loud, and then waved to her mother, who had come out to the front garden and was waving her arms about madly.

Mary looked worried. She was convinced that Lucy was about to cross the road on her own. The experience of living in London had taught Lucy a great deal about road safety, and the little girl cautiously stopped just near the edge of the road. Sam reached Lucy's side, catching hold of her hand as Mary opened the little front gate and hugged her daughter and granddaughter.

A familiar and delicious smell wafted through the open door. Sam's stomach rumbled loudly as she recalled that other than the pain au chocolat she had eaten that morning, she had been too preoccupied to eat anything else.

Lucy skipped through the front door, following her grandmother. Sam paused and took another look across the green to her new home.

'Yep, still perfect,' she said again, and went inside.

Lucy ran straight through the cottage and up the garden to find her grandfather, who was busying himself with the overhanging buddleia bushes. Beside him was a tray of autumn bedding plants that he had bought for Lucy to plant.

Sam's father had dug Lucy her very own vegetable patch and flower bed and had been preparing it for her for when they moved. Mary and John had gone out of their way to ease the burden of moving to Willow Green for their daughter and granddaughter. They had even rescued a year-old black Labrador from The Blue Cross animal charity as a companion for Lucy.

'Yet another perk of living in the country,' her grandfather had told Lucy.

They encouraged Lucy to choose a name for the dog, and Sooty was now bounding after the little girl as she ran around in circles. Sam stood chatting to her mother in the kitchen and watched from the window, smiling.

'Thanks so much, Mum. You and Dad have no idea how much you have helped with all the upheaval. I really am grateful to you both. I just hope we don't crowd you,' Sam said.

'Nonsense. It was one of the happiest days of our lives when you finally moved here. Besides, it's the least we can do, as I don't think we will ever forgive ourselves for deserting you.' Mary was so sad, Sam squeezed her mother's arm.

'Don't, Mum. We've gone there so many times, it just hurts.'

'But you needed us. We just abandoned you,' Mary said, tears filling her eyes.

'Mum, I said stop this. Matt made it virtually impossible for you to visit, and you know he would kick off in style every time I tried to bring Lucy here.'

'Yes, but we should have tried harder. We just gave up.'

'Mum, stop. Please.'

'Well, it's hard darling. We abandoned you and poor Lucy.'

'Look, we're here now. Let's not let Matt take any more of our time from us, please, Mum. Right now, I'm struggling as it is. Please don't do this,' Sam pleaded.

Mary smiled and apologised. She put the tea pot, cups and saucers on a tray. She also cut a slice of homemade cherry cake especially for Lucy.

'Come on,' called Mary, 'let's get this outside and give that poor dog a rest.' Sam dutifully followed her mother into the garden and helped set out the tray on the table.

Mary and John had inherited a beautiful, mature garden, but their own inspired handiwork had made the place their own. Only last year they had had decking fitted around outside the back door.

'A proper outdoor room,' John had proudly called it. With the many colourful pots and creepers dotted about, it really was a relaxing and peaceful place.

'Did Lucy manage to speak to her father?' Mary inquired when the two had sat down.

'Yeah.' Sam glanced at her mother, gauging her reaction. Mary nodded, hiding her true feelings for Matt.

'Do you think he'll cope with you two living here? I know you said how angry he was,' Mary asked.

'Pretty much so, I guess. Matt spends most of his life working, so he's never really spent too much time with Lucy. He'll be seeing Lucy this weekend.'

John appeared and gave his daughter a kiss and hug.

'Be with you in a minute, my darling. I just want to get these few in before I start on Lucy's patch with her. That is, if she can bear to be parted from that foolish dog for a second. I'm not really sure how well this bedding will get on; it's a little late to be planting them. Mid-August the label says, but well it's worth a try.'

John waved his trowel as he wandered back to his labours, taking the cup of tea Mary had poured for him.

Mary felt a surge of anger swell inside her, directed at Matt for hurting her family. It had always been about what he wanted, and never what poor Sam had wanted. Mary had struggled for the past few years with the shame and the guilt of giving up on her daughter and had had to seek counselling to cope with her feelings. She realised that she still had a way to go. Still, sleepless nights tormented her. She smiled now as she watched her daughter walking around the garden. She was so proud of who Sam had become. Not only had she grown into a beautiful, talented woman, but also a kind and wonderful mother.

Sam wandered around the garden. She was dreading letting Lucy go this weekend, but felt helpless. She knew it was crucial for Lucy and Matt to spend the weekend together. She also knew that it would not be easy for either of them without the comfort of having Sam there.

Sam could feel the little bubbles of excitement in her tummy. It was as though she were permanently on holiday. She was looking forward to working with Abigail, the new young singer who she had been asked to write for. She had seen pictures of the young woman and had listened to her demo. Abigail had covered a couple of well-known hits, but with her own twist of originality. She definitely liked what she heard.

Sam paused at the top of the garden and gazed lovingly at her father and daughter, their heads touching as they bent down, carefully planting out the autumn bedding. A beautiful full head of silver hair pressed against the red-blonde silky hair of Lucy. Sooty looked most put out at not being the centre of attention for once and was digging a hole to show his outrage. Sam marvelled at her father as she listened to him patiently answer one hundred and one differing questions that Lucy fired at him, one after the other.

When they had lived in London, Sam had tried bringing Lucy to see them, but sadly Matt would kick up such a fuss that it had only happened once or twice a year. He liked them to be at home at all times.

If ever her parents had tried to visit, Matt had made it so uncomfortable for them; this, too, prevented many visits. By the time Matt had started touring with Jasmine, the gap had grown so wide between Sam and her parents, which didn't help to bring them closer. She was so glad to be living near them now. Lucy could spend quality time with them and really get to know her grandparents...

It was a warm evening, so they decided to eat outside. Mary's pie was delicious, as was her homemade apple and blackberry crumble.

By the time they made their way home, they were full up and happy. Sam and Lucy held hands and skipped home, singing songs and laughing together.

Chapter 4

Opening the front door to the cottage still gave Sam goose bumps. She took in its beauty while Lucy sprinted through to the lounge and dive-bombed the sofa, shouting 'I love it here!' over and over again.

When Lucy had calmed down a little, Sam let her phone Matt. Then it was time for a bath and bedtime. Sam retold a favourite story, then tucked Lucy in and kissed her goodnight. At that moment, Lucy threw her arms around her mother's neck and squeezed as hard as her little muscles would allow.

'Oh Mummy, I love it here so much, and I love you too! Promise me we will never leave.'

Sam gazed into her daughter's shining eyes. She hated to make promises she couldn't guarantee to keep, so she simply said, 'I'm glad you like it here poppet, because I love it too.'

'When is Daddy going to come and live here?' Lucy asked as she lay back down on the pillow.

Sam could've wept. She gently started stroking her daughter's head.

'Oh Lucy, my darling, Daddy lives in London, doesn't he? We are going to live here.'

Lucy solemnly nodded her head.

'Daddy is keeping your bedroom just the same for you and he is coming to get you on Friday so that you can stay with him all weekend. Just think, you now have two bedrooms, don't you?'

'Yes, and two is much better than one, isn't it Mummy? And Mummy, will I get two lots of presents on my birthday and Christmas to keep in my two bedrooms?'

Sam laughed and gave her daughter a hug. 'I am sure that you will my darling, yes.'

She gave her another kiss and said goodnight. Sam knew she hadn't dealt with that particularly well, but she wasn't sure what to say.

Sam poured herself a glass of wine and sat at the island, over-looking the green. She smiled, watching her mother in her front garden watering the hanging baskets and window boxes. They had lasted well this year. Young lads were playing cricket, and people at the pavilion were setting up the tables outside ready for the evening.

Sam had wondered if she would cope with the quietness of village life, yet there was more activity for her to watch than in London. She watched people walking their dogs and chatting to each other as they passed. Further down the green, Sam could just hear the sound of older children playing a noisy game. She tried to gather her thoughts for the day: the usual sinking feeling of guilt, her constant companion, was still burning underneath. Still, she couldn't deny what a remarkable day it had been. Lucy had enjoyed a wonderful first day at school and had seemed to get on well with Mrs Holland, her teacher. She had made a new best friend. Sam, too, had met a new friend, and one she particu-larly liked.

Lucy and Matt had a good long chat on the phone before bed, and when Sam had briefly spoken to Matt he had seemed quite upbeat and positive and, for once, didn't turn on the guilt trip.

Matt and Sam met several years ago. Sam had been playing in clubs, promoting her songs. Cut Raw had received such interest that Sam was beginning to build up quite a following. Most of her gigs were sell outs. When she turned up at a popular London venue, Matt was the sound engineer, and over the next few months the two of them had become very close.

They had moved in together eventually, and for the next few years they got on well, inspiring each other creatively which, in the end, resulted in a powerful collection of songs. Before long, Sam was receiving attention from some pretty big record labels and Matt, as co-producer to her new work, was gaining the type of recognition that meant lots of bands and artists wanted him to work with them.

Together they were a powerful combination, about to dominate the world.

They bought a house in Muswell Hill, converted the cellar into a studio, and had just started working on a new album when Sam fell pregnant. Matt had not been happy, to say the least. He spent the next month trying to persuade Sam to terminate the pregnancy, convincing her that it was the wrong time for both of them and that it would wreck both of their careers if they proceeded to have the baby. Sam had tried desperately to convince him that they could work through this, but cracks began appearing in their relationship almost immediately.

Matt's goals and ambitions hadn't changed a bit, and while Sam thought that she still wanted the same, her hormones and body seemed to have other ideas.

Even though he bullied her day in day out, Sam refused to abort their baby.

Sam struggled. She felt emotionally exhausted. She also found that being pregnant didn't leave her with a great deal of energy, and she was unlucky to suffer with nausea throughout the entire nine months, making her feel permanently ill. Late night recording sessions were definitely off the agenda, igniting Matt's fury all the more.

She had tried to get out and sing, but the nausea and dizzy spells, combined with lank hair and weight gain, had sapped her confidence. Before long, she was finding excuses not to perform.

The situation hadn't been helped by the look of distaste Matt revealed each time he looked at her growing stomach, and one night while chatting to a colleague, Matt had let it slip that he actually found pregnant women revolting, a real turn off... Sam sank deeper into despair and tried to keep herself well and truly covered up after that.

By the time Lucy was born, Sam's confidence had plummeted so far down that just the thought of performing on stage terrified her. She made a life changing decision, one that Matt had never learnt to accept, or forgive for that matter... She told him that she no longer wished to be a performing artist, but had decided to concentrate on song writing for others. Matt had been furious and had accused her of wasting her ultimate talent. He reminded her that record company executives still raved about her, saying they hadn't heard a voice or songs so powerful in years. The more he protested, the more her confidence evaporated. When this tactic didn't work, he tried emotional blackmail, telling her that she was responsible for his career prospects and the dwindling interest in him had been due entirely to her letting everyone down.

Sam listened over and over as Matt bombarded her with reasons not to give up, but she had convinced herself that she didn't care about performing. She discovered as each day went by that spending time with her daughter and enjoying the simple things far outweighed the pleasures of being a performer and was far more rewarding.

Matt tried everything in his power to convince Sam to find a nanny and to "get a life", but nothing he could say would change her mind. He convinced himself that it was just the 'baby blues', and that within a few months she would change her mind. He even waved a recording contract under her nose, but to no use. After several months Matt gave up trying. He found it hard to hide his feelings. The woman he had fallen in love with no longer existed. She was gone and had been replaced by a replica: someone who looked a lot like Sam, but who put her energy and creativity into looking after his little girl instead of him and their music career.

Matt had had to accept the new reality: their relationship had never stood a chance. Whilst he shouldn't really blame her, he did, and he realised that he no longer knew her or understood her. The barrier between them grew ever wider. Matt had wanted the world, whilst Sam had just wanted him and Lucy.

She often wondered nowadays: if Matt hadn't have pushed her so hard so soon, would she have gone back to performing after Lucy's birth?

Sam had asked Matt on several occasions to take a little time out to be with Lucy so that perhaps she could spend some time in the studio and test the water again, but it had been too late. Matt had moved on and had reminded Sam about the perfectly good nanny he had found but Sam had rejected. Therefore, she only had herself to blame.

Unforgivably, he had also reminded Sam that it was she who had wanted to keep the baby, therefore he wasn't responsible for the situation she found herself in. Sam had argued that it was entirely reasonable to want Lucy to be cared for by herself or Matt when she was so young, but Matt refused. The longer time went on, Sam's former life in music drifted further and further away, and the harder it seemed to go back to it…

Life with Matt had turned into a grey, lifeless maze. Sam became trapped within the miserable walls. He didn't like her going out. He refused to care for Lucy, making it almost impossible for her to do anything. When she attempted to invite people to the house for a little company, Matt made it his mission to make the guests feel as uncomfortable as possible. She longed for her best friend, but Suzy worked morning, noon and night. Her skills as an interior designer had made her so successful that she was always in demand. Matt didn't like Suzy, and Sam knew it was because she was the only person who wasn't intimidated by Matt and would stand up to him.

Sam got up and poured another glass of wine, the evening light casting soft shadows around her comfortable kitchen. Willow

Green was ablaze with life, lights were glowing in people's homes, and later she would look out at the twinkling scene and think of Christmas.

Sam's thoughts drifted back again to that first couple of years after Lucy's birth and how nervous she had felt. She knew that Matt was bitterly disappointed with her attitude.

She didn't want to be bullied and longed for Matt to hold her and tell her that he knew how she was feeling. That he would help. Matt hadn't offered, he'd just kept pushing and getting angrier with her. She had wanted him to make love to her, anything to make her feel wanted, but he had rejected her.

Sam experienced what her best friend's life had been like for so many years. She developed an acute anxiety disorder, resulting in severe panic attacks and agoraphobia. One time she had been rushed to hospital because she thought she was having a heart attack. Matt had been furious to find out it had only been a panic attack and accused her of doing it deliberately to prevent him from travelling to New York to meet a business contact. Her punishment resulted in him sulking for days.

Sam tried desperately after that to avoid anything which could trigger or aggravate her condition, and so her world grew even smaller. She would make it as far as the shops and to nursery with Lucy but apart from that, she was pretty much house bound.

Matt had convinced Sam that not only had she ruined her own career, but that he too was being punished for simply being associated with her. Sam could see no way out and grew more and more miserable, guilt racking her every breath. Not only had she screwed up her career, but she had done for his, too.

The turning point came when Matt met Jasmine. He had returned home one Saturday night to announce that he would be working with the singer. Sam would never forget the look on Matt's face as he came face to face with Jasmine. Had he have punched her in the stomach, it would not have hurt her more. The look he gave the young woman was the very same look he used to give to Sam. Alas, those days were long gone. When he looked at her now, it was with contempt and bitterness.

To add insult to injury, Matt spent the next fortnight in rapture over the beautiful, talented singer, and it wasn't long before he had managed to worm his way into Sam's head, convincing her to allow Jasmine the opportunity to record over the vocals of Sam's last album.

When Sam explained that the lyrics were very personal, that she wasn't sure she wanted someone else to sing those particular songs, and that they were special to her, Matt had refused to listen. Growing impatient with her, he exploded.

'Why the hell not, Sam? You might as well get some use out of them, especially after all the hours I spent producing the damn things. It's not just your decision, you know.'

'But Matt, they're my songs, my babies,' Sam pleaded.

'No, the songs are not your babies. Lucy is your baby. The songs are a product of a lot of hard work on my behalf, so it is only fair that someone as amazing as Jazz can do them justice, and maybe earn back some money to make up for it all. Otherwise, it's all a waste of time.'

'But, I, I...' she stammered.

'Unless, of course, you're jealous. Is that it? Could've been you, Sam, you could be Jazz. You were stunning, you had the voice of an angel, but you blew it. Your choice, not mine,' Matt said spite-fully, and finished it with a disparaging look up and down her body as though to rub it in.

She knew she looked a mess, but her eczema had flared up and make-up only aggravated it. Matt didn't like her without makeup. He said she was too pale to get away without wearing any and his latest dig was to tell her was that people with Jasmine's colour-ing could easily carry it off, and hadn't Sam seen Jasmine without makeup and how naturally beautiful she was?

Sam's confidence reached rock bottom. She could see how much Matt resented her. She knew that he would never give up this latest battle, and so she agreed that Jasmine could re-record the whole album.

Jasmine had needed little convincing once she had heard the tracks and realised what little work it would take to scrap the original vocal and put hers over the top. She jumped at the chance and was brimming over with excitement. Sam's album had been sabotaged by Matt and her only involvement now consisted of making lunch, dinner or providing tea and coffee for Matt and Jasmine as they worked into the early hours.

Matt grew obsessive over his protégé. Within weeks he had ar-ranged for a photographer to take her pictures, and then went around to all the major labels to get a deal for Jasmine. When he succeeded in landing her a record deal, he naturally wanted to celebrate. Typically, it was all last minute, without a thought for Lucy. Sam had been unable to get a babysitter that late and so Matt had taken Jasmine out on her own. Sam cringed now as she remembered the look of delight on Jasmine and Matt's faces when they realised Sam would be declining the invitation. Matt virtually skipped out the door. He would have the beautiful young singer all to himself.

Sam had woken much later that night with a sense that all was not right, and she had crept downstairs. There she discovered Matt and Jasmine in a loving embrace on the leather couch in the studio. She hadn't said anything, but had slipped back upstairs and cried herself back to sleep.

The next morning, she asked Matt for a quick word before he started work.

'I, I... I saw you. You and Jasmine, last night. I saw you.'

He had looked stunned and was initially speechless. Matt, however, then reverted to type.

'And? So? You only have yourself to blame, Sam, you've driven me to it, you've been so uptight and I'm sick of it. Anyway, at least Jasmine wants me.' With that, he had turned on his heels and stalked off, leaving Sam to dissolve into floods of tears.

Fortunately, Lucy had been invited round to a friend's for a play date that day, so Sam had been able to nurse her broken heart in private.

She had felt so humiliated. Matt had done such a number on Sam's confidence that it wasn't long before she started to blame herself for his defect.

After all, how could she blame him? Since having Lucy, she seemed to live in jeans and huge sloppy jumpers, no make-up and her hair tied back. She never had any extra energy and couldn't be bothered to go out. Jasmine was young, vibrant, stunning, intelligent and full of life.

The next few weeks were atrocious. Matt seemed to think that now Sam knew about his affair, he didn't need to keep it quiet from her. She would often hear the two of them laughing together. Most evenings Matt would drive Jasmine home and not return until the early hours, if at all. Lucy had stopped asking for her daddy at bedtime.

When Sam had told him she couldn't take it any longer and that she wanted to leave, Matt had gotten nasty. He made it clear that there was no way he was going to let Sam take Lucy.

Things dragged on for a few more miserable months. Sam had learnt to cohabit with Matt and Jasmine, who was forever present in their lives.

Sam knew she was on her own and needed to build a new life for herself. Matt made it clear that he had no intentions of helping her, and so she had embarked on an online music programming course and online guitar lessons.

One busy yet enjoyable year later saw her equipped to work with the latest recording software. Her guitar skills had come on so well that she could strum a few tunes acoustically in public if she wanted to, but the main purpose of this entire endeavour was to let her put her songs across to potential artists. Her piano skills were excellent, but guitars were portable, and some songs were better suited to the guitar and not piano.

Because Matt was away, touring with Jasmine, Sam was able to record lots of songs. She also took advantage of the freedom to visit her parents and whilst Matt had sucked almost all the life out of her, Lucy and her parents were beginning to breath it back in. They had so much fun together; it seemed to rebuild Sam's spirits so she was able to cope better.

Her anxiety hadn't gone away, however, it was certainly better without Matt around.

Richard was another factor, and he was always present and encouraging. He introduced Sam to a band called Tremor. He'd been asked to approach Sam to write for them and having the house to herself meant she spent hours with them, learning all that made them tick to inspire the songs they needed her to write. They filled the house with so much light and laughter.

At this time, Jasmine was becoming quite well known off the back of Sam's songs: she may have lost her man, but her reputation as a great songwriter was supercharged and the royalties were pouring in.

Before long, her phone was ringing again. Sam's name was in circulation and this time it was several different companies asking her for songs to suit their artists and bands. She was even invited to work on a couple of film soundtracks, which was a challenge, and one she really enjoyed.

As Sam's confidence in her career grew, so did her appearance and strength.

By Lucy's fourth birthday, Sam made the decision to leave. She had organised a little tea party for her, but Matt let them down, breaking Lucy's heart. He'd decided to take a trip to Paris with Jasmine instead of attending the party.

When Sam tried complaining that he should spend it with his daughter, Matt blamed her. Because she had refused to work, he and Jasmine had had to record the album and promote it themselves.

Sam could not really complain, as being the main songwriter meant that she was earning more than the pair of them put together. This gave her independence, as the money now meant she could afford to leave and set up a home elsewhere.

She had to face up to the fact that she and Lucy were pretty much alone in a city she had grown to detest. She decided there had to be more. She wanted to be part of a family.

When Matt returned just before Christmas, she told him that she and Lucy were leaving. Matt's reaction surprised her; he sunk to his knees, broke down and wept.

'What did you expect, Matt?' Sam had asked quietly, once the tears had subsided. 'That I would be here for you when you were on your own? When there was nothing better to do? I have tried for four long years to make this work. You know how I hate London. I have wanted to move to the country for years, so please try to understand.'

'But Sam, I had hoped that you and I could work everything out, and that for Lucy's sake we could make a real go of it. I realised whilst I was away that I love you guys, and I need you.' Matt's practiced words never sounded so shallow and meaningless.

'For how long, Matt?' Sam cried. 'Until you get tired of me again and notice another Jasmine waiting to be discovered by you?'

Weeks of arguments and sullen silences had followed. Matt finally realised that Sam would not change her mind. His mood changed; he grew nasty and began making derogatory comments about Sam within earshot of Lucy. Lucy had become withdrawn. Suzy had been round a lot, she was worried sick about her best friend and her beautiful little girl. Sam was a bag of bones and lethargic. She had also began having night terrors and panic attacks, so severe that agoraphobia prevented her being able to leave the house again. Sam was diagnosed with PTSD and Suzy knew they needed to get away, so when Sam's dad phoned with the news that Wisteria Cottage had come up for sale, Suzy had leapt at it, convincing her friend that it was the perfect opportunity to start over, not that Sam had needed any persuading.

Fortunately, Matt and Jasmine had been away touring in Japan when Sam made all the arrangements, and by the time he returned a month later, everything was signed and sealed. He wasn't even able to argue that it was his money, as Sam had made enough through royalties to buy her own home.

'And now, here I sit,' Sam said out loud, raising her glass to salute Willow Green.

Chapter 5

Before starting work, she took another glance outside. Although it was dark now, she could still hear people laughing and drinking outside The Fox and Hounds. It was proving to be a beautiful warm September so far, and suddenly Sam longed to join the locals for a drink amongst the glittering fairy lights. She would give Suzy a call. She needed a really good giggle and knew that her friend would always provide that. Sam decided that first thing, she'd call her best friend and invite her over.

'Mummy, come on! Wake up or we will be late for school.'

Sam woke with a start as Lucy jumped up and down on her bed. The sunshine was radiating through the blinds, boasting of yet another beautiful morning. She checked out her alarm clock and realised that it was not quite seven.

'Lucy, my love, you don't need to be at school for another two hours, so why don't you get in and we'll have a cuddle?'

'Weeeeeeee,' Lucy squealed, diving under the covers. Before long the pair of them were giggling and singing songs, which Sam kept changing the words for whilst Lucy took great pleasure in telling her off and correcting her. They ate breakfast together, looking out over the green. Lucy squealed again when she saw her grandparents coming out of their cottage with Sooty. Sam felt the corners of her mouth lift.

They met up with Liz, Faye and Marcus and walked to school together. The children were so happy to see one another, and Sam realised that so were the mums.

'Are you still on for this evening?' Liz asked.

'We are, thank you,' answered Sam.

'Good, let's say four thirty. I'm doing party snacks so that we can all pick at them. Do you want to bring Lucy's PJs so that she can have her bath and stay 'til bedtime? I have some delicious wine that I thought you and I could sample. Paul should be home around seven, so he can drive you back when you're ready.'

'Don't be silly!' Sam replied. 'I can see your road from my bedroom window, it's not as though it's far.'

'Nonsense, it's a ten or fifteen-minute walk with tired little legs. He'll take you home,' Liz argued.

'Well, if you're sure he won't mind. What would you like me to bring?'

'Nothing really, only yourself and your daughter,' smiled Liz.

Sam had a productive day; she wrote a heart-wrenching melody. She already had a good outline for the lyrics and thought for a second that perhaps she should hand it over for Abigail.

Her heart sank at the thought of letting this latest song go into 'over production hell'. All the essence and subtlety would get lost by a dancy drum beat and millions of instruments. No, she decided, it would be tucked away in her 'best kept secrets' file, where she hid some of her most favourite and personal songs.

That was the hardest part of her job: letting go. She thought back to the songs she had given Jasmine previously, how they had been subtle, powerful, deep and meaningful, but by the time Jasmine and Matt had finished with them the songs had been remixed with a poppy dance feel by adding keyboards and a drum machine. They had been compressed within an inch of their lives and each and every song had lost most of its feeling. When Sam had plucked up the courage to criticise, Matt had been nasty, and merely said, 'If you'd have performed them yourself, then we wouldn't even be having this conversation. You wrote them and only you can give them their full potential so I'm sorry, but it's your bed and you are going to have to learn to lie in it.'

And so that had been that – like it or lump it. Sam's already broken heart took yet another blow and the wall she was gradually building around her had grown a little higher…

Grabbing a towel and Lucy's pyjamas, they made their way to the far end of the green and Lucy fell in love with the willow trees and announced that she wanted one in their garden so that she could build a den under it. Sam was captivated by Lucy's love for these beautiful trees and realised again the benefits for Lucy to grow up in the country.

Liz's house was lovely. It had a huge playroom and garden, which had a treehouse, a climbing frame and an enormous trampoline. There was also a wooden two storey playhouse, and Sam decided it was probably every child's dream garden: it catered for every childhood fantasy.

The kitchen table was bursting with party food. After the children had eaten, they tore off up the garden to play and Liz poured Sam and herself glass of wine.

'Come on, it's so lovely. Let's go sit in the garden,' Liz said.

They relaxed in the still-hot sunshine, sipping their wine and nibbling the hummus, pitta bread and grapes that Liz had put aside for them.

'Oh Liz, this really is lovely,' sighed Sam. 'I keep pinching myself that I've actually moved here.'

'I am so glad you did. I'd already feel pretty lost if you were to leave, you know. How sad is that?'

'Not at all,' interrupted Sam, 'but I think I am the lucky one here. You've made us feel so welcome. I kind of figured that I would be spending most of my time socialising with my parents, so this really is a pleasant surprise. Mind you, not that I don't like hanging out with my parents…'

The two new friends continued to chat in the afternoon sun, getting to know one another. Then, Liz remembered something.

'Oh, I meant to ask you earlier. You know you said you wanted to convert your attic into a studio? Well, we know someone – he's Paul's best mate, Dominic. He's an excellent all-rounder and I know he knows all about soundproofing and stuff like that. He did the old theatre up – you should check it out, you know. Anyway, it's wonderful what he's done. Would you like his number?'

'Oh yes please, that sounds promising.'

'Well, I really think Dominic is your man Sam. He is a wiz with electrics, too. He would be perfect.'

'Thanks, he sounds great. In fact, he sounds rather like the guy dad told me about, I'm sure he said his name was Dominic. I had asked this guy called Eddie, from London. He's someone I've worked with before. He and Matt set up our studio there, but he's snowed under with work, said there is nothing he can do until December, and I really need it up and running sooner.'

'Oh, he's great alright!' Liz grinned. 'So, did you manage to avoid Sue today? Only I know she was searching you out, desperate to invite you the girly night she's planning?'

'Yes, she called me over after school.'

'Did you refuse to go?' asked Liz.

'Yes... but I'm cross with myself. She actually looked quite hurt. Problem was she started talking about my songs and everyone turned round to stare and I didn't cope with it at all well, I literally walked off.'

'Oh no! I promise it didn't come from me,' Liz assured her.

'No, I know, it was Lucy. She got everyone to Google me. Apparently one of the children messaged their mum... to be fair, I had already told Sue I wrote songs, so I guess it was only a matter of time before people knew, but someone posted something on Facebook. Willow Green's parents' network or something.' Sam was embarrassed.

'Ah, bless her little heart, she is obviously proud of her mummy. Surely you're proud of your career? I mean, you are amazing,' Liz said. Sam blushed scarlet.

'Thanks, and yes, I am proud, but I struggle with it all. I have a bit of an anxiety issue, and that really is between the two of us.'

'Oh Sam, I'm sorry. I had it. It was when I first moved to London. I would completely freak out. My legs would stop moving and I would get stuck in the middle of a road. Eventually I was put on anti-depressants and beta blockers.'

'Did they help?' Sam questioned.

'Not at all, just made me sleep and eat. I piled on the weight, then I did need anti-depressants because I was so miserable about my weight,' Liz said. Sam was amazed at her new friend's ability to make the hardest of subjects sound light.

'Gosh, it's not until you talk about these things that you realise so many others suffer or have suffered. I never took them, but in hindsight I think maybe I should have done,' Sam replied.

Both women looked up when they heard the door slam. Faye screamed with delight and ran into the house. A very handsome man in a suit appeared; Sam realised that this must be Paul, Liz's husband. After he disentangled himself from his daughter's arms and threw his son affectionately up into the air several times, he came over and gave Liz a kiss.

'So, you must be Sam?' he smiled, shaking Sam's hand before getting down on his haunches. '…and you have got to be Lucy, I've heard so much about you. Faye tells me you have only lived here for a little while and already you are her favourite friend in the whole wide world. So, tell me Lucy, do you love it here?'

Lucy nodded vigorously and grinned. Sam decided she liked Liz's husband.

'Why don't you join us for a drink, love?' suggested Liz.

'Yeah, let me get changed and I will, excuse me everyone,' Paul said and then went indoors to change.

'He seems nice,' Sam said approvingly.

'Yeah, he's a gem, but he can be a pain as well at times. Then again, can't we all?'

Paul joined the women for a quick glass of wine before Faye

insisted that she and Lucy have their bath. Of course, it turned into a soapy, drawn out, messy affair and by the time Lucy was dried and dressed in her pyjamas, it was almost eight o'clock and beginning to get dark.

After a noisy farewell, Paul drove Sam and Lucy the short journey home.

Sam felt relaxed. Like his wife, Paul was very comfortable to be around. He walked them both to the door and then shook Lucy's hand to say goodbye, which made Lucy burst into giggles yet again.

'Lucy, it has been a pleasure meeting you and your mummy and I do hope to see you both very soon.'

He turned to Sam and said goodbye. Sam thanked him for the lift and was about to go in, when Paul said, 'Oh, I nearly forgot. Here's Dom's number, Liz said you need him to fit your studio. Did Liz tell you he completely renovated the old theatre? He even rewired the entire place. He really would be the best man for the job, but then again, he's always busy so...'

'Thanks Paul, I will do. I kind of need it up and running ASAP.'

'Ah. I'd let him know it's urgent, if I were you,' Paul called out as he walked back to his car.

When they got inside, Sam called Matt so that Lucy could say goodnight, and then she phoned Dominic's number. It went to voicemail, so she left a stuttered message, put Lucy to bed and then ran herself a bubble bath.

She decided a soothing mug of Horlicks would be nice to finish the evening off perfectly, so she lay back in the bath and sipped it whilst going over the day's events.

Funny, Sam mused: when she was living in London she had always avoided going back over her day and had tried to keep busy to avoid thinking very much at all. Living in Willow Green seemed slightly unreal, almost dreamlike. She wanted to savour and then memorise every moment, keeping it safe forever.

Her phone rang.

'Hi, is that Sam?' asked a husky voice.

'Er, yes, is that Dominic?' she wondered.

'Yeah, sorry to call late, but you said it was urgent.'

'Don't worry, I'm in the bath.' Suddenly Sam's cheeks burnt as she realised what on earth she had just said. His silence made what she had just said seem a hundred times worse. Sam sat bolt upright in the bath. 'What I mean is I'm not in bed.' She flopped back noisily into the warm bubbles, blushing scarlet.

Oh no, he must think I'm some crazy loopy woman, Sam thought. She decided if she remained silent for a few seconds, she may salvage a little dignity from this call.

'Right uh… so you're interested in soundproofing and installing a studio in your attic?'

'Yes, that's right. Do you think you would be able to fit me in? Only Paul said you're pretty busy.'

'Yeah, Paul called. Yeah, it should be doable if I work evenings and weekends, if that's okay with you? I need to see the space first, though. I can scoot round tomorrow evening after I finish work to take a look if you like?'

'Oh thank you, that would be wonderful. What sort of time?' she asked, still slightly distracted by his sexy voice. She was already trying to picture him, although desperately telling herself he would not be as gorgeous as he sounded.

'It's going to be sometime after eight, but I can't give you a definite time in case I'm running late. Is that okay? It's Wisteria Cottage, right?' he asked.

'Yes, it is, eight-ish sounds fine. I shall see you then.'

And that was that: he was gone.

Sam was quite shocked by the erratic feelings she was experiencing since moving here, and now she was getting all girly over some friend of Paul's. It had been several years since Sam had felt desirable. She smiled as she thought of Ace, one of the guys she was writing for in the boy band. All the other guys teased him because he apparently had a thumping crush on Sam. She found this all very sweet and flattering, however, her instincts made her feel motherly towards them all and certainly nothing else. She laughed out loud now as she remembered Suzy's reaction when Sam had told her about Ace.

'*It would do you good to get yourself a toy boy,*' her friend had exclaimed. Suzy pointed out that, in any case, at twenty-eight Ace was hardly a boy but a gorgeous young man.

Gorgeous he might be, thought Sam, but it would be the last thing that either of them needed.

Sam adored Suzy and since moving they spoke each day. In spite of the difficult life she led, Suzy made sure she kept the conversations light, bright and breezy as she sensed her friend's worries and fears.

Chapter 6

By the time Matt came round the following afternoon, Sam had worked herself into a stupor. She anticipated him resorting to his usual behaviour, criticising her, putting her down and turning her into a gibbering wreck.

She had tried distracting herself. She cleaned the cottage, recorded a few ideas and had somehow squeezed in a frantic trip to town to get her food shopping.

She hastily showered and dressed in a new powder pink gypsy skirt and matching vest. Glancing in the mirror, she was satisfied with the way she looked.

Sam watched Matt climb out of his snazzy new sports car. Lucy was going to love riding in that, she thought. He looked as handsome as ever, bouncing with his familiar cocksure strut.

She took a huge breath and opened the door.

'Wow, country life seems to suit you. All your freckles are beginning to join up, you're so brown,' Matt teased. Then he grabbed her and squeezed her tight. 'Whoa, and check out your waistline. Looks like all those wobbly baby bump bits are finally going. You'll be back to your amazing self before too long, I can see.'

Sam escaped his clutches, repulsed by the way he was squeezing her and inspecting her body like a slab of meat. She noticed a faint smell of alcohol which concerned her, knowing he was driving Lucy back to London.

As they walked up the lane, Matt talked nonstop about the new album he was about to work on and how he wanted Sam to get involved in the production side of it. Sam made all the right noises, but she knew deep down that if she was going to build a new life for herself and Lucy here, then she would have to limit her time with Matt. Whatever he thought, she certainly had no intentions of working with him for the foreseeable future.

At school, Sam noticed the other mums gawping at Matt. She could hardly blame them: he was so handsome, and his boyish charm was quite something when he turned it on. She was glad to see Liz and introduced Matt to her. Sam was surprised by how frosty Liz was towards Matt. The atmosphere was quite strained until Lucy came bounding out and ran into Matt's arms.

Lucy dragged him through the playground and in to show him her classroom.

Sam watched them skipping hand in hand and she felt a huge lump creep up into her throat. Sensing her sadness, Liz squeezed her arm.

'You ok?' Liz asked.

'Yes, thanks. Just forgot how wonderful he can be with her.'

'Well, I'm sure we'd all be perfect parents if we only saw our children once a week,' Liz said pointedly.

Sam was shocked by what Liz had said. Mrs Holland was waving her over, asking for a quick word.

'Miss Tate, Lucy told us all that you write songs?' she asked.

'Oh, has she? Right, yes I do.' Sam's heart sank to her toes; she had an idea what was coming next.

'Well I was wondering, I don't suppose you could pop in one day and perhaps join in a little music with the children? I know it would mean so much to them.'

'I'll see what I can do, Mrs Holland, but it won't be for a while I'm afraid. We have only just moved here, and I have so much to sort out.'

'Of course, whenever you feel ready would be wonderful, just let me know.'

Sam felt terrible; she knew she hadn't come across as particularly positive.

Sam walked up to the notice board, feigning interest. Her eyes were drawn to Matt and Lucy, who were now playing hopscotch together in the playground. Their easy relationship was something else that haunted Sam's thoughts. How could another man have such a natural relationship with her daughter? Would another man play hopscotch and skip like a girl with Lucy? Risking the chance to make an absolute fool of himself, like her daddy would?

Most of the other mums eyed the pair curiously and smiled, but Liz just looked disapproving. Sam felt her new friend was definitely out of sorts when it came to Matt.

The three of them walked home, and Matt carried Lucy on his shoulders whist she taught them both a new song she had learnt at school that day. Sam managed to keep up the happy façade.

Matt asked to stay for a quick cup of coffee, much to Lucy's frustration. She sat on her little suitcase by the front door, huffing and puffing about being bored and ready to go. Sam pretended to find it funny but was relieved when they went, as she felt it all a strain.

Seconds later, there was a knock on the door. Sam opened it to find Liz looking sheepish outside.

'Sorry, I was rude,' she blurted out.

'Yes, you were. Very.' Sam smiled. 'Have you been lurking around in my bushes waiting for Matt and Lucy to leave?'

'Sort of,' Liz said, brushing down her clothes while squirming with embarrassment.

'Well it's obviously important to you, so you had better come in,' Sam said, standing back to let Liz past.

Sam made a pot of tea, trying not to laugh. Liz looked ridiculously guilty and had some sort of twig or a leaf sticking out of her hair, left over from her hiding place.

'I am so sorry about that, Sam. I really was bang out of order.'

'Luckily for you, Matt has rhinoceros skin when it comes to disapproval. He genuinely believes that any woman who doesn't adore him is either gay or has anger issues,' Sam reassured.

'Wonder which one he would have placed me in.' Liz groaned in embarrassment. 'Look, Sam, anyway I can only apologise. I think I was channelling a lot of anger at your ex.' Liz looked up to see Sam staring out across the green. 'Oh Sam, only a few days I've known you and I've already managed to upset you.'

Sam turned around and burst out laughing.

'Please don't be sorry. To be honest, I find it rather refreshing to meet someone who wears their heart on their sleeve. You remind me of Suzy.'

Liz looked relieved and took a deep breath, astonished that she hadn't blown her new friendship.

'I just can't believe how amazing you are, how forgiving.'

Sam dragged her fingers through her red-blonde hair. She was finding it all a bit intense. Without speaking, Liz reached across the table and squeezed Sam's hand.

'Has there been anyone else for you, if you don't mind my asking?'

'No. No, I don't mind you asking, and no, there hasn't been anyone else for me. I am not sure I would know how to have... well, a relationship. Once I'd given birth to Lucy, Matt seemed to look upon me as just a mummy. I was no longer a woman to him. Apparently for some men it's quite normal.'

'I know what you mean, Paul and I went through that for a while. It was horrible, I felt so rejected.'

'Well you appear to have sorted it out now,' Sam said, smiling.

'Not without couples' therapy and an awful lot of weekends away. It worked out well, because Paul's parents could have the children and spoil them rotten and we got to have the best sex in years.' Blushing, Sam flinched.

'Oops, sorry. Too much info. Sorry, you must really think me bonkers. I'm hiding in the bushes, stalking you one minute, attacking your ex the next, and then I'm telling you all about my sex life. I wish I could say I'm not usually this upfront, but it would be a lie.'

'Not at all... I think you're hilarious. Right, c'mon, do you fancy a slice of carrot cake and a fresh cup of tea? Mum brought it round earlier.'

'Ooh, yes please. I like your mum. She's really mumsy, isn't she?' Liz smiled.

'Yeah she is. I'd be lost without her, well, Mum and Dad to be honest. Since finding out about the breakup, they have been nothing but supportive.'

They sat in silence for a few moments savouring the carrot cake, and then Liz asked Sam, 'Are you working tonight?'

'No, I have your friend Dominic coming round to take a look at the loft.'

'Ooh, lucky old you,' Liz said, folding her arms as if giving herself a hug. 'I forgot to tell you how drop dead gorgeous he is.'

Sam laughed and felt the butterflies from the night before returning. She tried to calm down and told Liz, 'After being with someone as handsome as Matt, I don't really go in for all that good-looking charmer type… although I do think your Paul is very handsome,' she added cheekily.

'Oh, you haven't met delectable Dom. He'd even outshine Brad Pitt or George Clooney.'

'Yeah, right.'

'Oh dear, Sam, you have no idea,' said Liz in a somewhat superior tone, before she reached over and patted her friend's cheek in the most patronising manner. 'Prepare yourself. Sleep deprivation here you come.'

Sam shook her head but couldn't stop giggling. She knew that Liz was being mischievous and silly, however, she decided a little makeup couldn't hurt, and instead of putting her hair up she allowed it to hang loose in a beautiful shaggy mane down her back. She was pleasantly surprised with her appearance when she checked herself in the mirror, just before opening the door to delectable Dom.

Delectable was one word, but utterly mind blowing would fit better. Sam tried to get herself together to invite him in but she almost choked on her greeting, making her cough and splutter. Her cheeks were burning up. She noticed he must be over six foot tall; he was lean, yet muscular; he had short dark hair, and the sexiest darkest brown eyes she had ever seen.

Sam decided that Matt wasn't quite so handsome after all, and that Liz may have been right.

Even Dominic's clothes looked right. He wore a pair of jeans he obviously worked in, and she could see little sneaks of brown hairy legs peering out through the holes in the knees. His crisp white t-shirt was fitted and revealed a muscular torso. His huge, masculine boots, and even the pencil stuck behind his ear, were making her all hot and bothered.

Matt's face was boyish and good looking, but Dominic's was all rugged, male and quite intimidating. Sam realised that other than saying hello she had said nothing else, and it seemed an eternity had passed.

'Um, would you like to come in?' Sam asked, scarlet in the face.

He stepped inside and started unlacing his boots. She watched his big, strong hands set to work. As he took the boots off, he revealed thick masculine walking socks. Sam's mind was spinning now.

Sam led Dominic upstairs and tried to sound as calm and as grown up as possible, but she found herself rambling on about the weather and Dominic hardly got a word in. He made the cottage feel a little claustrophobic… or was that just her hormones, she wondered?

Once he had established what Sam wanted him to do, he started measuring walls and making notes.

Dominic kept referring back to the architect's drawings of the attic conversion, and Sam suddenly felt quite in the way.

'Can I get you a cup of coffee, or would you prefer a glass of wine or a beer, Dominic?'

She tried to act casual, in the hope that she sounded more like the thirty-five-year-old woman she was, and not like some besotted teenager. *Talk about scare the poor man away before he even starts working for you!*

'Beer would be good, thanks,' he said in that deep, sexy drawl.

He asked to take a look at her current studio so that he could measure up all the recording equipment, and just for a second Sam hesitated as she opened the door, dreading that once he saw the gold disks, he would judge her as some egocentric self-obsessed woman.

For years Sam had shied away from letting anyone into her personal space. She feared they would dig around, desperate to find any intimate details of the artists she had worked with. She was quite surprised to find that Dominic didn't seem remotely interested in her working life, if indeed he even noticed.

Dominic met Sam back downstairs, over an hour later. She offered him another beer, but he refused.

'Thanks, but I need a clear head.' He paused and smiled. 'I need to go and look at another job, so I'll get the quotes back to you as soon as possible.'

She let him out and hugged her arms close to her chest, smiling. Sleep was a long time coming. Her poor mind kept racing over and over, with Dominic featuring continually in her thoughts.

Chapter 7

By the time Matt dropped Lucy off on Sunday morning, Sam had managed to calm down, but only just. She'd convinced herself that her reaction to Dominic on Friday night had just been a blip. Too much country air, or something like that.

It had only been forty three hours since she had seen Lucy, but Sam thought she had changed so much. She looked grown up somehow.

Lucy was delighted to be back with her mother and keen to show off her jewellery, handbag and new clothes. Sam made all the right noises while thinking to herself that it was all highly inappropriate. She kept this to herself as it wasn't Lucy's fault, it was Matt's. It materialised that Matt had had to work, so Jasmine had taken Lucy shopping in the West End.

Sam couldn't decide what annoyed her more: the shopping spree or the fact that Matt had chosen to work whilst having Lucy.

He's only got her for the weekend! she thought.

Her mobile rang and Liz's cheery voice sounded out on the other end.

'Hey, where are you?' she called out.

'Hi Liz, at home. We're about to go over to my parents, we're having lunch.'

'What time are you there 'til?'

'Oh I guess around five, why?'

'We thought we'd exploit the barbecue whilst this gorgeous weather lasts. Why don't you and Lucy pop by afterwards?'

'Ah, thanks for the invite, Liz, Lucy needs an early night. But I hope you guys enjoy yourselves.'

'Okay, but shout if you change your mind.'

Sam couldn't work out what had surprised her more: the fact that Liz hadn't asked about Dominic or that she was disappointed Liz hadn't. Either way, the conversation unsettled her. She knew that her mischievous new friend was up to something. There was no way on earth Liz would miss an opportunity like that.

By the time Sam and Lucy left her parents, they were exhausted. Lucy and Sooty had run around the garden all afternoon and they had been persuaded to stay for tea. Mary had bathed Lucy and had got her all ready in her pyjamas so that she could get straight into bed and snuggle down for her story.

Sam loved story time because no matter what had gone on in the day and no matter how challenging Lucy had been, especially since her weekend in London, the minute they were snuggled up, her thumb would go in and she would twiddle her mummy's hair. She would be Sam's little angel once again.

Once the story had reached its happy ending, Sam turned the night light on and made to leave. Lucy called out, 'Mummy?'

'Yes, my angel?' whispered Sam.

'I had fun at Daddy's, but next time can you come too?'

Sam swallowed the huge lump in her throat.

'Oh, my angel. I'm sorry, but it's not really that simple. Darling, do you remember I explained to you before we moved here?

Mummy and Daddy care about each other very much, but we will not be living together anymore, will we?'

'Then can I just go for one sleepover next time, please? Because I miss you too much.'

Sam stroked Lucy's hair, wondering what to say next.

'We will talk to Daddy about all of this my darling, okay?'

Sam felt awful. Matt would find this hard to take, and no doubt blame her. Sam knew she needed to speak to him about the shopping spree and that it couldn't be put off, so she took a deep breath and called his mobile.

'Hi, Sam,' Matt answered.

'Hi, can you talk?' Sam asked.

'Sure. What's up?'

'Matt, look… I really don't want to sound a bore, but Lucy must have come home with around five hundred pounds worth of clothes and shoes and things after her weekend with you guys. I'm trying desperately hard to make Lucy aware of the value of stuff and…'

He didn't let her finish.

'Oh, lighten up Sam. The kid's only four.'

'It doesn't matter that she's only four, Matt, she needs to have it taught to her now.'

'Look,' said Matt, getting irritable now. 'I can afford it, so why shouldn't she get spoilt? You're more loaded than I am. You could buy her a vineyard in the South of France if you wanted to.'

Sam thought that Matt was being ridiculous.

'And what sort of message would that give her?' she challenged.

'You get to have Luce all week, so don't begrudge me spoiling her for the few hours that I do get to see her at the weekend.'

'But it wasn't you who took her shopping Matt, was it? It was Jasmine.'

'Ah, so now we're getting to the truth. It's Jazz you have a problem with.'

'Oh, Matt, you're not listening. I do not have a problem with Jasmine. I do have a problem with my daughter coming home dressed as though she's about to enter a tacky beauty pageant, wearing make-up and laden down with hundreds of pounds worth of clothes.'

'I don't believe it. My first weekend having her and already you're trying to ruin it. Don't you think you've already taken enough from me, Sam?' he shouted.

'I've taken nothing. I left you the house, the car, the studio. I'm starting all over again with my own savings, so please don't try to make out you're the loser in all this,' she argued.

'I meant Lucy,' Matt said slowly. 'You took my daughter from me, Sam. How do you think that has made me feel?'

Sam was shaking. Matt's words were like a dagger to the heart. She had never felt so guilty, anger reared its ugly head.

'Oh, right, and you expected me to remain living in a city I hated, with a man who no longer wanted me, and who treated me as no better than a pair of old slippers he could squeeze into when nothing else felt comfortable. Hey, and let's not forget the best part, Matt, allowing your mistress to stay over in our studio whenever you wished?'

'You know Jazz and I only got it together once you made it perfectly clear you didn't want me anymore. To tell the truth, Sam, you didn't pay me the blindest bit of attention once Lucy came along, did you?' He had the audacity to sound hurt.

'Lucy is a child. You are an adult. I'd have thought you could cope with having to share my affection.'

Sam was getting very tired now and drained by the encounter, but Matt continued with one criticism after another. One thing Sam did know about her ex was that he would never back down, not whilst there was still air in his lungs. She decided enough was enough.

'Look, Matt, sorry to be rude but there's someone at my door,' she lied. 'Let's finish this later.' Sam managed to cut the call short whilst he was still mid-rant.

Lucy was having an awful night's sleep, and when Sam went into her room for the fourth time she discovered that the poor little thing had wet the bed, something she hadn't done in a long time. Sam gently bathed her, wrapped her up in clean pyjamas and tucked her into her own bed. By the time she had finished stripping Lucy's bed and had returned to her own, she discovered the little girl fast asleep. Lucy looked so tiny and vulnerable lying there that, not for the first time, Sam cursed Matt.

Lucy seemed much more settled by the following morning. The bed wetting incident was put out of her mind. All her chatter was about going to school and seeing Faye. They had breakfast together, and then met Liz and the children on the common. It was another glorious morning, and once they had dropped the children off, they decided to pop to the Enchanted Cafe for a coffee and a Danish pastry.

Sam listened and laughed as Liz told her all about the highs and lows of the barbecue. She regretted not going, as it sounded lots of fun.

'So, have you forgiven me yet?' Liz teased.

'What for?' Sam said, munching on the pastry.

'For being off with your ex.'

'Oh, to be honest with you, I think you managed to hit a couple of raw nerves. Anyway, it's had me doing a lot of soul searching over the weekend,' Sam explained.

'Are you sure it wasn't delectable Dom who got you peeling back the layers? So come on, out with it, Sam; this is driving me nuts. Did he get you all hot and bothered?'

'I'm amazed you have haven't asked before,' replied Sam, smiling.

'Oh look, it's your mum. We can't talk about him now.'

'Yeah I text her and asked her to meet us,' Sam said.

Mary waved as she came in and joined them. Sam smiled; Liz was just hilarious and she adored her. She had come to realise that Liz was indeed a special friend. It seemed that they were having a significant effect on one another.

Morning coffee stretched to early lunch, and by the time Sam got home it was almost one o'clock.

As Sam arrived at school, she noticed Sue talking to a couple of others.

'Hello Sam, how are you?' Sue came cautiously over. 'We've just been organising a splash party for the children after school tomorrow. We thought we would make the most of this beautiful weather. I would love for you and Lucy to come along; Liz and the kids are coming. But I understand if you would rather not, I just didn't want to leave you and Lucy out,' Sue asked.

Sam could see how nervous Sue was. Again, she felt bad that she had been so offhand the other day and said that they would love to come to the splash party. Besides, Lucy really needed to meet other children in the village and make new friends.

'Thank you for asking us. Do you want me to bring anything?'

'Just bring your cosies and a bottle of plonk; I'm going to do the food. Oh, and please can you bring a towel? I never seem to have enough to go around.' Sue looked so genuinely delighted that Sam had agreed to come that it made Sam feel even worse.

'Where do you live, Sue?' Sam asked.

'We live at Greyfriars – you can't miss it, it's at the top end of the common.' Sue announced the name of her house with such pride. Sam wasn't at all surprised, however, as Greyfriars really was a spectacular looking house.

Sam continued working whilst she waited for Dominic. Her dad had called him earlier to ask him to help set up her new lights around the arches. She needed the lights running along the path now that the nights were drawing in. John was going to set them up for her, but he had pulled a muscle in his back and so had gone ahead and asked Dominic, unaware of the effect he had on his daughter.

She heard his truck pull up and composed herself.

'Hey Sam,' he said.

He just gets more handsome, Sam thought, her heart racing.

Sam's choice of lighting was spectacular. Metres of LEDs, falling like a curtain to create a tunnel lit by a thousand stars. She'd bought the several wrought iron arches to attach them to and had paid extra for the garden centre to fit them along the path.

She took him up to the beach hut. There were a couple of sockets that weren't working and she blushed, realising it was all a little childlike. Dominic sensed her embarrassment.

'I bet your daughter loves it here, it's so cool,' he said kindly.

'She does, but I guess I pretty much monopolise the space.' Sam noticed him staring at the paper littered all over the floor. Lyrics, notes, scribbles and random sketches, revealing the voyage that each and every song must travel on.

'Did you want me to run the lights up to the veranda?' he asked.

'Ooh, yes please. Will they reflect on the river?' she asked, blushing yet again.

'Yeah, they should do.'

'Thank you so much Dominic, I know you're busy. Would you like a coffee?' Sam asked.

'No thanks, I need to get some supplies.'

They walked in silence and as they got to the door Dominic stopped, as though he wanted to say something. Forgetting to breath, Sam was lightheaded. Making direct eye contact, he searched for the words. *Oh wow, here goes, he's going to ask to take me out.* Sam was afraid she would pass out.

'Um. Sam?' He said frowning.

'Yes.' *Here goes, here goes.*

'Did you want chrome sockets? I can't remember what we agreed.'

Sam blushed puce. Terrified he would read her mind, she quickly pretended to check her phone.

'Ah, yes, chrome, thank you Dominic , ooh let me, um, ooh I need to get this,' she lied.

'No worries, see you later Sam.' And he was gone.

Chapter 8

Sam was still cringing an hour later. She had a restless day and was not in the mood for work this evening, so she asked Liz if she'd like to pop over for a glass of wine once the children had gone to bed.

At eight thirty, Liz arrived.

'Wow, you look gorgeous. How come you're so organised? I've only just managed to get Lucy down.'

'I threatened to sell them on eBay, it always works.'

Sam giggled. 'You're funny, you do know that, don't you? Come on in. By the way, I got the quote from Dominic and I've decided to go ahead.'

'I knew it!' squealed Liz. Sam looked puzzled.

'Knew what?' she asked. Liz looked at her watch with glee.

'Fifteen minutes and I won. I bet Paul that you would mention Dom within the first half hour. Paul said that not everyone was as sad and depraved as me, but yes, yes! I won.' Liz punched the air to celebrate her victory.

'I said I received his quote,' reminded Sam. 'I shouldn't read too much into that if I were you, you're bound to be disappointed.'

'So why did you go scarlet when you said it, then?' Liz mocked. 'Oh Sam, don't look so worried. I may be a chatterbox, but you'll never find a more loyal friend. So, lust away in private for all I care, my friend, he is gorgeous and so are you. Wow, just think what beautiful children you two would have.'

'Oh, wow,' cried Sam. 'Your imagination is something else! I think it's time I opened the wine.'

Sam put some music on and went into the kitchen. She smiled as she listened to Liz singing tunelessly along with the popular track. She could feel the little fizzy bubbles bursting inside her; all this laughter was doing her the world of good. Since having Lucy, she seemed to have lost her sense of humour completely. She wasn't blaming Lucy for this, as it had nothing to do with her and it was more about Matt.

Liz's awful singing was getting louder so, worried that she would wake Lucy, Sam hurried through to the lounge with the wine, a couple of glasses and some nibbles, hoping this offering would calm her down.

'I hate to admit it, but you're right,' Sam said, raising a chilled glass to her lips.

'Of course I'm right, I'm always right, but what about this time?' Liz said, smiling smugly.

'I can't stop seeing his face. I'm finding it almost impossible to concentrate on anything. Pathetic, aren't I?'

'Not at all, I find it rather sweet. Do you want me to put in a good word for you?' Liz suggested, with a wicked glint in her eye.

'No!' Sam wailed.

'Well, as long as you're sure. Dominic's a hard nut to crack. When is he starting the work?'

'I'm not sure. He called by earlier and set up all my lights, Dad asked him. The quote for the attic looks reasonable, and he thinks he will get it done in the next couple of weeks which will be perfect. Are you sure there's nothing wrong with him?' Sam hadn't intended on asking that last question, but spoke before she thought it through, making Liz burst out laughing.

'Right, so he's gorgeous and single, therefore he must be either gay or weird, right?' Liz feigned insult.

'No, it's not that, no. That sounded awful, it's just… I don't get it, I mean he's something else, *and* he's single.'

'Okay Sam, I'm gonna give you the Dominic talk, but I'm warning you, if you had the hots for him before, well, this'll give you the hots with bells on.'

'Oh dear, do I really want to hear this? I guess I was hoping you would put me off him. I really don't need any distractions right now, and he is so damned distracting.'

'Yeah, tell me about it.' Liz drained her glass dramatically. 'Okay, so the brief story is that Dominic and his brother Luke – and yes, he is just as hot as Dom – anyway, some years ago, they both went off and joined the army. Well, I don't think it was the army, but it was one of those military jobs. Anyway, Dominic had been posted out in Afghanistan when his father had a massive stroke. Dominic was offered compassionate leave to begin with, but his father's condition was a lot worse than they'd first suspected, and so he needed long term care. Anyway, Dominic left the military and came here to take care of his dad.'

'But what about his mother? Why couldn't he have got carers in?'

'Oh no, his mother left when the boys were at boarding school. Dom was nine and Luke seven.'

'Boarding school at seven? Poor little lambs,' Sam said, genuinely appalled.

'Tell me about it. Anyway, their dad was in the army, well the military, way high up, some sort of officer… no, he was an admiral. Anyway, so he was posted all over the world. That was his excuse not to have them, and their mum was lovely, but fragile by all accounts. Paul said that Dom and Luke shut down from their first day at school.'

'So, in spite of being abandoned at boarding school, he then gave up his own career to nurse his father?' Sam groaned.

'Yeah, Dom knew that his dad was way too proud to be taken care of by nurses and carers. He knew it would kill his father off to have someone wash him and care for him, so he did the honourable thing and took care of him by himself.'

'But what about his brother?' wondered Sam. 'Why couldn't they have shared the load?'

'Dom's the eldest. Only by a couple of years, but it seems there was no way he was going to let his baby brother forgo his career to save his own.'

'Liz, that's awful. Does he still care for his father?'

'No, Mr O'Donnell died last year. Dominic is thirty-seven now and has pretty much missed his chance. He was such a good army bloke, or whatever it was he was in, got lots of medals and things. Paul knows a lot more because he and Dom have known each other since they were little squirts.'

Sam felt so sorry for Dominic that she could feel the tears welling up. She busied herself pouring more wine, but Liz noticed her expression.

'See, I warned you that you'd go all gooey, look at you.'

'Oh, but Liz, it's so sad.'

'Yes, it is,' sighed Liz. 'I think, like you, Dom's a survivor. He knew he had to stay here and sort things out. His father made him promise not to sell the house as it was handed down through the family from way back. Unfortunately, there were a few debts to pay off, so Dom had to work his butt off to clear them. Then there were loads of renovations to do on the house. It was in pretty dire straits.'

'So, where is the house?' Sam asked.

'It's the Manor.'

'Ooh, the Manor, now that's a beautiful place.' Sam had often admired it on her many walks around the village. It was a huge Georgian house, and certainly looked amazing from the outside.

'Yeah, and you should see the inside. He had Paul and I round for dinner a few weeks back because he'd finally finished the downstairs and oh, Sam, you should see it, it's amazing. Although I often think that Dom would be happier in a tree house, he doesn't really go in for grandeur.'

Sam laughed at Liz's turn of phrase.

'Do you think he will sell it?' Sam wondered.

'Not sure, it's Luke's and his, but to be honest he's so into that honour thing that he will probably keep it. Could be a great family home if he ever gets married and has kids.'

'Has he ever gotten close to getting married?' Curiosity was getting the better of Sam.

'Yes, he was engaged to his long-term girlfriend Susannah, but she did a bunk once the admiral got ill. I think she liked the idea of living with some highly decorated officer, but not some carpenter who had to care for his sick papa.'

'Gosh, I'm surprised he's not bitter.'

'Oh, he's too emotionally switched off to hold a grudge. However, he sure as hell put a few walls up after that.'

'Hmm, I can imagine. So where did the girlfriend go?' Sam enquired.

'No idea. Look, I may be married, but delectable Dom gets me all hot and bothered. A few years back I developed such a crush on him that I use to fantasise Paul was him. Even called Paul Dom once, you know when we. Anyway... I mean, how awful is that!'

'Liz, that's terrible. Poor old Paul, did he freak out?' Sam asked, quite appalled.

'No. He only went and told Dominic about it. Guess it was the only way to deal with it.'

'Oh, that's hilarious. How did Dominic take it?'

'He found it all highly embarrassing at first. Then of course the two of them teased me relentlessly, but it kind of worked I guess. I see him as a member of the family now, albeit in a drop-dead-gorgeous-cousin kind of way.'

Sam shook her head. 'Oh, you do make me laugh... Right, change of subject. I definitely need a change of subject.'

'Lucy?' Liz said.

'Lucy, yes Lucy. Well, if I'm honest, she seems a little unsettled. I had hoped she would be able to breeze through most of this, but she clearly hasn't. She told me tonight that she isn't keen to stay at Daddy's for more than one night unless I go, too. Matt'll be furious, but to be honest he's to blame. Do you know, Liz, he worked most of the weekend whilst she was there? Don't get me wrong,

Jazz is nice, but she's not brilliant with children. She'd be better if Lucy was a teenager or a chihuahua.'

'Oh, the poor little lamb,' Liz said, not knowing whether to be amused or furious on Sam's behalf.

After a moment's reflection, Sam turned to Liz and said, 'It's strange, you know. I am such a private person. I never usually discuss my personal life with anyone except my friend Suzy, and yet here I am spilling my guts to someone I've only known for a few days.'

'To be fair, Sam, I am quite an exceptional person.' They both laughed at this latest revelation of Liz's. 'Look, we all need to talk. If you hold all this inside, you'll become emotionally constipated. Besides, to be fair, I have bombarded you with questions. This is all new and raw, and I'm a firm believer that if you leave stuff like this to fester it can do you a great deal of harm.'

Liz took a deep breath and reached for her glass of wine.

Sam smiled; she loved the way Liz seldom came up for air, ranting along and merging one rambling sentence after another.

'Emotionally constipated?' Sam repeated. The two friends giggled. 'You have a great way with words. I think I'm going to use that line in a song, you know,' Sam said.

'Ooh, does that mean I will get one of those shiny disks you have? And will I get those royal things you were talking about?'

'Royalties,' Sam corrected, laughing at her friend.

'Are you taking your swimming costume to Sue's tomorrow?' Liz asked suddenly.

That was another thing Sam loved about Liz. Her ability to completely about turn in the middle of a conversation. She was like one of those bouncy balls you throw, having no idea where it would end up. With friends like this, there was never a dull moment.

'No, but I'm taking Lucy's. She's really looking forward to it, so I need to make an effort. She missed out on a lot in London because I was so anti-social.' Sam hung her head.

'I find that hard to believe, especially in your business. Why the big change?' Liz asked and poured them both another glass of wine.

'I don't think I had any idea just how miserable I was in London. Since moving here I've felt nervous and excited, but so happy all the time, and even if I'm having a bad moment, I just look out of the window at the view. How can you not feel happy and refreshed looking at that?'

Sam nodded to the window and Liz glanced outside and smiled. She, too, felt blessed living in this perfect village.

'Did you ever ask Matt to move away?' Liz asked.

'All the time, but Matt loves London for all the reasons I hated it, so we stayed put.'

'Oh what a surprise,' exclaimed Liz. 'So, he got to live his dream whilst you lived the nightmare, what a gent!' Liz downed her glass of wine in temper.

'You really aren't keen on Matt, are you?' Sam asked, staring at her friend.

'No, I'm not. I think he stands for a lot that's wrong with people. He's running as fast as he can on his own treadmill, he's locked inside his own little selfish cocoon, pretending to sacrifice his time working for his family. He's just another selfish fool who would rather do what he wants than build secure foundations for his family. I'm not talking just financially, either. Anyway, I think his head is so far up his backside that he must stink of it.' Liz put her hand to her mouth, sure she'd overstepped the mark.

'Oops. Sam, I think I've drunk too much, are you cross with me?'

Sam shrugged. 'No.'

Sam sat silent. She had taken in all that Liz had just said. She wasn't sure whether she agreed or disagreed, but one thing was certain: Liz had a knack of drawing Sam's attention to Matt's faults, and she was becoming disturbingly aware of just how many he really had.

Chapter 9

The following day was Sue's splash party. While Lucy and the other children found plenty to do, Sam found herself sat with the other mums in a constant state of hysterics. Sue and her friends really were a scream. Sam discovered that all this laughter was working wonders for her stomach muscles.

Combining laughter with all the walking was great therapy, and she was doing well.

'Ooh, before I forget, we are throwing Tessa a baby shower on Friday night and I've got some hilarious games planned. I don't suppose you two can make it, can you?' Sue said, looking from Sam to Liz whilst all the others chatted excitedly about the event.

'I'll need to sort a sitter for Lucy, so can I get back to you?' Sam said.

'Yeah I'll need to check out Paul's plans, too,' Liz said, then they all became aware of another conversation taking place.

'Wow, wasn't it weird?' Shannon asked Dee.

'No, it was fabulous for a while. I haven't had a proper snog like that in months.'

'Dee pulled a twenty-eight-year-old,' Shannon pointed out to the rest of them, before eagerly turning back to Dee.

'I would like to say that my husband left me a couple of months ago,' Dee added quickly, looking to Sam. Sam worried that her face had given off a wrong reaction, so she said how sorry she was to hear it.

'Oh, not at all, Sam, it's the best thing that could have happened to me.'

'So, are you seeing him again?' Sue asked. Dee quickly continued to tell the tale.

'No, I don't think it would be a good idea. He's awfully sweet but I really don't want to get caught up in anything heavy. Besides, he may have looked fab, but his conversation wasn't that great.'

'What about the guy you met on the internet? I thought you were keen to meet up with him again,' Em asked now.

'Ooh, now he really was gorgeous,' Dee said, smiling.

'So, what happened?' Shannon asked.

'I'm afraid, ladies, he had a weird affliction. Every now and then he did this strange shaking thing with his head and made an odd growling noise when he did it, like this.' Dee demonstrated the bizarre act and everybody roared with laughter.

'Surely you're not going to hold that against him, are you, I mean if he really is that gorgeous?' Sue asked, appalled.

'Trust me, ladies, I was most disappointed. When he kissed me, he did it again. He shook my head so hard I felt like Bertie when he catches a rabbit and shakes it to death. Had whiplash for days.'

'Bertie is Dee's Jack Russell,' Liz kindly explained to Sam.

'It was weird having someone else's tongue in your mouth, y'know, not your husband's,' Dee said.

'Well, if Tom put his tongue in my mouth, I'd jolly well bite it off, I can tell you,' Sue announced, sending everyone into hysterics yet again.

'Oh no! That's awful, poor Tom. Surely you guys still kiss, don't you?' Pauline asked.

'Of course we do, but I never got on with that French kissing, it always made me feel queasy. I'll never forget years ago, Justin Bradshaw laid on top of me and put his tongue in my mouth for a kiss. A load of his saliva dribbled straight into my mouth, and I didn't want to offend him so I swallowed the lot. It was disgusting. Traumatised me for years.'

Everyone squealed and screamed, making the children stop what they were doing for a second.

Sam collapsed back in her chair. She could not believe how hilarious Sue and her friends were and how starved of fun she had been. Sam started to daydream. In London, most of the friends that she and Matt knew had been very obsessed with music, and evenings were spent discussing the music scene and films and the industry in general. Apart from Suzy, no one else seemed to know how to have simple fun. Sadly, Suzy's PTSD kept her housebound most of the time. Sam had got to see her less and less. Matt's idea of humour had always involved anecdotes of the rich and famous celebrities he had worked with, and oh dear, they had become deadly boring after a while.

'You okay?' Liz asked, concerned.

'Yeah, I'm really enjoying myself Liz, can you believe that!'

'Told you you would, didn't I?' Liz cried.

'What about Lorenzo?' Pauline asked.

'Who's Lorenzo?' Liz asked.

'He's Dee's personal trainer at the Georgian,' Sue explained.

'Personal trainer, *please*, she only goes to lust after his bulging biceps, don't you darling?' Pauline teased.

'Well, I do enjoy the spa also. Besides, I think it's helping with my depression,' Dee said.

'She doesn't even have depression. She only became a member of the club because of Lorenzo,' Pauline told them all.

'Does he know you have a soft spot for him?' Sue asked.

'Wouldn't do any good. He's got a girlfriend,' Dee said dramatically.

'What's his girlfriend like?' Pauline asked.

'Stunning.' Dee was unable to hide her disappointment.

'Oh dear, guess it's time you leave then,' Sue, practical as ever, suggested.

'Good heavens, I'd never make it through the week without the Georgian.' Dee was appalled at the suggestion.

'But you'd save a lot of money, you could join the recreation centre, it's only ten pounds a month.' Sue made another helpful suggestion.

'Exactly. And why, oh why, my dear Susan, do you think that is?' Dee said, making everyone laugh.

'Well, it's good enough for the rest of us.' Sue looked cross now.

'Be that as it may, my friend, but it is not good enough for me, I'm afraid. Besides it doesn't have a pool or jacuzzi and it isn't situated in the most breath-taking location where my mindful meditation is at its most vibrant.' Dee tried to justify herself now. Everyone was laughing.

'It's extravagant, Dee, and it isn't as though you use it very often. Personally, I much prefer the recreation centre,' Sue lied.

'It is not extravagant, it's about three pounds a day.' Dee snapped.

'Well, I think you would be better off coming with me to the recreation centre,' Sue snapped back.

'Ah okay, so I was going to invite you for a spa day again next week as I have my new guest passes, but clearly you'd rather not come.' Dee was smiling now, and so was everyone else.

'Don't be ridiculous, of course I will come.' Sue snapped.

Dee turned to Pauline and high-fived her.

'Knew it!' she laughed.

The following morning Sam woke with an almighty hangover. Her head was splitting from the wine and her stomach muscles were so tender from all the laughter. Sam felt glad that she had given Sue and her gang a second chance; they were actually a good bunch of women after all.

When Sam and Liz had gathered the children to go, Sue had sheepishly put a bottle of wine in Sam's hand and said, 'Please take this, Sam, as a welcome gift and a peace offering for my appalling behaviour last week.'

Sam threw her arms around Sue and gave her a huge hug, then giggled all the way home.

The rest of the week panned out in a peaceful haze. The weather was still beautiful, but there was an autumnal feel and a definite drop in the temperature. Lucy had finally got into a steady sleep pattern and now woke up around seven thirty, happy to watch a couple of cartoons before trying to rush Sam out the door to school.

Working in Wisteria Cottage was far more productive than anywhere else Sam had lived or worked. She found her life, too, was developing a pattern. After dropping Lucy at school each morning and walking home, she would make a pot of tea, have some toast and read the paper. She would then work until three in the beach hut, breaking only for a quick lunch.

By Friday, Sam decided to go to Tessa's baby shower and Mary and John were only too happy to babysit. She had managed to finish two songs and had arranged for Dominic to start first thing on the studio. Matt was coming to collect Lucy in the morning, so hopefully Dominic would be well underway by the time he arrived, as Sam didn't feel good about Matt meeting him.

When Liz arrived, Wisteria Cottage was like a mad house. Lucy was jumping up and down on the sofa, John was shouting at Sooty, who was barking excitedly and trying to pounce on Lucy, Mary was noisily attempting to ask Lucy about her day at school, and then the phone started ringing. Mary grabbed it, shouting over the din to Matt. Sam's music was zinging around the cottage. While not quite blaring, it was pretty loud all the same. Liz smiled because it was blissful, happy chaos – something she recognised from her own home – and she knew it was a good sign.

Sam came downstairs; she looked beautiful. Her hair was twisted up with a couple of curls escaping seductively around her face. She wore a fitted long pink dress, which really flattered her, and the denim jacket she wore over it finished the outfit off perfectly. Her mum handed her the phone and whispered, 'It's Matt.'

'Hi Matt,' she said.

'Hey, so I hear you're off out. Blimey Sam, twice in one week – what the hell has got into you, you taking happy pills or something?'

Sam knew that Matt was just joking, but it irritated her all the same. She passed him onto Lucy, planting a kiss on her little head as they were already running late. She then grabbed a bottle of wine off the rack and the little gift she had bought for Tessa's baby shower. The two women started off excitedly across the green. As they walked past The Fox and Hounds they spotted Dominic sitting outside, reading the newspaper with a pint.

'Hey delectable Dom, we can't stop. How's it going?' Liz teased.

Dominic looked up and smiled. He started exchanging familiar banter with Liz. Sam waved to Dom and told him she would see him in the morning. He smiled but said nothing, unnerving her a little.

'Wow, did you see delectable Dom eye you up back there? Talk about lust you all the way up one side and then back down the other!' Liz squealed once they were out of earshot.

'I think you are over exaggerating.' Sam blushed, pleased to have her suspicions confirmed.

'Seriously, I know Dominic, and that was full on serious appreciation he had going on there.' Liz linked Sam's arm in excitement.

'I think you really should consider taking up creative writing, Liz. You really have the knack.' The women laughed, and by the time they reached Sue's front door they could hear screams and whoops coming from the other side.

'Oh,' cried Sam. 'How on earth are the children going to sleep with all that noise?'

'Sue's mum has got them and Tom's away, so…'

Just then the door opened and a very tipsy Sue was standing there, a sugared dummy around her neck and furry rabbit's ears on her head.

'Quick, you two, get in here and calm this bunch of animals down. It's all going crazy.' Sue pulled the women in, and then someone else thrust a glass of wine in their hands.

The scene was one of total mayhem. The blinds were drawn and the music was thumping. Through the glow of lamplight,

Tessa was on her knees, hands tied behind her back, leaning over her huge bump and trying to eat something which looked quite disgusting from a nappy, and there were other women squirting one another with strap on breasts which doubled up as water pistols.

'Oh, let's go get another drink, Sam. We're sure as hell going to need one,' Liz said, leading Sam into the kitchen. Sam was astounded. She had never met a bunch of women like it in her life. She knew their behaviour was inappropriate, but she couldn't help but find them hilarious.

The evening got rowdier and rowdier, but between the outrageous party games and the endless rounds of nibbles and drinks, the women managed to catch up.

'Did you hear that Benji's mum and dad have split up?' Sue announced to the group.

'Oh no, poor little Benji. They only moved here last year, didn't they? What happened?' Izzy asked.

'Well apparently she just disappeared, leaving poor Dave with Benji.'

'Does Dave know where she's gone?' asked Emily.

'Apparently there's a flat somewhere in London and she's meant to be shacked up there.'

'Is there anyone else?' Pauline asked.

'Yes, Beth found some old boyfriend on Facebook and she met up with him again. Then that was it, a month later she was gone.'

Sue held up her hands and looked around the room, genuinely appalled. Sam realised that perhaps Sue's gossip wasn't always malicious or done to shock people. She seemed quite sad for the family, as did everyone else. They really weren't a bad bunch after all, Sam thought.

'So, what's Dave like? I've not met him,' Pauline asked, reaching for another handful of nuts.

'Well that's the mystery,' answered Sue.

'He's a gem of a guy and a bit of a dish, too. In fact, I think he's a really good catch,' Sue said.

'What about the other guy, did you get to see him?' Pauline asked.

'Yes. Funny little man, really. I bumped into them the day she left, packing his car up. Yes... funny little man and he couldn't have been any more different to Dave,' Sue repeated.

'How come?' Liz and Sam asked.

'Well, Dave's handsome and masculine and... well, the funny little man looked like a tree hugger, you know the ones who wear sandals all year round with perfectly clean feet, but crunchy underneath. He had those 'daddy long legs' eyebrows too, and he kept picking his nose and examining his pick as though it were a diamond. Quite disgusting!' Everyone squealed in disgust.

'Oh Sue, I love your descriptions. Ooh, Dee! Maybe you and Dave could get it together,' Pauline said with a mischievous twinkle in her eye.

'Oh no, no way. I've just got rid of one 'has been', I don't want another one thanks, especially someone else's cast off 'has been'. Anyway, I'm going to be celibate for a while,' Dee grinned. Strangely, everyone found this last remark hilarious.

The evening was a huge success; there were plenty of baby gifts for Tessa. The games were fun, if quite bizarre, thought Sam. She was astonished at how many were invented just for baby showers. By the end of the night her head was hazy and her stomach muscles were aching, so she welcomed the cool walk back home to Wisteria Cottage. There were still a few people gathered outside the pub, but Sam noticed Dominic's truck had now gone. She felt a tiny bit disappointed.

Mary and John stayed for a coffee with Sam before making their way home across the cool, lamp lit green, Sooty trotting excitedly beside them. Sam went in to check on Lucy who looked so angelic, curled up with her arm round Winnie the pooh. As soon as Sam's head hit the pillow she too fell into a deep peaceful sleep.

Chapter 10

Lucy woke her mother later than usual the following morning and Sam panicked as she saw the time. It was five to eight and Dominic was due at eight. She scrambled out of bed, threw on some yoga pants, her bra and t-shirt, then quickly scrubbed her teeth and ran downstairs. She could hear his footsteps on the path and then a knock at the door.

'Hi,' he said smiling, looking towards her neckline.

Sam put her hand to her neck. She felt a label sticking out under her chin. She not only had her t-shirt on back to front, but it was inside out too. She blushed scarlet, but he just grinned at her.

'I need to carry the wood in, so is it okay if I wedge the door open?' he asked.

'Yes, of course. Shall I make a coffee? Lucy and I always have a bacon sandwich on a Saturday morning, would you like one as well, Dominic?'

'Yeah, that'd be good, thanks. Is Lucy okay with this door open, Sam?'

'Oh yes, I didn't think. Thanks, I shall have a quick word with her.'

By the time he'd carried the wood and tools upstairs, Sam had made a pot of coffee and a plateful of bacon sandwiches. She assumed that Dominic would want to eat them upstairs and took them up to him but no, he followed her back down, perched on one of the bar stools around the island and started chatting to Lucy.

He asked her what she thought of school and which was her favourite bit of the day. He asked about Sooty, but he didn't ask her about London, and the move, or Matt.

Sam was grateful to him for being so sensitive. Whenever Lucy veered in that direction, Dominic would gently steer her away from it. He had clearly overheard Lucy's protests about her impending trip to her father's, either that or perhaps Liz had said something. Either way, Sam was grateful for his thoughtfulness. The bit she loved the most was that Lucy couldn't quite pronounce his name properly, and instead called him Domnic. She noticed he smiled each time she got it wrong.

The first time she said it, Sam had tried correcting her.

'Darling, its Dom-i-nic, not Domnic.'

'That's what I said, Mummy. Domnic,' Lucy said, and then raised her eyes to Dominic as if to say, "Silly Mummy". Sam and Dominic found this hilarious.

This happy, domestic scene was not helping Sam. She'd made a promise last night to focus on Dominic's faults in a desperate attempt to put herself off him. The problem was the blasted man appeared to have none…

After eating a couple of sandwiches and having his fill of coffee, he went back upstairs to start work. When Sam told Lucy that she needed to get her suitcase ready as Daddy would be here in half an hour, Lucy had other ideas, and much to Sam's amazement she threw herself down on the kitchen floor screaming at the top of her lungs.

'I told you,' Lucy wailed. 'If you don't come, I'm not going.'

Sam attempted to remain calm and in control.

'But darling, you know I can't come too. Mummy doesn't live with Daddy anymore. Lucy, we explained all this to you, didn't we sweetheart?'

'Well I'm not going, and you won't make me, Mummy. Will you please promise me you won't make me go? Daddy can stay here tonight, Mummy. He can, can't he, Mummy?' Sam's heart broke as the little girl stuck her thumb in, sucking frantically and hiccupping at the same time. Poor little angel was in bits.

Sam couldn't seem to get Lucy to change her mind; she had got in such a state that the poor little thing could hardly breathe. Lucy had never behaved like this before and had clearly been affected by the breakup.

She told Lucy to go up to her room so she could have a chat with Matt when he arrived.

He arrived on time for once and took a good look at her.

'Wow, Sam. You look rough. Good night, then?'

Sam realised that she still hadn't put her t-shirt on the right way and wondered just how awful she must look. Matt pushed past her and walked into the lounge.

'So, you got the chippy here, I see. Does he know what he's doing?' he asked, looking up the stairs.

'Matt, please keep your voice down. Of course he knows what he's doing,' Sam said, embarrassed in case Dominic could hear.

'Has he ever worked on a studio before? See, I know what these guys are like, Sam. They can hammer a few nails in and fix stuff, but when it comes to the putting together a studio, well it's a whole new ball game.'

Sam felt her blood boil. 'Matt, thank you, but Dominic has experience in this area. He converted an entire theatre, fitting all the sound equipment and lights. I'm pretty sure he can cope with a small recording studio, don't you?' She realised that she was being quite assertive, something that would irritate Matt.

'I think you'd better pop upstairs and see Lucy, because she is refusing to come with you today. I'm sorry Matt, but I'm not sure she is feeling one hundred percent,' Sam lied.

By the time Matt came back downstairs, he looked so drained and utterly rejected.

'Can I get you a drink?' Sam said gently. 'Maybe if we get her downstairs for a bit she'll perk up and change her mind.'

'No, I really don't have the time, I have a meeting at two,' Matt said briskly. 'Sam, I don't understand. Lucy was fine when I dropped her off last Sunday, what's happened since then?' he asked.

'What are you implying?' Sam folded her arms defensively, not liking where this was heading.

'Well, you were clearly miffed with me for letting Jazz take her shopping. Call it a coincidence Sam, but it just seems a little weird, that's all. Now she doesn't want to come home with me. Why the hell couldn't you have called me before I left?'

'Matt, I suggest you and I have a chat about this later. Lucy might hear us, and I think she has been through enough for one day. If you want, why don't you see if she will come home with you for a few hours at least?' Sam suggested.

'Not a lot of point really,' sighed Matt. 'I'm in a meeting, and then I have a session booked for a few hours. The plan was to meet her and Jasmine for dinner this evening.'

Sam bit her lip; she couldn't believe it. He'd made arrangements to work all afternoon. He clearly had no intentions of putting himself out for Lucy at all. The man was so selfish. Sam took a breath and tried again.

'Okay, how about you collect her in the morning, and she can stay for the day and come home early evening?'

'Yeah, that's a plan, but not too early. I need to finish a mix. I'll probably get up early, Jazz will be at the gym, so maybe about eleven, if that's okay. Unless you can drive her down to us?'

'Sorry, Matt, but I'm still struggling with driving too far, my anxiety…'

Matt burst out laughing.

'Driving too far! It's like twenty odd miles from London. Driving too far. Wow Sam, you clearly do have issues.'

Sam was mortified, Matt was shouting, and she knew that Lucy and Dominic would be able to hear.

Matt looked her up and down with distaste, and with that he stormed off back to London in a huff.

Sam stood for a few minutes trying to calm herself before going up to see Lucy. She was fuming with Matt. How dare he make her feel responsible for Lucy not wanting to go with him? She took a deep breath. In all fairness, Matt was just being himself. The only difference was that he had to make a real effort to see Lucy now they had moved. In London he could pop in and out whenever he fancied it. Sam never went anywhere, so he'd had it easy. Sam realised that she and Lucy had always had to fit in around Matt's schedule.

She went upstairs and found Lucy playing with her dolls in the dollhouse. Sam looked for Ted, the little boy doll, but it wasn't there.

'Sweetheart, where's Ted?' she asked as she knelt beside Lucy.

'I hid him in the wardrobe. I'm pretending he's Jasmine.'

'But why have you hidden Ted? I mean, why are you pretending that Ted is Jasmine and why do you feel you need to hide her?'

Sam sat down beside Lucy and gently stroked her hair.

'Because if Daddy didn't live with Jasmine, then we could all live together again.'

Sam pulled Lucy into her arms and gently rocked her.

'Oh, Lucy, my poor little angel, Jasmine isn't the reason Mummy and Daddy don't live together. Mummy and Daddy have decided that we don't want to live together anymore. Mummy and Daddy love you, Lucy, and we both want you to live with us, but it isn't that simple. Daddy likes living in London and he works there, doesn't he? Now I've wanted you and me to live in a village for so long, Lucy. Look at me, my angel,' Sam asked. 'Do you miss London and our house there?' Sam asked, feeling the tremendous weight in her heart as she dreaded Lucy begging to return there. However, she was pleasantly reassured by the little girl's response.

'No, I don't like the house, Mummy. It is creepy, and there are ghosts,' Lucy said quickly.

'Sweetheart, there are no ghosts in that house. I don't remember it as dark and creepy,' Sam added.

'It wasn't dark when you were there, Mummy, but it is dark now. Daddy and Jasmine keep all the lights off.'

'How about we ask Daddy to leave more lights on for you, if you find it creepy? It's such a big house, I expect it can seem, I don't know, a bit dark I guess.'

Sam was struggling to reassure her daughter, especially as she had never really liked the house either.

'No, Mummy. It scares me, and Jasmine won't let me sleep in with Daddy even if I'm scared. She gets all cross and huffy and puffy, so Daddy says I can't.'

'Listen, my angel. I shall have a word with Daddy, I promise, okay?' Sam looked straight into Lucy's sad eyes. 'Right. Now, how about you and I go across to see Grandma and Grandpa? They'll be surprised to see you, they were only expecting me. I'll just go tell Dominic where we're going then we'll be off.'

Sam told Dominic they were going out, that he was to help himself to tea or coffee and that she would have her phone with her if he needed her.

When they arrived, John took Lucy straight out for a walk with Sooty and Mary made Sam a cup of tea.

'Right, my darling, sit down and drink this. Tell me, what's happened? You look awful and so does Lucy,' she said gently.

'Thanks, Mum, that sure makes me feel better,' Sam muttered. 'To be honest, I'm not sure how much of this is due to Matt, or if it's all down to the self-infliction of Tessa's baby shower.'

'Ah yes, the party. I heard some of them stumbling home around two. You and Liz escaped early. Must have been a hoot, though. So, tell me, what is happening with Lucy and Matt?' Mary asked, concerned.

'Lucy refused to go and stay at Matt's today unless I stayed, too, and I feel awful because I know he thinks it's my fault.'

'Well, I'm sure it makes him feel better each time he blames you for everything. It kind of passes the buck really, doesn't it? I think it's time Matthew took some responsibility for his atrocious behaviour, to be perfectly honest with you... So what is wrong with easing Lucy – and you too Sam, come to think of it – into the new set up for the first few weekends? Lucy could maybe go up for the day, it's not as though London's far, is it?'

'No, I know. I did suggest that he take her home this morning and bring her back later, but he said he was working anyway.'

'Oh, for heaven's sake,' Mary exclaimed. 'Is there no way he can schedule his work around the little time he spends with her?' Mary was clearly angry now.

'Well that's just it really, because Matt has only ever really fitted Lucy in around his work. I guess living and working in the same house was convenient, at least he got to see her.'

'Oh, right, so you're expected to just hang around like a spare part, are you? Putting your entire life on hold in the hope that Matt will grace you with his presence for a few minutes a day? I'll tell you something, Samantha, it's about time you jolly well stand up to that man.'

Sam burst out laughing.

'What's so funny, why are you laughing?' Mary demanded.

'It's just you haven't called me Samantha since I was at school. It just sounded really funny, that's all. Look, Mum, please don't stress over this. Truth is that I have stood up to Matt. I left him.'

Sam was becoming aware of the anger she felt towards Matt. It was like someone had opened an economy-sized can of worms and they just kept wriggling out. Memories of the bad times kept flooding back. She remembered when Lucy had been tiny and was teething; the poor girl had been crying most of the day. Matt dealt with it by cocooning himself inside his soundproofed studio, leaving Sam to cope with it all.

Sam had suffered badly with post-natal depression. She had believed for so long that she was a useless excuse for a mother who could not care for her daughter or please her man. In order to try to inject some light into her life, she had tried to make friends, but it just didn't seem to go beyond the initial stage.

Sam recalled an occasion when she had organised a girly night at their place with some of the mums from Lucy's nursery. They had all sat down to eat when Matt appeared and insisted on having the television up loud to watch football. Sam had been so embarrassed; her efforts at being more sociable were ruined. Matt didn't even particularly like football; he was obnoxious and smarmy and had flirted with one of the mums, making poor Sam feel useless once again.

After that occasion, she didn't try again. When she addressed the incident with Matt, he, of course, denied being deliberately rude, saying that the rhythm of the footsteps and constant chatting had interfered with his work. His creative flow was always disturbed by having strangers in the house, so he'd had to wait until the house was empty of its guests...

Mary finished clearing the cups and sat back down. She smiled at her daughter then squeezed her hand.

'You've been miles away and you look so sad, my darling. It really will be fine, you know. The main thing is you're making a fresh start. You're settling into village life. Even if Matt tries to control you, he can't anymore.'

Sam squeezed her mum's hand and got up to stretch her legs.

'I love this kitchen, Mum. It's beautiful isn't it?' she said, changing the subject.

'Yes, we love it. Mind you, yours is beautiful. By the time you have been able to put your own stamp on it, the cottage will be unique and quite something. Which reminds me, I noticed Dominic's truck first thing. I take it he'll be there all day?'

'Yes, he thinks he'll be done next week. I can't believe how good he's been. He managed to fit me in even though he is fully booked up until Christmas.' Sam's cheeks were glowing, and Mary giggled.

'Yes, he is really rather splendid and dashing, isn't he?' Mary replied. Sam burst out laughing at the old-fashioned description of quite possibly the most beautiful man she had ever set eyes on.

'I thought you were meant to be working today?' Mary asked, smiling.

'Yes, I was going to camp out in the beach hut all day, I love working there. Anyway, never mind, Lucy is hopefully going to Matt's in the morning so I may be able to get some done then. It's more this evening, because I have Abigail coming round to work on a couple of songs and obviously it disturbs Lucy. I don't have a soundproofed studio yet, but hey ho, only a few more days.'

'Sounds exciting! I still can't get over what an amazing job you've done to the path, it's like a tunnel lifted directly from fairy land,' Mary said, smiling.

'I know, it didn't take him long to do that. Oh Mum, it's going to look fantastic up there. You should see the lighting I've chosen, and I'm getting my sofa delivered Monday – it's one of those L shaped, antique leather brown sofas, and it's so comfortable.

Oh, and in a couple of weeks Dominic is going to come back to section a tiny area so I can get a mini kitchen put in with a coffee machine and a fridge, so that when I'm working I don't need to keep popping back downstairs. Also it gives guests the freedom to make their own drinks.'

Mary listened intently. It was so good to see the sparkle back in her daughter's eyes again; funny, she thought, she hadn't noticed it had gone until she saw it flicker just now.

'Listen, darling, why don't you and Lucy come here for dinner this evening, and then you can leave Lucy here for the night if you wish? You and Abigail can work in peace, and then you can pick her up in the morning,' Mary suggested.

'Oh Mum, that'd be great, thanks so much. Are you sure you haven't overdosed on me and Lucy yet?' Sam joked.

'Never in a million years, my darling. Your father and I love having you both here. You know, it was quite frustrating for us with you living in London, we didn't feel able to help much.' Mary looked out to her garden; it was a lovely afternoon. 'Sam, why don't you go and finish those songs off? I can sort something for Lucy for lunch and then at least Lucy can see you this evening.'

Sam jumped up and put her arms round her mother.

'I love you, Mum. That really would be amazing, as I have so much to finish. I will pop over and walk Sooty with her later to give you a break.'

Chapter 11

As Sam made her way across the green, her heart started racing as she saw Dominic leaning into the back of his truck.

'Hi, I'm just going to make a coffee, do you fancy one?' she offered, trying desperately to keep her voice sounding calm and not at all squeaky.

'Yeah, that'd be good thanks, Sam,' he said.

Sam was just putting Dominic's coffee on a tray with some biscuits when Liz knocked at the door. Sam let her in and offered her a drink, too.

'So, I see delectable Dom's here,' Liz said.

'Shh, he'll hear.' Sam went bright red as Dominic was indeed listening, stood in the doorway with his arms full of wood.

'Oops, sorry Dom, but I guess you're used to being treated like a huge, juicy steak, aren't you?' Liz joked as she went up and kissed his cheek.

'Yeah, if you say so Liz, although only by you,' he said, teasing her.

'Well, you really are my choice of rump. Tough on the outside and all red and juicy on the inside. Right, Sam?'

'Oh no, don't drag me into it,' Sam said, squirming. Dominic was laughing and shaking his head.

'I hear that Paul is going to come and play squash with you,' Liz said.

'Yeah, we used to play a lot.'

'Well maybe Sam and I could join you for a game of doubles, girls against guys. I could do with giving you a good thrashing. What say you, Sam?' Liz had a wicked gleam in her eye.

'Yeah right,' Dom said, smiling.

'What do you mean 'yeah right', you chauvinist?' Liz said, feigning fury.

'Realist, more like,' he said, shifting the weight in his arms.

Sam had almost forgotten to breathe. *Wow, that smile*, she thought. The man just grew more beautiful by the second.

'Did you hear that, Sam, did you hear what he said? Well, say something then,' Liz demanded.

Sam stopped her daydreaming. 'Oh, I think you are coping admirably Liz,' she said, smiling at Dominic.

'So, when are you going to get yourself a woman then, Dom?' Liz asked. Sam desperately wanted to hear what he had to say.

'Why are you so desperate to marry me off?' he asked with a playful look on his face.

'Because, darling Dominic, you are depriving some poor woman of a good man and beautiful children,' Liz announced with feeling.

'Yeah, right. You really need to get a job or a hobby; you have way too much time on your hands. Right, I'd better get back to work, see you later.' Dominic kissed Liz on the forehead, making Sam sick with envy.

'I'll bring your coffee and biscuits up in a second,' Sam said to Dominic, but Liz quickly put her mug down and snatched the tray.

'Oh no, you won't. I'm going to follow him up, and that way I get a bird's eye view of your gorgeous behind, Mr O'Donnell.' Sam shook her head in disbelief.

'You know what, Liz, that's sexist and wrong on so many levels. How would you feel if I spoke to you like that?' he said.

'I would think all my Christmases had come at once,' Liz said, always needing the last word.

When Liz returned, Sam was sat gazing across the green.

'So, what time did Matt collect Lucy?' Liz asked.

'Lucy refused to go.'

'What? Oh, the poor little lamb. Is she okay?'

'Oh Lucy's fine now, having the time of her life. To be honest, she spent most of her time alone with me in London when the guys from Tremor weren't around, so I think she's embracing a little independence from me. She's gone for a walk with Dad and Sooty. It's Matt I felt sorry for, he looked so rejected.'

'Well, I know you think I'm a Matt-hating psycho from hell,' said Liz, 'but if you don't mind me saying this... had Matt bothered to make the visit a little more memorable for Lucy last week, then perhaps she'd have wanted to go back this weekend. Sorry, Sam, but you must see that this is his own fault.'

'I know. Anyway, she will see him tomorrow morning for the day, and he's going to bring her back tomorrow night.'

'Does she know yet?' Liz asked.

'Yes, she said she'll go as long as he promises to bring her home tomorrow night. Thing is as well, Mum has said she can sleep over there tonight so that I can work. I know Lucy will jump at that, but it kind of makes it even worse that she doesn't want to stay at Matt's, especially when Lucy tells him where she is at bedtime.'

'Can't you ask her not to tell him?' Liz asked.

'No, I don't encourage her to lie or keep secrets,' Sam said.

'Ouch, that made me feel awful. Well, this is a big deal for her, Sam, she's only young. I guess she can see you from your parents' house, can't she?'

'Yes, she can. Dad has even bought her a pair of 'walkie talkies' so she can be in constant contact with me, so I'm not sure how much work I'll get done.' Sam smiled.

'If you get finished early enough, why don't you come across to the pub for a drink after?'

'I may do if I get done early, thanks. I've been dying to have a look in there. It's been torture watching everyone filter in and out. Look, I'd better go and get some work done, but do you think I should make Dominic a sandwich for his lunch?' Sam asked.

'Dom!' Liz bellowed, making Sam jump out of her skin. 'Do you want some food for lunch?!'

'Got it covered, thanks,' he shouted back.

Sam was jealous of the relaxed relationship that Liz had with him, and wished she wasn't quite so intimidated by the man.

'He's very quiet, isn't he?' Sam whispered.

'Not usually, but I'm not surprised he's quiet around you, the poor bloke. You're so jittery and nervous with him, he probably thinks you're going to jump his bones any second.'

'I am not jittery around him,' Sam argued.

'Oh please, you so are. You kept going bright red and you spilt your coffee twice, you looked about fifteen. Anyway, it's all very sweet,' Liz said. She linked her arm through Sam's for the second time since they'd met, something that only Suzy had ever done before, yet Sam found it comforting. 'Do you know, Sam, I think you are really going to love living here. I wish you'd moved in the spring, though, because it really is stunning here then, and in the summer they put on the Blues musical festival and a folk festival. The annual village fete is always a laugh, too, it's just so Midsomer Murders. Mind you, you wait until Christmas. It's pretty special then, too.'

Liz is off again, thought Sam, smiling.

'What made you go into this song writing, by the way? I mean it's not exactly normal, is it?'

Sam laughed. She loved Liz's directness.

'No, I guess not. Normal it isn't. I suppose I kind of grew into it. I always loved making up nursery rhymes and stories. Mum and Dad limited how much time the television was on and I guess that helped because Mum would persuade me to create something or write something, so… I guess I can thank them.'

'Yeah, that makes sense, I guess.'

'Dad has the ultimate record collection, and we spent hours listening to music together and discussing what we liked about each song or band or artist. I tried so many different jobs, but I can't really describe how writing makes me feel.' Sam felt at a loss for words, but Liz seemed to understand.

'Well, however it makes you feel, keep writing you, and don't forget to call if you get time for a drink later.'

Sam spent a blissful afternoon in the beach hut. She popped across to see Lucy and stopped for a cup of tea. She noticed the little girl had the rosiest cheeks. That was another reason she loved living here: Lucy seldom asked to play on her gadgets and seemed to prefer being outside all the time, a very different lifestyle to London.

After dinner, Sam helped with the washing up, said her goodnights and headed home. She had seen Dominic leave at six thirty and was relieved that she wouldn't need to see him again until the morning. She couldn't cope with too much excitement in one day; she wasn't sure her poor nerves could take it.

When she got in, she found the key as promised, posted back through the door, so she went up to the attic to see how it looked. Her whole body burst with goose bumps. It looked and smelt wonderful; the light oak panels gave such a warm glow. She was delighted she had gone with the oak, knowing that Matt would criticise it. Sam didn't care, the whole point of this studio was for her to be creative, for writing and producing demos. She'd worked in enough studios made with all sorts of materials to know that this is what she wanted, and she was having it.

She had a candlelit bath with a cup of tea and listened to some soothing music. Tears pooled in her eyes. For the first time in years Sam, felt at peace, happy and safe.

Abigail and Sam spent the evening working on the songs. They were sounding wonderful.

Abigail's voice was so beautiful, but what surprised Sam more was how mature the young woman was. She had all the enthusiasm that Sam had once felt, yet her expectations were realistic. Her feet were firmly on the ground. The time flew by, and when Abigail left it was one in the morning and the village was bathed in a starry light. Sam waved Abigail goodbye as she sped off back to London. She noticed a voicemail from Liz.

'Hey you, sorry you can't make it. Paul and I are over here with Dom and he's been asking questions about you, so make sure you answer the door in a sexy little number in the morning and you may score lucky. Anyway, sweet dreams, Maestro. Speak soon.'

Sam couldn't sleep. Her mind was racing. She kept thinking about Liz's message… Dominic had been asking questions about her, so she decided to get up and carry on with the songs. Once she sat at her piano her fingers took on a mind of their own and, before she knew it, she had written quite possibly the most beautiful song she had ever written. She quickly set up a couple of tracks on her Mac so that she could record the piano and a rough vocal. Then after she finished, she nervously played it back.

She was shocked by the pain in her voice. Sam realised that she could never give this song to another soul. She decided to call this one "The Master of Disguise", and this, too, would be placed in her best kept secrets file, waiting for her to find the courage and confidence to record in her own right again.

It was already getting light by the time she fell into bed and drifted off to sleep. It seemed only seconds before she could hear knocking. She looked at her mobile and realised she'd overslept yet again! 'What the hell is wrong with me?' she said out loud. It was eight o'clock sharp, and that could only be Dominic banging on her door. She quickly jumped up and grabbed her dressing gown, ran to brush her teeth, then giggled as she remembered Liz's words last night about striking lucky. She caught a glimpse of herself in the mirror and groaned aloud. Poor Dominic would be horrified by her latest appearance, and not remotely attracted to her. 'Oh, not again,' she thought as she raced downstairs.

'Sorry Dominic, I overslept,' she said lamely. Dominic appeared most amused.

'No worries. I need to grab a few bits from the truck, so can I wedge the door open again?' he asked.

'Yes, of course. Shall I make some tea, or would you prefer coffee?' she asked.

'Coffee, please.'

'We always have a full English breakfast on a Sunday,' suggested Sam, 'would you like one too?'

Dominic smiled, making her heart flip. 'You have some pretty cool rituals. Breakfast would be great thanks, Sam.'

Oh dear, Sam cringed. He probably thought she had OCD, what with their bacon sandwiches on a Saturday and a full English on a Sunday. Oh, and he'd said her name... she had never heard her name sound so dreamy before, spoken in his deep husky drawl.

Dominic came downstairs to the delicious smell of cooked breakfast. Sam sat opposite him and found she'd suddenly lost her appetite. She kept staring at his brown hands as he ate, and his beautiful mouth. She'd kind of hoped he would eat with his mouth open, anything to put her off of him but alas, his manners were impeccable.

Dominic looked up and stared straight into her eyes, 'How long did you and Lucy live in London?'

'All our lives until we got here. I hate London,' she added as an afterthought.

'Yeah, can't say I'd like to live there, but it is a beautiful city,' he declared and then silently finished his meal. He carried his empty plate over to the sink and ran it under the tap. Sam watched how relaxed Dominic was around her, and wished she felt the same, but she was a bag of nerves.

'Right, I'd better get on, thanks for that. I should be finished here about eight but if it's going to be later, I'll let you know. I expect you'll need to get Lucy ready for school tomorrow, won't you?'

'Oh, you're so thoughtful, Dominic, thank you. Is there lots more noisy work left to do?' she asked, trying desperately not to look at his mouth, imagining what it would taste like if he were to kiss her.

'Well, there are only a few more bits of drilling to do, so I should have that done by three. After that, there's just the setting up. I should be able to get round in the week and next weekend to put the kitchenette in. Was thinking, you said you wanted a toilet and sink put in, too. It may be an idea to kill two birds with one stone if you think you want to go ahead with it.'

'I think that would be a good idea, if you're sure you have the time? Thanks Dominic, and thanks again for fitting me in.'

Lucy was full of fun when Sam got to her parents'. They had all gotten up bright and early, walked Sooty and then returned for a huge breakfast.

'My goodness, this young lady can eat,' John said.

'Yes, she takes after her mother, don't you, Luce?' Sam cuddled the little girl tight and showered her face with little kisses. 'Right, young lady, we need to say goodbye to Grandma and Grandpa because we are running a bit late. Your dad will be here any minute to collect you.'

Lucy told her all about Sooty, who had snuck up in the middle of the night and somehow squeezed himself next to Lucy on her bed. When Grandma woke up this morning, she found him still lying there beside her granddaughter. Matt would hear all about the sleepover too, and it would no doubt hurt his feelings even more.

Oh, hey ho, storm's brewing! Sam thought.

Matt arrived over an hour late and Sam was just about furious by then.

'Daddy!' Lucy squealed as he walked through the door. She ran to him and jumped into his arms.

'Hey, princess. Man, have I missed my little kitten. You hungry? Only Jazz and I are gonna take you out for lunch.'

'I slept at Grandma's and she made me the biggest breakfast, didn't she, Mummy?'

Matt glared at Sam and Sam decided she wanted them both gone.

'She did, darling. Now, do you have everything ready? Matt, can you get here for six, please, and would you mind making sure she's had a bath? Only it starts getting late otherwise.'

Matt ignored Sam and carried Lucy's bag out to the car. Sam gave Lucy an enormous hug before saying their goodbyes.

Sam had a productive day and enjoyed chatting with Dominic over a late lunch. She made some sandwiches and a nice salad and the two of them tucked in before going back to work.

Matt didn't drop Lucy home until seven forty-five and Sam wasn't at all surprised to hear that Lucy had not been bathed, but she didn't care because Lucy was in really good spirits and had spent a wonderful afternoon with Matt and Jasmine. She had agreed to go again next weekend, as long as Matt promised to leave the lights on and let her sleep in with him, if she wanted to. Matt promised to in front of Sam, so they all felt happier.

'Mummy, is Domnic still here? Can we see him?' Lucy asked. Sam smiled and stroked her cheek.

'Yes, my angel, let's go up and see what he's done.'

Chapter 12

Sam followed Lucy up to the studio and caught her breath. Lucy squealed, 'Wow, Mummy, it's magical, look!'

Dominic had turned an empty shell into the warmest, cosiest studio that Sam had ever seen. The light oak panels were now glowing in different colours from the many multi coloured spotlights shining on them. The huge mixing desk was all boxed in perfectly. He'd lifted all the dust sheets and the cream carpet was still intact, without a single mark. Sam wanted to hug him, but then went scarlet at the thought of it.

'Oh Dominic, it's just amazing,' was all Sam could manage to say.

Dominic got down on his haunches.

'Hey Lucy, how you doing? Do you want to do the honours?' He handed Lucy a remote control and showed her which button to press. All of a sudden, the blinds drew back automatically, revealing the three huge skylights. Then he whispered to Lucy to press another, and the skylights started to open. Dominic got her to press a third button which started the glitter ball spinning slowly round. Lucy's eyes grew wider and wider as the twinkling lights reflected everywhere. It truly was magical.

Lucy was jumping up and down, unable to contain her excitement. She kept pressing the controls again and again. Dominic ruffled her hair affectionately, making Sam's heart skip a beat.

'Dominic, I don't know what to say. I mean I knew it was going to be good, I could see it in my head, but you've gone above and beyond my wildest dreams. Thank you.' Sam could hear herself babbling. She couldn't trust herself to shake his hand without him feeling how nervous she was, so she gently punched his arm. Dominic stared down to where she'd hit him. The tension between the two of them appeared to be getting more intense.

By the time Lucy had played in the studio, had her bath and a hot chocolate, it was almost nine thirty.

'Come on, little one, you really need to sleep now. You'll be exhausted in the morning if you're not careful.'

Sam tucked her in. There was no need for a story tonight and Lucy didn't seem to mind.

'Mummy?'

'Yes, darling?'

'I love living here so much.'

'Me too, my angel.'

'Mummy, please can we have a dog? You did say when we moved to the country that we could get one.'

'I know that I did, darling, but you get to play with Sooty whenever you want, don't you?'

'I know, Mummy, I just miss Sooty too much and I'm not allowed to hold him on the lead because Grandpa said he is too strong for me.'

'Well, Grandpa is right. You're still just a little girl, Sooty might pull you over. I'm not saying no, my darling, but we will look into it, okay?'

Lucy yawned sleepily, and murmured, 'Thank you, Mummy, I love you.'

'I love you too, my darling.'

Sam kissed her goodnight, switched on the night light and then crept back upstairs to the studio. She had the room to herself, and joyfully played with the controls to her heart's delight.

She reached over and switched on the computer, turning on the security monitor and positioning it so she could see Lucy fast asleep with her thumb in her mouth. Sam put on her headphones and prepared to lay down the new song she wrote last night.

The computer had various drum programmes and loops to play around with and once she had found an appropriate drum beat, she recorded it, then plugged in her electric piano and played along with the drums. The song already had a ghostly feel, which was how she had wanted it to sound. Tomorrow she would put her vocal down to celebrate and christen her lovely new studio.

That was enough for one night, Sam thought as she switched the power off in the studio. She made herself a Horlicks for bed and grabbed her book.

The following week was one of the happiest Sam had ever had in her life. She spent her days working in the beach hut, and then she'd collect Lucy from school. They usually ate with her parents, and then popped back to Wisteria Cottage for hot chocolate and story time before Sam went up to the studio to work in the evening.

She hadn't yet invited anyone up to see her work space; she needed to spend time there alone. Dominic still had a few bits left to do but it was fully functional and stunning. Lucy was her only visitor, and she spent all her time playing with the remote control and the disco ball. Sam shook her head; Matt would never have allowed her to create a studio like this. Their studio in London had been impressive, but masculine and not at all cosy.

When she wasn't in either the beach hut or her studio, a favourite place to work was at her piano. She had placed it on the landing under the large bay window, overlooking the village green. Sitting there now, staring out of the window, she sighed and closed the lid.

Living in Willow Green was proving to be a distraction to hard work. Thinking practically, Sam knew the piano should ideally have to move in order to increase her output. Deadlines were looming, and she must not get distracted by the beauty of the place, but how could she move it from this beautiful spot?

Sam felt her heart race every time she saw Dominic's truck fly through the village. She was aware that she missed his presence around her home. She missed the sound of his whistling tunefully along to the radio and she missed their chats over coffee.

The odds were stacked against Sam getting a grip, and Friday night would bring her a whole new challenge.

Playing the damsel in distress went against all of Sam's new, independent principles, but on Friday night everything went disastrously wrong. A knight in shining armour had not been on the agenda for her new life in the country, but a knight was precisely what she needed.

John and Mary had gone on holiday. They had treated themselves to a cruise for ten days. Sam had offered to take care of Sooty for them while they were away, and so around eleven o'clock Sam let Sooty into the garden to tend to his toiletry needs one more time before bed. She was about to call him back when she heard an almighty piercing screech. She ran outside and found the dog being mauled by next door's tomcat.

She managed to peel the cat off him and got him to the back-door. Poor Sooty was bleeding badly around his ear and along the side of his face. His left eye looked as though it was closing, and she also noticed a little blood seeping from his paw. She led him into the kitchen and grabbed a towel to wrap around his head, then she reached for her phone, but for a few seconds Sam just stared blankly at the screen.

She couldn't call Liz, as she and Paul had taken the kids to London to see a show and were staying in a hotel overnight. She knew there was no point in calling Sue or any of the others, as they were having a jolly tonight at a cooking demonstration and judging by the WhatsApp messages she'd been tagged into, they were all pretty obliterated by now. She had no choice: she had to call Dominic.

It took a while for him to answer and when he did, he sounded a little tired. She was worried she'd woken him up, or worse, that he may have been with someone.

'Sam, everything okay?' He asked.

'I am so, so sorry to disturb you this late, but there's no one else I can call. Sooty's cut himself really badly and I'm supposed to be looking after him while Mum and Dad are away. Lucy's in bed; I don't want to wake her and worry her, and I can't leave her, but Sooty seems to be bleeding a lot and he's limping and...'

Dominic cut in. 'No worries, Sam, I'll be round in five minutes. Can you call the vet and let them know to expect me, and find out where I take him?'

'Yes,' replied Sam. 'Mum left the details in case of an emergency. Thank you.'

'No worries.'

Sam called the emergency number for the surgery and was informed that the vet would get there in time to be ready for Sooty's arrival, so she kept the poor dog calm while watching the ticking of kitchen clock.

Dominic arrived in five and a half minutes. Sam opened the door to him and her knees buckled.

Wow, he just keeps getting better, thought Sam.

He stood there with his hands on his hips and smiled. He looked quite dishevelled, as though he'd just got out of bed.

'The vet will be at the surgery by the time you get there. They said to go around to the back entrance; there'll be a light on. Do you know where Nine Lives is? It's just off the high street.'

'Yep, I know it. Right mate, let's get you looked at.' Dominic was so calm and focused. He dropped down on his haunches and gently stroked Sooty's head, before lifting the large dog effortlessly into his arms and carrying him out to the truck. Sam gave him a couple of towels to prevent any blood getting on the seats, but he didn't seem bothered at all: his only concern was for the dog. As he was about to get into the truck, he stopped, lent on the roof and turned to look at Sam.

'D-did I wake you? You sounded pretty tired.' Sam was desperate to know.

'No, I was working on some quotes. They usually give me a headache.' Dominic glanced down at Sooty. 'He's gonna be okay you know, Sam.' With that he was in, and off.

She was shaking with the suddenness of the incident. She checked outside, as she had heard a crash, and one of her pots was smashed to pieces. There was blood around it and she wondered if that was where Sooty had cut his paw, as there was so much blood. After washing Sooty's blood off the kitchen floor, she went up to check on Lucy, who was fast asleep and, much to Sam's relief, blissfully unaware of the drama that had unfolded downstairs.

Sam felt the familiar signs of panic grip her as she thought of Lucy and the drama she had endured by moving her away from all that she knew. Sam reasoned that it was highly unlikely that Sooty would die from his injuries; however, she knew there were the occasions where infection could set in and the animal had to be put down, especially after a particularly nasty scrap with a cat.

She slowly padded downstairs and tried to control her emotions. She put another log in the wood burner and waited for Dominic. By the time she heard him pull up outside, it was nearly one thirty in the morning.

She opened the door, and she and Dominic both burst out laughing. Sooty sat on the welcome mat looking such a pathetic sight. He was holding his paw up, showing its bandaged state. He also had a shaved area around his face, which appeared to have been stitched, and the most comical plastic collar around his neck which resembled a lamp shade. For some reason, it was decorated with daisies. If dogs got embarrassed, then poor Sooty most definitely was, Sam thought.

'It's just a precaution, and he didn't have any plain ones left, I'm afraid!' Dominic explained. 'It's just for a few days, until the stitches start dissolving.'

'Oh Dominic, look at him, he looks so pathetic. Look, come in. Would you like a drink? I've just put another log on the fire.'

Dominic crossed the threshold and took his boots off, and Sooty limped in behind him. Sam's heart started racing again. They had a glass of wine and Dominic filled Sam in on all that the vet had to say. Sooty got as comfortable as he could and they all sat in cosy silence, enjoying the warmth of the wood burner.

Sam could not believe how relaxed she felt sitting here with Dominic. She loved the way he never felt the need to talk unless he had something worthwhile to say.

After all the stress, they both decided they were starving, so Sam put together a cheese board and some dips. She brought it into the lounge with a couple of glasses of port.

'Do you know what? I have never drunk so much in my life as I have since moving here,' Sam confessed.

Dominic rubbed his face. 'Yeah, it's the country air.'

'Oh, good, so does that mean everyone drinks too much around here?' she asked, relief in her voice.

'Well, when you look at it, it's only a village, but it has three pubs and two decently stocked stores – the Co-op allegedly ran out of gin during the summer – so I guess something or someone must be keeping them going.'

They ate, chatted about the finer points of village life and laughed, a lot.

Dominic was an exceptional man. He didn't like to talk about himself much; instead, he chose to ask questions and seemed genuinely interested in what she had to say. Sam felt quite disappointed when the time came for him to go, but she walked him to the front door.

'I'm going to leave the truck if that's okay, Sam. I've had far too much to drink. I will scoot by in the morning to get it. Listen, any problems with Sooty, give me a shout, but I think he will be fine now.'

Just for a second, Sam fantasised about him leaning forward and gently placing a kiss on her lips but alas, he bent down to make a fuss of the dog and was gone.

Chapter 13

Sam had to brave a trip to London the following Friday. Her anxiety made it impossible for her to travel far these days, but her ever patient manager Richard had kindly offered to collect her and drive her there. He knew all about Sam's anxiety and did all he could to work around it. Sam was constantly overwhelmed by his kindness.

She had also registered with the local doctor's surgery and her mum had advised her to register with Dr Bhakta, who just happened to be the most unbelievable GP. She had spent several sessions with Sam, helping her come to grips with her anxiety and giving her tips and advice on how to deal with it.

She had meetings all day to discuss Tremor, the five-piece boy band she had been writing for.

Matt had agreed to collect Lucy from school and take her home, then Sam could collect her later. Liz had kindly taken Sooty for the day so she could have a clear head and not worry.

The recent success of Tremor had been unexpected to some, but not to Sam. She knew they had every ingredient required to make a band these days. She'd been working with them for some time now and knew they had all the guts and determination to carry them through.

When Matt and Jasmine had been away on tour, Sam had the boys virtually camp out at her house so she could get to know them. Sam had written 'My Crazy Lover' for them. She got the idea after spending a riotous evening in their company. The boys sat around, telling outrageous anecdotes, laughing hysterically and drinking together.

One tale in particular caught her attention. Buzz told them all about his older brother being madly in love with some girl who kept taking off around the world. Each time she came home she would tell him she would marry him and stay this time, and they would throw an engagement party, but then she would always get itchy feet and take off again, and he was left to send back the gifts and so 'My Crazy Lover' was born.

Ace was the oldest member of the band. He was twenty-eight and had one of the most expressive voices that Sam had ever heard. His voice had a maturity, and there was a depth of passion and pain in one so young which gave his voice a heart-breaking edge. Ace sang the sweet melody whilst the others weaved in and out with harmonies. Darcy rapped his frustration over the middle section to such a powerful effect that the combination of the bittersweet words and melody bolted the song straight to the top of the iTunes charts.

So now, Sam was surrounded by record company executives keen for her to sign up and write enough songs for the band to record a whole album. Sam made it clear that whilst she was happy to write one, maybe two more tracks, she would not commit to more, much to everybody's annoyance.

Steve Jones, who ran the publishing house, was the king of manipulation and flattery. He cleared his throat and attempted to change Sam's mind.

'Thing is, Sam, the boys want you. We tried putting other writers forward, but they want you.' Steve thrust his hands forward and grasped the thin air.

Sam smiled at his reaction. 'That's really sweet, Steve, but I don't want to make big commitments right now. Besides, I think it would be good for the guys to work with other writers as well. I'm not saying I'll only write another two, but I will only commit to one or two at a time, okay?'

Mike Thurston piped up. 'I'm pretty sure, Sam, you're aware of how many people want to write for these guys. They are going to be huge you know!'

Sam agreed readily. 'Yes, Mike, I've always thought they have what it takes, and I'm sure their popularity will continue to grow. I love being with them and I'm looking forward to writing for them again, I really am, but two tracks at a time. Now that is my only offer, gentlemen.'

When it was clear they were not going to get any further with Sam, the meeting drew to a close and they shook hands on the deal. Sam was happy; she had been firm and got what she wanted.

The traffic was heavy across London, so by the time Sam and Richard got to Matt's to collect Lucy they were exhausted. Lucy and Jasmine were playing table tennis on the Wii and Matt was slumped in the chair, acting like a poor, wounded victim. Sam found herself becoming increasingly irritated by his behaviour these days.

By the time they arrived home, collected and walked Sooty, it was nearly seven o'clock. Sam had wanted Richard to stay for dinner before turning back to London, however, he'd arranged to take his wife and daughter out, so turned straight back. Sam thanked him profusely for taking her to the meetings; he reminded her that it was in his best interest to! Sam missed Richard's wife,

Hayley, and Lucy adored Maisie, their twelve-year-old daughter, who was an angel with Lucy. She would call them tomorrow and put a date in the diary for them to come for dinner.

Sam bathed Lucy, made her a hot chocolate and read a story. Around nine, there was a quiet knock at the door. Sam's heart leapt to her mouth, thinking it could be Dominic. She opened the door and there stood Ace. Sam threw her arms around him.

'Ace, what a lovely surprise! I've been talking all about you today, were your ears burning?'

'Hey, Sam. Sorry to just turn up like this, but I needed to see ya.'

'That's fine. Come on in.'

Sam thanked God that Lucy was asleep. She knew the little girl would never have gone down once she saw Ace, because she absolutely adored him. Before they moved, Matt and Jasmine had been away a lot, giving Sam the luxury of having the house and studio to herself. The boys had virtually moved in, and Lucy had been besotted with them all, but particularly Ace. During her heart-breaking sobs leaving London, it had been Ace who she'd said she was going to miss the most. He had a way with Lucy. Sam knew he had younger step siblings and had helped raise them, which gave him the advantage with Lucy. Sam was reminded of how Matt disliked Ace and had assumed it was a clash of personalities, however, now she realised why.

'Can I get you something to drink? Have you eaten?'

She realised by Ace's reaction that he hadn't for some time, and Sam couldn't help mothering these guys.

'How about an omelette and a lager, does that sound okay?'

'Yeah, that sounds great. I've missed your omelettes, you know.'

Ace sat at the island and watched Sam as she cooked his omelette. They chatted about the new song Sam was writing for them, but she was aware there was something that Ace needed to get off his chest.

'Okay, Ace, so how about while I cook, you tell me what's wrong?'

'You know Bryan Montgomery?'

'I do,' Sam said carefully.

'He's asked to manage me.'

'Okay and what about the others, what do they think?'

'Yeah, that's just it. Problem is it would be just me, not the guys.'

Sam grimaced; she'd seen this happen so many times. She picked up her glass and took a sip of wine.

'Ah, right. No doubt he's filled your head with lines like, 'It's all about you, Ace' and that 'the guys are holding you back', right?'

'Yeah, how'd you know?' Ace replied in surprise.

'Look. This is just my opinion, okay, so you can take it and use it however you like.' She paused and took another sip of wine. 'I think Bryan is partly right. In a certain way, you do have the strongest voice and you also happen to be "mustard".' They both burst out laughing: it had been Ace who had taught Sam his use of the word mustard, describing someone who is extremely good looking or 'hot', as Ace would call them. 'However, you've just signed a deal to record an album with the guys, and whilst I'm sure Bryan can get you out of that contract, you'd be letting a lot of people down. Mud sticks. Trust me, Ace.'

'Thing is, Sam, I want to go it alone. I never wanted to do the band thing,' Ace confessed.

'I suspected as much, but what's stopping you planning a solo album whilst working on the current one?' Sam fired back. 'You're still young, and there's no reason you can't have the music career you want. One that's right for you.'

Sam added the finishing touches to Ace's supper while he took in her words. She really felt for him; he seemed quite vulnerable this evening, pouring his heart out to her.

The other guys were gorgeous, and she loved them all dearly, but they were quite immature, whereas Ace had a maturity greater than his years. Sam knew something of Ace's background. He lived with his mum in a flat way out in the suburbs. His mum suffered from severe anxiety, preventing her from leaving the house very often. With no father present, it was down to Ace to get his brothers and sister to school and back, get the groceries and, depending on how his mum was, meant most evenings he needed to cook for them all, too. Not once had Sam heard him complain about the hand life had dealt him, and she knew his driving force in music was to get his mum, his siblings and himself away from there.

Sam knew that it would be a while before the boys saw any profits. The record company had put a lot behind them. She knew Bryan and knew that whilst he probably was desperate to sign Ace, however, as good a manager as he was, he could be fickle and impatient. If Ace didn't deliver expectations, Bryan would drop him pretty smart. Sam knew she needed to persuade Ace to stick with Tremor, and vowed to help him work on his solo career which, if he played his cards right, could be launched in a couple of years. She spoke in depth of her concerns at him leaving the band so soon, but also of her offer to help him plan and schedule his solo career.

By the time Ace left, it was late. She hoped she'd been able to convince him not to let the rest of the band down, as she genuinely believed he had one hell of a career ahead of him.

Sam was exhausted; it had been such a gruelling day. She turned off the lights and took her usual mug of Horlicks up to bed, but she didn't even get to take a sip before falling fast asleep.

Two months into her new life in the country, Sam's world took an unexpected and unsettling turn.

Ronnie Driscoll called, making her an offer she may well find easy to refuse. However, she could not ignore it, no matter how desperately she wanted to.

'Just one song, Sam, that's all they are asking for,' Ronnie pleaded.

'Ronnie, I can't. It's been way too long. Besides, you need to go through Richard.'

'I did. He refused to put you on the spot, so he said he wanted me to ask you. Sam, you need to think about this. It's a massive opportunity for you. Look, it's not every day you get an award like this. Think about it, please. Give it some thought, for me. Christmas is only a few weeks away, Sam, take that time to think… Just explore the idea, Sam, please. That's all I ask.'

Sam had sat in the kitchen in the same position for a couple of hours. Her coffee remained untouched and was now cold when Dominic turned up to fix a faulty connection. He could see she had been crying.

'Is Lucy with her dad?' he asked gently after he had fixed it.

'Yes, she's gone for the weekend, although she will probably want to come home tomorrow, but we are giving it another go.' Sam was embarrassed that she had been crying. She reflected on the many embarrassing occasions she had experienced with this man; he had witnessed first-hand the difficult relationship between her and Matt, and also the torment for Lucy, yet he simply dealt calmly and quietly with each new situation.

Sam thought about the difference between Matt and Dominic. Matt would fall apart if he couldn't find a clean ironed shirt to put on, whereas Dominic appeared unflappable.

'Sorry, Dominic, I was miles away.'

'Yeah, I got that. Look, if you don't have plans tonight then do you fancy scooting out for something to eat?'

'Oh um… I was meant to be… No, that sounds lovely. Yes, thank you so much.' She couldn't believe it, she had fantasised about him asking her out for days – and now he had.

'No worries. I'll pick you up at seven?'

'Perfect.'

The prospect of dinner with Dominic was far more daunting than the show held in front of thousands of people. Sam must have tried on her entire wardrobe, checking out look after look before deciding to pop into town to buy something new. She chose a beautiful multi coloured jumper, knitted in the softest of angora. With her boot cut jeans and converse trainers, Sam hoped she looked casual and not at all as though she had tried too hard.

Dominic picked her up at seven. He was driving a particularly smart Mercedes. When she asked where they were going, he simply said, 'London.'

Her heart sank, but she did her best to hide her reaction. London always gave her claustrophobia these days and triggered the worst panic attacks.

The car soon swallowed the miles and before long, they were almost beside Tower Bridge. Sam had discreetly needed to take her flower remedy during the journey. She knew Dominic had noticed but hadn't mentioned it. She really appreciated that, as she was embarrassed by her anxiety. Matt had been mortified once when she had had an attack in a shopping mall and refused to take her out again after that.

They parked and walked around a corner and Sam's heart leapt, for she was greeted with the most perfect sight.

Chapter 14

'Oh wow, this is beautiful. Where we are, Dominic?'

'St Katharine's Dock.'

'Dominic... It... it's perfect. I had no idea that London had somewhere so beautiful.'

'Yeah, I think it's one of those places that you need to explore to appreciate all it has to offer, don't you think?'

'Mm.' Sam was speechless as she looked around her. The marina reflected the sparkling lights of the London skyline and Tower Bridge, in all its glory, stood proudly in front of her, appearing like the perfect fairytale palace.

Sam shivered. Fear gripped her again. She could feel the starts of the panic attack looming and goose bumps were tingling up her arms. Dominic cursed himself for bringing her here, she was clearly struggling. He remembered Luke coming home with PTSD and battling with panic attacks; he knew Luke had been given lots of strategies to cope and if all else failed, then a shot of whiskey always nipped them in the bud.

'Do you fancy going to The Dickens?' he suggested and nodded to a beautifully lit up place which strangely looked like a ship but was actually an 18th century warehouse. 'Thought we could get a drink. The food's good and the view's even better.'

Sam was so relieved. She knew in the safety of the pub she could do her breathing exercises and get a soothing glass of wine. She excused herself to the bathroom and ran ice cold water onto her wrists, then she very calmly did her yoga breathing, touched up her makeup and went back to meet him.

Their meal was delicious, and Sam realised she had done her usual trick of people watching, staring out over the little marina and saying nothing. She tried picturing the people who lived behind the glass of the luxurious apartments. Were they the owners of the stunning boats moored in the dock, gently swaying in the water?

'Sorry, Dominic. I'm not the most stimulating company, am I?' she said, embarrassed.

'On the contrary,' replied Dominic, leaning back in his chair, 'it's actually refreshing to be able to sit without the need of constant conversation.'

'Do you know, when I lived here, I never ventured out much. I had no idea that this was here. I mean, look at this place. How come I never came here before, and how many other beautiful secrets does London have?'

'It's a stunning city,' he said, looking out onto the marina. Just for a second Sam thought he looked sad, lost somehow.

'Liz said you left the forces to care for your father?' Sam asked.

'Yeah, she said she'd mentioned it.'

'That was a kind thing to do, Dominic. I imagine a lot of people would have shoved him in a nursing home and forgotten all about him,' she reasoned.

'I'm not so sure. His sister went into a nursing home and it was the making of her. She played bridge one day, bingo another, and became local champion at backgammon. Before that, she had sat at home bitter and lonely whilst her daughters bent over backwards trying to please her. I should have let him go, but he was so proud, you know. I just couldn't do it to him.'

Sam was keen to know more of Dominic's story.

'Liz said that your brother joined the army, and you left so he could stay. I think that's pretty amazing, you know.'

Dominic made it fairly obvious that he wanted to change the subject.

'I'm going to settle the bill, Sam, then how about we take a walk around and cost up all these boats?'

'Ooh, yes please. I could do with a walk, and thank you Dominic, the meal was wonderful.'

They wandered around St Katharine's Dock, taking in the evening's ambiance and wondering which boat they would buy. They approached a gallery. It had large, illuminated windows and plenty of paintings and prints on show. They stared in at the window at the work on display. Sam was jolted by one particular portrait of a woman… She was stood in a black camisole, black stockings and holding a glass of red wine. Sam was moved by how sensual the woman looked. There was something so strong and powerful in the woman's eyes that said, 'Don't you dare touch me, don't come near me and don't you dare even speak to me.' She grabbed Dominic's arm in excitement.

'Wow, Dominic. Look at her.' Sam told Dominic about her immediate reaction to the portrait, but he disagreed.

'No, I think she's disappointed. She looks pretty unimpressed,' he said lightly.

'Oh no, surely nothing that simple. No, there's more to her, just look.'

'Maybe he's late or maybe he just didn't bother turning up,' Dominic suggested.

'No, she's too hurt, too angry. There's too much there.'

'You're right, it is a stunning painting.'

Sam looked at her watch. She had been analysing the same picture for the best part of half an hour and she was still fascinated by it.

'Sorry, Dominic, but I can't take my eyes off of her. It's as though she wants someone to take the time to really work out what's going on in her head.'

'A bit like you then,' Dominic said.

Sam suddenly turned and looked up at him as though he had slapped her face. He said nothing else, just looked at her. Suddenly she felt as though a light had finally been shone on her life. She felt understood; someone had seen inside.

Dominic didn't flirt with her, chat her up or try to seduce her, but Sam knew that tonight was a turning point in their relationship. Tonight he had a serious air that blew her mind. She knew that Dominic was as attracted to her as she was to him, but she was relieved he was a gentleman. When they finally got back to Wisteria Cottage it was late, but they opened a bottle of wine and Dominic lit the log burner. The lounge looked magical. Sam chose to curl up on the sofa whilst Dominic sat on the floor in front of her, legs stretched out, leaning against the cushions. Staring at the back of his dark hair did not help to diffuse the fire in her.

Sam was so nervous that she was worried she would make a fool of herself. Dominic put another log on the burner, and the sparks lit up the darkened room. He came over and sat next to

Sam on the sofa. Leaning against his hand, he stared directly into her eyes and then lazily stared down at her mouth, slowly and tantalisingly. Sam had stopped breathing; the moment was so perfect. Then Dominic seemed to read Sam's thoughts and, as though psychic, asked if she'd like a little more to drink.

'I would.' Sam breathed again.

'You fascinate me, Sam. You are so beautiful and talented, and yet you are so troubled. Your eyes give you away, you know. Why didn't you tell me you suffered from panic attacks? We could have stayed local.'

'Yes, but then I would never have gone to one of the most beautiful places I have ever seen.'

'No, but you would have felt safe.'

'To be honest, I find it all really embarrassing, the anxiety and panic attacks. They are disabling, and I suppose I don't like anybody to know about them.'

'You'd be surprised how many people suffer them, you know. Loads of guys who come out of the forces are plagued by them. I've seen some of the most decorated men and women unable to leave their homes 'cuz they're having a panic attack. It's nothing to be ashamed of, you know.'

Sam found her voice and tried to explain to Dominic. 'Thing is, it was all so subtle. It's only really since we moved here to the village that it's occurred to me just how bad things had got.'

'Is that why you were upset earlier?' Dominic asked.

'No, that's another issue.'

'Do you want to talk about it?' Dominic asked. Sam decided that she did.

'Thing is, I have been asked to do a show. I've won an award for my songs and this is so cringy… but…' She stared at Dominic to gage his reaction and was relieved to see that he didn't bat an eyelid. 'Well, it feels like there's this voice inside of me begging me to do it. Problem is, it's as though I am not in control and I have no confidence to do it. It's so conflicting and exhausting; I have so much work to do, and that isn't helping. I know what you're thinking, that on the grand scale of things there are people starving in the world and I'm stressed over one show and a few panic attacks which will naturally go hand in hand with it.'

'No, I wasn't thinking that actually.' Dominic glanced at her. 'I was thinking that it's a shame that if it means so much to you, you deny yourself so much release and pleasure. What's the worst that can happen?'

'I guess I could have a panic attack and freeze and let everyone down,' Sam replied ruefully.

'Yeah, you could. Then again, you might not. Who knows? After all the stuff you've experienced, it may give you a new edge.'

'But what if I panic and bottle out?'

'What if you get to the side of the stage and find you can't wait to get back out there?'

'But what if I still love it?'

Dominic started to laugh. 'Then that's good, surely?'

'No,' wailed Sam. 'That means I'll want to do it more.'

'Would that be so bad?' he asked.

'What about Lucy?' Sam asked.

'What about Lucy?' He replied and shrugged his shoulders.

'How will she cope? How will I cope, come to think of it, if I launch my career again? There's lots of work involved in producing music, and I, I... I don't travel at all well these days.' Sam seemed to be grasping at straws, using the same old arguments to prevent her from moving on.

'Sam, Lucy will cope. You have your parents here, and she's got her dad. I imagine Liz'll be queuing up to have her. I don't know much about the music industry, but I do know there's people who don't do the touring thing. Why don't you just take one step at a time and see how it goes?'

Sam let Dominic's words sink in for a moment. Of course he was right. She shifted position on the sofa and searched frantically to change the subject.

'Do you mind me asking if you ever regret leaving the army?' She felt relieved she had found something else to talk about.

'No, I don't mind you asking, and yes, I had a lot of regrets, but not now. I like where I'm at and who I am these days.'

Mmm, me too, thought Sam.

As though he had read her mind, Dominic smiled, reached across and kissed her lips, so gently, as though savouring every moment. He ran his fingers through her hair and then he cupped his hand round the back of her neck, making Sam melt.

Sam felt overwhelmed. It had been a long time since someone had touched her like this, and it felt like all her senses would explode at any moment.

Matt had told Sam she was frigid, therefore she had convinced herself that perhaps she was, but there was nothing frigid about her thoughts and fantasies this evening. Dreading that Dominic would read her thoughts, she decided to offer him a cup of coffee.

'Can't actually say I want one, but if you need a distraction then I will drink one.'

Sam laughed, got up and went into the kitchen. Dominic followed her, sitting at the island.

'Oh, Sue tells me you are going to build their annex,' Sam said.

Dominic nodded. 'Mm! should be a good project, I like the particular architect who's designed it.' He said, smiling fondly, as Tom, Sue's husband, was the architect who had designed it.

'Do you like her husband?' Sam asked, handing Dominic his coffee.

'Yeah,' he said, smiling.

'I met him last week – he turned up after school and grabbed Sue's bottom and wouldn't stop squeezing it. She asked him what on earth he thought he was doing, in her loudest, poshest voice, and he said he was practising for the next time she's drunk.' The two of them were laughing hard now. 'Honestly, it was hilarious.'

'Tom's hilarious. He's my brother's best mate, which is a good thing, as Luke seriously needs lightening up sometimes.'

By the time the coffee had been drunk it was nearly 4am, and the first birds were beginning to sing. Sam peered out of the window and over the green.

'You do realise that people will see your car, don't you? I am going to be the talk of the village again.'

'Yeah, Liz said you had a hard time when you got here, being a newcomer I guess. Villages can be a bit like that, y'know, close-knit, but it does have its plus points.'

'So do you like living here?' Sam asked.

'Well it suits my needs, to be honest, and there are some pretty good people living here. They tend to give me my space, which is what I really need.'

'Yes, I heard you're about as sociable as me,' Sam laughed. 'Although I have never mixed so much since living here.' Sam couldn't take her eyes off of him. She was often reminded of how many women lusted after him.

'Dominic, can I ask you something?'

'Course.'

'Well, does it irritate you that any woman you come across seems to flirt with you?' She asked, thinking of the waitress earlier, who couldn't concentrate on anything but Dominic's mouth.

Dominic laughed. 'I think that's a slight exaggeration, don't you?' he said, smiling.

'Can I ask you something else, then?' Sam continued.

'You can,' Dominic sighed.

'Why aren't you with someone? Is it because you still love your ex fiancé?'

Dominic laughed out loud and then looked at her mouth. He ran his tongue across his lips and Sam had never wanted to kiss anybody so badly in her life.

'I wasn't into anyone until recently.'

Sam looked away, her cheeks colouring.

Dominic stood up to leave and her heart sank. Reading her mind once again, he reached across and pulled her roughly to him. This time, his kiss was not at all gentle. It was passionate and demanding and she felt light headed in his embrace.

'It's been a great night, but I'd better scoot before I can't, don't you think?'

Sam leant against the front door watching Dominic walk away, willing him to turn around. Alas, he didn't. Her only hope was that he would call in when he collected his car later that day. Snuggling up in bed, sleep came easily and she slept in until eleven.

Sam drew back the curtains and looked out the window. Dominic's Mercedes had gone. Tingling at last night's memory, her heart flipped over when she checked her phone and found that Dominic had sent her a text.

'Cheers for a good night, Sam. Hope your head's ok. Dx'

She decided to drink a coffee before replying, and when she did, she plucked up the courage to invite him to dinner that evening. Dominic rang within seconds.

'You just got up?' he asked.

'Yes, I can't believe it. What time did you get up?'

'Eight thirty,' Dominic admitted.

'Good heavens! You must be exhausted,' exclaimed Sam.

'Oh, I'm ok with sleep deprivation. Look, Sam, dinner would be great, but I'm going down to Cornwall. I should have mentioned it, but I'm meeting a couple of mates and we're going diving for a few days. it's been booked for a while, but I'll give you a shout when I get back Friday. Won't be 'til eleven, eleven thirty that Ok?'

'Yes, of course,' Sam replied, trying to sound cool. 'You have a good time and be safe.'

'Sam?' he said.

'Yes?'

'I had a really good time last night, 'n I wish I wasn't going away, to be honest.'

'A bit of male bonding will do you good, you've been working morning, noon and night to get everyone sorted by Christmas,' she said.

'Yeah, think a bit of bonding with you would do me more good. See you Friday.' And he was gone.

Chapter 15

By the time Friday arrived, Sam was a bag of nerves. The prospect of seeing Dominic again was driving her crazy. Combined with her own excitement was Lucy's, who was having a sleepover with Faye. The little girls were fit to burst, and Sam knew that neither the girls nor Liz would get a lot of sleep that night. Sam was actually relieved that Matt was having Lucy to stay the following night, as she did not cope with a lack of sleep and could be quite the little monster. Also, she secretly thought of spending the weekend with Dominic. He had sent her a text saying that he was leaving Cornwall soon and should be with her by eleven thirty, he also added that he had got her a present.

Sam couldn't settle or concentrate on her writing and so had another long bath.

When the doorbell rang at nine o'clock, she almost choked on her glass of wine, totally unprepared if it was Dominic. It was Ace. He had clearly been drinking and was leaning heavily on the doorframe. Sam looked over his shoulder for his car, but thankfully couldn't see it.

'Ace, please tell me you didn't drive?'

Ace smiled and swayed slightly. 'Nah, I got the train from King's Cross and then took a cab here. Can I come in, Sam? I'm bustin' for the loo.'

'Of course, be my guest,' said Sam.

Sam put the kettle on whilst a very tipsy Ace staggered his way to the toilet. Sam felt butterflies in her stomach. She knew that Ace turning up drunk unexpectedly at this time of night was not good news. She feared he had blown it and thrown in his notice with the band and record label, but surely, she thought, she would have heard about this immediately?

She made some strong coffee and put three sugars in Ace's.

'Jeez, Sam, you trying to rot my teef? I just spent the best part of three hundred quid gettin' them whitened.'

Sam just laughed and pointed Ace towards the sofa. He gladly collapsed into its soft contours and drank his coffee. They sat and talked for a while and when Sam could see that Ace had calmed down and sobered up slightly, she asked him to explain.

'So, are you going to tell me what this visit is all about? I imagine you have far better things you could be doing on a Friday night.'

'See that's just it, Sam, no I haven't. I just wanna be here with you.' Ace was still slurring his words, but Sam was touched by the sentiment.

'Listen, Ace, you know you are welcome here anytime, don't you? The thing is, I have so much work I need to do, I would appreciate a little notice next time,' she added, smiling.

Ace shook his head; he had a confused look on his face. Sam quickly tried to put forward some practical suggestions.

'Look, is there something you want to do, Ace? Have you got some ideas, maybe you want write something?'

Ace turned and stared at her, putting down his empty coffee cup unsteadily. Sam saw something in his eyes that she had seen in Dominic's a few days before. It scared the hell out of her, as she knew there could only be one outcome.

'Sam, I wanna be with you. I wanna spend all my time here with you. You keep bangin' around in my 'ead and I wannit gone but I just can't shake it.'

Sam took a deep breath and focused. 'Ace, do not believe for one second I am not flattered.'

'Oh no, Sam,' Ace interrupted, 'don't tell me you're gonna patronise me.' Ace buried his head in his hands and started groaning.

'I would never patronise you, I am trying to be honest,' declared Sam. 'Of course I'm flattered, you idiot. Look at you, you are stunning. You're talented and you have a voice that makes me melt. You are unbelievably amazing with my daughter, who adores you. Added to that, you are funny, kind and intelligent, and way older than your years. Oh, and add a really sexy cockney accent into the mix. So do not think for one second that I have not been attracted to you, Ace, because I have been... but that's all it is.' He looked as though he was agonising over her words, but she continued. 'You have spent your childhood caring for your mother and your siblings. You have struggled financially for years, and at last you have been given an opportunity to have a life you and your family deserve.'

'Yeah, I know all that, and I wanna share it with you and Lucy. You are all I want. I mean it, Sam, we would be so good together, you know.'

Whoa, here it comes, thought Sam. 'Ace, I spent the last few years in a relationship with a man whose career took him away from us for hours every day. Lucy and I only got glimpses of him here and there, and I will never put myself or my daughter through that again. I'm finally learning to enjoy my space and independence, but the next time I have a committed relationship, I want it to be with someone I see every day and who I can curl up beside each night.'

'Cool, then I'll quit and you and me can write and live here together,' Ace replied.

Sam could see he was serious. 'Ace, listen to yourself, please! You are not thinking clearly.'

It became clear to Sam that there was no getting through to Ace tonight; she would need to speak to him again when he was sober. She had also checked the time and realised that Dominic could be back soon.

'Listen, I am going to call you a cab to take you back to London. I'll put it on my account. You must go and sleep this off, get a clear head and I'll call you tomorrow, okay?'

'Why can't I crash in the spare room? We can talk more tomorrow morning, go for a walk 'n stuff?' he demanded.

'Under the circumstances, I think that would be a very bad idea. I am calling you a cab now, okay?' Sam ended the conversation, stood up, strode over to her mobile and made the call.

By the time the cab arrived and she helped him to the door, it was late. Dominic had pushed it to get back earlier than expected and couldn't wait to see her. He pulled up and saw Sam at the front door, smiling at a younger man. She was holding his hand, and then the young man reached out and grabbed Sam, kissing her full on the mouth. Unfortunately, Dominic didn't stay long enough to watch Sam push Ace away furiously.

Dominic got home and headed for the brandy, something he hadn't done since his father's funeral.

Sam was bitterly disappointed that Dominic hadn't bothered coming round. She'd text at midnight to make sure he had got home safe and received was a curt reply.

'Yeah cool thanks'

By the following Friday, Sam was hurt and bewildered. She could not believe that he hadn't shown up or text her. If nothing else, she had at least thought of Dominic as a friend. She couldn't believe that he could have sat and encouraged her to talk about her fears and feelings only to go and trample all over them.

She knew that the last thing she needed in her life was another man to disrespect her, hurt her and keep her guessing. She couldn't help but feel foolish that she had put her trust in yet someone else.

She drafted several texts to him asking him to justify himself, and yet never sent any. This, too, made her feel foolish and needy. Old wounds soon opened, pouring out all her insecurities and anger. After spending a couple of days in pieces, she found the anger and strength to get back up.

She decided that she would focus on Lucy and her work and try everything she could to forget about the man she thought Dominic was.

Lucy seemed to be flourishing at school. It was only three weeks before the Christmas holidays, so school life consisted of nativity plays, Christmas carols and the imminent arrival of Father Christmas.

She was able to stay at Matt's for the whole weekend now and she actually looked forward to it. Sam was able to relax more and enjoy her free evenings without feeling so worried or guilty about Lucy.

Saturday night was the annual Christmas night out for the school mums. Liz had persuaded Sam to join in, convincing her it was always a scream. The women were meeting at the pub for a drink first, and then a mini bus would drive them into town. They were going to a Chinese restaurant which doubled up as a disco. Sam was reluctant to accept initially, as she didn't fancy the late night. Parties weren't really her thing, but she felt she needed a change of scenery. Since her night out in London with Dominic she hadn't socialised after dark, choosing to lose herself in her writing.

Sam wore her favourite skinny jeans and a black, chunky jumper. Her hair was freshly washed and fell luxuriously around her shoulders. She wore a pair of pink cowboy boots which she kept for special occasions, and they added a little colour to the look.

She spotted Dominic's truck was outside the pub as she walked over to meet her friends, and for a split second she debated whether or not to go in.

'No, you won't drive me away, Dominic,' she announced out loud and entered the pub with her head held up high.

Sam had forgotten the effect he had on her and gasped as she saw him, immediately drawn to him like a beacon. He was perched on a bar stool at the end of the bar with a pint of beer, reading the newspaper. He did not look up. Just for a second, she fantasised about tipping his pint over his head, but Sam was too proud to allow him to see how much he had hurt her.

Pretending not to see him, she looked for Liz and Sue, everyone was sitting around a large table. Ordering a glass of wine, she joined them. Dominic still hadn't looked up.

'Ooh, check you out, Miss Sexy Boots. They're gorgeous! Where on earth did you get them?' Liz cried.

'Brighton – a shop on The Lanes, a good few years ago now mind you, but I really love them although I hardly wear them. You look stunning by the way, Liz,' Sam remarked.

'Why thank you, my most favourite new friend, and talking of stunning, have you clapped eyes on delectable Dom tonight? Now that is what I call stunning, although he's a right miserable old sod these days. He hardly acknowledged me when I walked in. Paul said that Dom is so angry at the moment that he keeps thrashing him at squash as well, and Paul's pretty good.'

'I've no idea what's wrong, Liz,' Sam confessed. 'To be honest, I haven't really seen much of him since he finished the studio.'

Liz stared at Sam suspiciously.

'Mm! Not sure what's going on with you two. Doesn't help that you have been ignoring my calls either! All I know is that you went out one evening and then you've both been as miserable as sin ever since. Oh no!' Liz almost levitated in her seat. She thought she had solved the mystery and was really animated now. 'Please don't tell me that he sucks in bed? Oh no, that's it, isn't it?'

Sam laughed nervously. 'Sorry to disappoint you, but things didn't go that far. I'm afraid I've never been particularly liberated in that way and it takes me a lot of getting to know someone before I'm able to get into anything heavy. Besides, he didn't try, he was a gentleman.'

'Oh poor you, how dull!' Liz mocked.

Sam giggled. She loved Liz, the woman was hilarious. 'Listen, how about we talk about you? I have been cocooned inside my house now for days and I need to get out of my head, quite literally.'

'Oh yes, me too, let's get annihilated,' Liz whispered.

'No, not drunk. I mean I need to be distracted from the clutter in my head. The songs keep pestering me like some persistent stalker. So quick, tell me how the kids are, how is Paul?'

'Oh, y'know. Paul is Paul and the kids are a pain in the backside. So there, over and done with anyway, back to you and Dom. When are you going out again?'

Sam's heart felt quite heavy. Glancing over at Dominic, she still could not work out what had happened between them. The same questions had been rolling around in her head ever since. The night they had spent together had been perfect and so utterly romantic. He had been attentive and loving and, unless her instincts were completely shot, he was really into her. So had something happened in Cornwall, she wondered? Had he met someone else down there? But he'd text her that Friday saying he would see her that evening? Perhaps his mates had persuaded him not to get involved with a single mother who was carrying a great deal of baggage. Who knows? She just knew it still hurt like hell and seeing him again tonight wasn't helping to get him out of her system. Liz was still pressing the point.

'Well?' Liz demanded an answer, her urgency brought Sam back into the present.

'Liz, please let's change the subject. I really don't feel comfortable talking about Dominic, particularly as he is just a few feet away.'

As if he had heard, Dominic suddenly looked up and stared Sam straight in the eye. Holding her gaze for a few moments, he nodded, but Sam glared at him, so he shrugged and then casually went back to his newspaper.

After that, Sam felt furious and wanted to go home, but having made a commitment she didn't like to go back on her word, so she climbed aboard the mini bus, went with the others to the restaurant, ate Chinese food and drank far too much cheap wine.

Returning home, feeling too tipsy to work, she curled up with a blanket on the sofa and watched The Bodyguard, her favourite movie.

She woke up feeling thirsty early the next morning, so she made a streaming mug of coffee and went out to the beach hut to work. Fortunately, the timer Dominic had installed meant it was already warm and inviting. She wished they'd stayed and eaten at the Fox, it's wine and food were delicious and she could see why they had won the food and drinks award for the last three years running. Alas the wine at the Chinese restaurant had been quite awful and her head pounded.

The beach hut weaved its magic wand and before long its healing presence had soothed Sam. After a couple of productive hours writing, she cooked herself an early roast lunch and lit the log burner. After lunch, she indulged in a long soak in the bath. Sam felt a surge of strength as she made a resolution to stop being caught up over Dominic. Her day of self-exploration had worked wonders and she felt a huge weight lift.

That was the beauty of being used to having one's heart broken, she thought, you really did learn to live with it and multitask around it.

Sam's serenity soon disappeared. Matt was really twitchy when he brought Lucy home and Lucy was acting up and being extremely grumpy; there were little unshed tears threatening to fall. Sam tried to keep the atmosphere as light as she could, tickling the little girl and showering her with kisses.

'Mummy, please can I see Sooty?' Lucy begged.

'Let's just see Daddy off, sweetheart, and then we'll call Grandma, okay?'

Lucy squeezed her mummy's hand and then went to leave the room. Sam called after her.

'Hey Lucy, Daddy's about to go, so how about you stay here and say goodbye?'

Lucy scowled at Matt, who looked equally perturbed, so Sam tried another tactic to keep the atmosphere sweet.

'Right, you two, before Daddy leaves how about we all sit down and have a drink and a piece of Grandma's Victoria sponge?' Sam asked.

'Sam, how about you call your mum and see if Lucy can go across and see that dog?' Matt asked, looking shifty.

'Sooty!' Lucy shouted at her father. 'His name is Sooty!' Matt glared at her.

The last thing Sam wanted was to be left alone with Matt, but she could see that he needed to speak to her, so she called her mum. Sam and her mum had developed a ritual to allow Lucy to cross safely to her grandparents. She would take Lucy over the road on her side and Mary would cross the opposite side and meet her granddaughter as she tore across the green, waving like crazy.

Matt scowled as Sam came back in.

'Lucy loves it here. All weekend she's gone on and on about the village, the school, you, your parents and that stupid dog.' Matt was clearly agitated.

'It's early days, Matt, bear with her, please,' Sam reasoned.

'Why didn't we do this? We could have sold up and got something here, kept an apartment and studio for me to stay in London and I could have come home on weekends,' he announced.

Sam was stunned by the revelation. She turned her back on him to distract herself and put the kettle on.

'Do you fancy a coffee?' she asked.

'Er, do you have something stronger? Sorry, but I really need a drink. Maybe we could go across to the pub?' Matt asked hopefully.

'I can pour you a lager or a glass of wine if you like?'

'Okay, a glass of wine would be good, thanks.'

She poured a glass of red, handed it to him and was surprised that he downed it in seconds. Matt looked up at Sam and offered up his glass for a second round.

'Matt, you're driving,' Sam exclaimed. 'You can have a small glass.'

Again he downed it, and then slumped down on the chair. Matt put his head in his hands and then, acting completely out of character, burst into tears. Sam was astonished and didn't quite know what to do. She tried reaching across to hold his hand, but some inner voice refused to let her, so she just sat in silence, waiting to see if he would talk.

Eventually he did talk.

Chapter 16

'Jasmine is pregnant.'

'Oh Matt, that's wonderful news. Congratulations.' Sam was amazed to discover that she genuinely meant every single word.

Matt stared at Sam as though she had just stepped off of a space ship.

'Congratulations!? Wonderful news!? Are you out of your mind? For Christ's sake, she is about to record another album. We were about to approach a couple of record companies in the States and she is insisting on going ahead with the pregnancy. I need you to talk to her, Sam.'

'Me?! What on earth for? What do you expect me to say? It's none of my business.'

'Tell her what a mistake she's about to make. Convince her to get rid of it. Tell her how you messed your career up. Sam, please! Tell her she can always go back to having a baby someday. You need to get through to her, you know what it's like to lose everything. Please don't let her make the same mistake.'

Sam sat for a few moments in silence. She was lost for words, but she eventually got up and, uncharacteristically at this early in the day, she poured herself a glass of the wine and took a large gulp. She sat beside Matt and reached for his hand. He looked up and seemed to have aged in the last few minutes.

'Listen, Matt, I need to say this and you need to listen, okay?'
He nodded tearfully. 'Matt, having a baby is not like buying a car.
You can't just go back and buy another at a later date. This child,
your child, is already growing inside Jasmine and she will already
be emotionally, physically and spiritually attached to her baby, I
have no doubt.'

'But she's young, she can have another baby,' he argued.

'Yes, but not this baby. If she decides to end this pregnancy
then she may regret it so badly, Matt. There's no going back from
that place, you know.' She stared at him and squeezed his hand
tighter. He looked annoyed. 'Look, Matt, you tried persuading me
to have an abortion, but when you look at Lucy can you honestly
tell me that the world would have been a better place without
her? Tell me, Matt? Aren't you pleased I stuck to my decision and
continued with the pregnancy? Can you imagine your life if we
didn't have her?'

'Of course not, but Luce is special,' he protested.

'And your next child will be, too. Please don't ask Jasmine to
abort this baby, not if she really wants to have it. I don't think it's
fair Matt, I really don't.'

'But what about her career? What about the album?'

'There is nothing stopping Jasmine from having a baby and
a career. It is the twenty first century, after all!' Sam was getting
angry with Matt, but being the kind natured woman that she
was, she didn't want to hurt him. However, Matt's attitude wasn't
helping.

'What the hell is it with me and women? Why do I pick the
ones that want to trap me?'

They both looked at each other now, shocked. There it was: the truth was out. He said it. Sam's heart hardened, she felt anger boil up inside her.

'Sam… I, I didn't mean…'

'Trap you? Trap you?! How dare you. You really are one self-centred man. This is not about Jasmine's career, is it? It's all about you. Maybe it's time you stopped riding on the coattails of your girlfriends and made your own path. How dare you, Matt!'

Matt was taken aback at the venom in Sam's words.

'No, I wasn't meaning you, Sam, it came out wrong. I… I just meant…'

'I know exactly what you meant, Matt, and yes, you did mean me. I did not trap you. Let me remind you: I was on the pill, but had had a stomach bug when you and I went up to Scotland to do that show. If you recall, I kept on saying it wasn't a good idea, but we had been drinking and one thing led to another and yes, I got pregnant and no, it wasn't the right time, but thank heavens I did – else we wouldn't have Lucy.' She stared at Matt, seeing if he was taking it in, and when she was satisfied that he was listening, she went on. 'Jasmine can have a career and a baby and you can make sure of it by helping her. See the thing is, Matt, you weren't there for Lucy and me, not really.'

'What are you talking about? I didn't leave your side all through the birth.' Matt sounded hurt but Sam simply laughed at him. There was not a flicker of amusement in her eyes.

'Well hallelujah, you managed to stay for the duration of labour. You welcomed your daughter into the world and that's when you then took off – you carried on with your own career, not thinking once of mine.'

'Rubbish. I continually tried persuading you to go back to work, and you know I did.'

'Persuade? You bullied me. You told me I needed to get a childminder. All I wanted was a few hours a week to write and for you to take care of Lucy, but you wouldn't, Matt, not once! I didn't want a stranger raising our daughter, I wanted her father to take some responsibility for the childcare.'

Matt glared at Sam; he clearly had no intention of accepting any responsibility whatsoever. Sam had heard enough. She was tired and sick to death of her selfish ex-partner.

'Matt, the woman you are supposed to love is pregnant with your child. You seem convinced that I trapped you in a domestic hell of nappy changes and feeding routines and now Jasmine's doing the same. I do not care about the finer details, but I do care about Jasmine, and I care about your unborn son or daughter. If you continue as you are, then you will no doubt do to Jasmine what you did to Lucy and me. You will cast her aside for another, younger model who you believe will conquer the world with you… Poor Jasmine will spend hour upon hour alone with a tiny baby, wondering when the hell you will show up to offer a spare crumb of affection and attention. Y'know, Matt, I cannot bear to think of another woman being made to feel like that.'

Sam could see that Matt was struggling, but he needed to hear this. She owed it to not only Jasmine and his child, but also to herself and Lucy. Sam had always regretted never standing up to Matt, always avoiding doing anything to upset him with the risk of him going off and sulking for hours on end. She wished she had been braver and perhaps he would have given more to her and Lucy but… He was looking like he was about to leave, so she carried on.

'Matt, don't repeat patterns. I've already seen the photos that Keira Hunt is putting on Facebook of the two of you…'

'What! You? Facebook?'

'No, I'm not on Facebook, but Richard showed me. It's not fair, Matt. You don't have to seduce every prodigy that you get to work with. You're in an influential position, stop taking advantage of them please, and show Jasmine some respect.'

'What photos?' He looked worried.

'The photos of you and Keira in a club. If Jasmine sees them, she will be hurt tremendously.'

'Don't know what you are talking about. Someone would have photoshopped them. Keira is just a kid.'

'She's nineteen, and by the way you were looking at her in the photos, trust me, there was nothing but lust in your eyes.'

Matt had heard enough and shook his head. 'Guess I should have realised I wouldn't get any help from you,' he sneered.

'Matt, you know it really would help if you could just accept some responsibility. Playing the victim isn't useful or attractive.'

'Victim! Woah, Sam, if anyone ever played the victim, it's you. You spent the first years of Lucy's life playing the downtrodden victim. I was looking at some old photos the other day, and you know what? In all of them, you had a face like a slapped backside.'

Sam sensed that things might escalate, as Matt always turned nasty when he didn't get his own way.

'You're right, Matt, I did look downtrodden with a face like a slapped backside because I was downtrodden. I was a victim. You

173

treated me atrociously, and you have no idea just how miserable I was for years with you.'

'Oh please, you loved every minute of it. It gave you loads of angst and drama for you to write your miserable songs, you…'

'Enough, Matt. Enough.' Sam raised her hands and put them to her ears. 'I no longer need to listen to you. One more word and I will walk out and you can wallow in the miserable bed you've made.'

Matt fell silent, unsure how to reply to Sam. He wasn't used to her standing up to him. Sam had never, ever stood up to Matt before and he didn't like it.

'Now then, I'm interested in our daughter,' Sam said quickly. 'Something is clearly not right between the two of you, so do you think you can enlighten me please?'

Matt was clearly itching to carry on the outburst, but something had changed in Sam's manner and he could clearly see that she meant her last words. He had taken a while to admit it to himself but over the past few weeks, this new, confident, happy Sam was actually driving him out of his mind. He had never wanted Sam more than at this moment, and Jasmine getting pregnant had blown his chances of getting back together with her.

When Sam was home, the house had been organised, clean and tidy. Meals were always delicious and the house felt warm and cosy, but Jasmine was a lousy cook and ordered takeaways most nights. She was untidy, the house had rubbish piled up on every available surface. The lounge and their bedroom resembled students digs after an all weekend party, and she had even started letting her own appearance go, too.

It had irked him that Sam had been genuinely happy about the baby and for Jasmine and himself. It suggested to him that she had indeed moved on. He noticed how she never looked at him in a loving way any longer, but spoke to him as she would a colleague, not a man she was once in love with.

Matt had presumptuously spent a couple of weeks last month looking at apartments in London. In his mind, he had already decided to sell the house in Muswell Hill, buy a smaller place and move out here with Sam and Lucy. Studio space was easy to rent in London, he reasoned. He could pick it up when he needed it. He had also taken for granted Sam's once loyal and unconditional love, assuming she would welcome him back with open arms. He had planned the whole damn thing when Jasmine dropped her bombshell.

He glared across the green over to Sam's parents' house. He blamed them for taking Sam away from him, enticing her with their roses and clematis and their picture-perfect cottages in the perfect village. Lucy had complained all weekend that London stank and was too busy and that there weren't enough animals, flowers and trees.

Sam pressed him to answer her question.

'Matt! Talk to me, what happened with Lucy this weekend?'

'It was Jasmine,' he said sarcastically.

Well, I didn't think it would be your fault, Sam thought to herself, but remained silent.

'She announced Thursday night that she was pregnant and then, just because I didn't crack open a bottle of champagne, she sulked for the entire weekend and shut herself in the spare room. Lucy had to do puzzles and Lego on her own most of the time.'

'Do you mind me asking why you couldn't have entertained her instead?' Sam asked irritably.

'Someone has to work, Sam, and keep the bills paid, seeing as I have two families now.'

'Oh, Matt! This is getting silly now. You know you pay absolutely nothing towards Lucy. I pay all my own bills and have done so since moving here. I seem to remember paying a lot of our bills in London, too, by the way. I can't comment on what Jasmine does or does not contribute, and quite honestly I have no interest in that, but for the sake of your relationship with Lucy, you must spend a little more quality time with her when you have her.'

Matt stood up, grabbing his keys, and made to leave. He was shouting now and his eyes were bulging. 'I'm not going to stay around here and take any more of this. This is all your fault, Sam. If you hadn't rejected me, then I wouldn't have needed Jasmine and then all this wouldn't be happening.'

'Oh, poor you.' Sam started laughing, although she was angry. 'Get out, Matt. Get in that ridiculous car and go.'

Matt stormed off with a wheel spin. Sam watched the dust settle on the road outside and took a deep breath. She strode across the green. It was getting dark and the street lights were starting to glow. Sam could hear Lucy's familiar squeals of laughter as she knocked on her mum and dad's front door.

'Mummy, look at Sooty,' Lucy demanded.

Sam's eyes rested on Sooty. He looked adorable, with red tinsel around his collar and some little gold bells dangling from it. Lucy kept hugging Sam as she made her way inside the cottage. Mary insisted they stay for dinner, which Sam was so grateful for. She and Lucy needed distracting from Matt and the toxic cloud he walked under; its poison was penetrating everything around it.

So Sam tucked into her second roast that day, and by the time they walked home it was pitch dark. The village was peaceful and they felt calm, relaxed and full up. Sam had not needed to say anything to her parents. Instinctively they knew that something had happened with Matt. They just poured wine and filled the evening with anecdotes and tales about the village and villagers, keeping both Sam and Lucy highly entertained and distracted.

Lucy didn't mention Matt, Jasmine or the weekend she'd spent with them, and so Sam decided she wouldn't either. Instead, Lucy chatted on and on about Sooty and once she was fast asleep, Sam made the decision to keep to the promise she had made to Lucy some time ago.

Sam got herself comfortable on the sofa, MacBook in hand, and Googled the ideal dog for them, entering what she did and didn't want in a pet. After a little searching, there appeared a scruffy little dog on the screen. The Border Terrier.

With its otter-like face, it really is the most beautiful looking animal and the ideal companion. Adaptable and easy going. Happy to run in the fields all day or to curl up indoors. The Border Terrier likes a varied lifestyle and is good with other dogs and children.

Sam spent the next two hours reading all about this fascinating breed, and by midnight she had tracked down a local breeder who had a litter ready for homing in two weeks. Sam emailed the breeder requesting a visit so that she could meet her and discuss the pups on offer.

The following morning, having walked Lucy to school, Sam decided to check her emails. The Border Terrier breeder had got back in touch and she had attached photographs of the cutest puppies Sam had ever seen. There were two dogs and one bitch left.

The breeder had prepared a questionnaire for Sam to answer. She asked about the house and the garden, her lifestyle and career, and had she owned a dog before? Sam was astonished at how many details the breeder was asking for. She called her mum to ask if she'd had a similar interrogation when buying Sooty.

'Oh, darling, some of these breeders are obsessed. Mind you, my love, it's good that they do care where their little darlings go. Don't forget Sooty had been rescued, but even the rescue centre insisted on coming to check the garden and fencing, so don't be surprised if yours will do the same. Why don't I come with you this afternoon and have look at them? I imagine they will be snapped up before long. Border Terriers have become quite popular.'

'Thanks, Mum. I'll call her now and see if we can pop over.'

The breeder asked Sam to email the questionnaire to her immediately and unless there was a problem, then they could visit after lunch. Fortunately there wasn't a problem, and Sam and Mary drove over and instantly fell in love with the little girl dog.

After an hour of chatting and questions, Trisha, the breeder, said that on the condition all checks were satisfactory Sam could indeed have the dog. Sam paid a deposit and agreed to bring Lucy back at the weekend. Trisha had asked that she be allowed to visit Sam the following day at home in order to check the property for any hidden dangers. Sam happily agreed and felt reassured by Trisha: she was a typical, "no nonsense" animal lover, and she had promised Sam continual support in rearing the puppy should she require it.

Sam didn't think for one minute that they wouldn't be allowed to have the little dog, but she decided not to tell Lucy until tomorrow just in case Trisha changed her mind, as she said she had three other families who wanted her pups.

It was going to be so difficult keeping the secret from Lucy.

Chapter 17

Fortunately, the following day Trisha pronounced herself delighted with Wisteria Cottage. The safety and security of the garden had passed her stringent tests. Her only recommendation was to fit a strong lock on the front gate, as Border Terriers were renowned escape artists. She confirmed that her pup would thrive in the environment, particularly as Sam worked mainly from home.

Sam picked Lucy up from school. It was a cold, damp and wintery afternoon, and so they hurried along the lane to Mary and John's for tea. When they got home, it was already dark. Sam ran Lucy a bath and, while Lucy was splashing around, Sam crept into Lucy's bedroom and placed a card on her pillow.

After bath time, Lucy went to her bedroom to get her story book. Sam casually followed, hardly able to contain her excitement. Inside the card, she had printed out a photo she had taken of the pup on her phone. In the card, she had written "Happy early Christmas, darling, love from Mummy". Sam had assumed it was obvious, but when Lucy opened the card, her dear little face looked so confused. Lucy walked tentatively over to Sam with the card.

'Mummy, this is a pretty dog. Whose is it?'

Sam pulled the little girl into her arms, holding the photo up high.

'Lucy, this is our puppy. We are getting…'

Of course, she didn't get a chance to finish. Lucy squealed with delight and jumped up and down on the bed. She squeezed Sam so tightly around the waist that Sam felt herself well up with tears. She was relieved she had made the right decision, however, why on earth she decided to tell her daughter just as she was about to go to sleep, Sam would never know. She was still cursing herself at one in the morning when Lucy appeared for the hundredth time with the little photo, too excited to sleep.

On Saturday morning, Sam and Lucy went back to Trisha's to see the puppy. It was love at first sight; it seemed to distract Lucy from the thought that she was staying at her dad's that night. She had agreed, although needing reassuring that it was just the one night.

The puppy was an instant success with mum and daughter and was already responding to Lucy's excited voice. Over cups of tea and lemonade for Lucy, Trisha asked what they were going to call the pup.

'Little Dog,' announced Lucy proudly.

'Gosh, that's an unusual name, why Little Dog?' Trisha asked, while catching the appalled expression on Sam's face.

'Well Sooty is black and Mummy had a black rabbit she called Sooty, so I called him Sooty, and she is little and a dog, so I will call her Little Dog.'

Sam looked with pleading eyes to Trisha.

'Do you know, Lucy, my Border Terriers are actually classed as Red, like a fox.'

'Okay, I could call her Little Fox then, although it may muddle people because she's a dog really,' said Lucy between slurps of lemonade.

Again, Sam made frantic faces behind Lucy's back, but she really couldn't say anything as she had promised Lucy she could name the dog.

'Tell you what,' said Trisha, kindly, 'what do you think of the name Red or Ruby? Only her pedigree name is 'Little Red Ruby,' you know.'

Trisha looked at Sam for approval, who sighed with relief.

'Okay, shall we will call her Red, Mummy? Do you mind, or would you prefer we call her Little Dog?'

Sam had secretly been thinking of Ruby for the pup, but now Lucy had chosen Red, she realised that she preferred it and it somehow suited the funny little dog.

Trisha shook hands with Sam and sealed the deal. Lucy kissed the puppy for the hundredth time before saying goodbye.

Sam was relieved that it was Jasmine, not Matt, who came to collect Lucy. She was still somewhat bruised by her encounter with him and didn't want to have to see him anytime soon. Jasmine was an hour early, and Lucy was still over at John and Mary's reliving the morning's events at Trisha's.

Sam was taken aback at Jasmine's appearance. She was so exhausted and confused that Sam put a comforting arm around her and persuaded her to come in for a cup of tea. Poor Jasmine felt so sick.

'I have some peppermint tea and a ginger cake, how about you try it? It really helped me when I was pregnant.'

Jasmine's expression said it all. She sank into the sofa and turned to Sam.

'Yeah, right, Matt said he told you. Think he was hoping you would talk me out of it. So, if that's what you are about to do, then go ahead. It won't be hard 'cuz I've already had enough, Sam. I'm seriously considering it as an option.'

Sam brewed a pot of peppermint tea and placed it on a tray with two pretty teacups. She carried it through to Jasmine in the lounge.

Sam asked how Matt had been behaving and was disappointed to hear that their talk had little effect and not done any good at all. Apparently, he had sulked in the studio most of the week and spent every evening asleep on the couch. Sam knew Jasmine genuinely wanted this baby, as her whole being lit up when she spoke about it. It wasn't the sickness and tiredness that was putting her off, but Matt the bully. Sam knew he was doing his best to manipulate Jasmine into having an abortion.

'I'm so sorry, Sam, like you need to hear me go on about this. I stole Matt from you in the first place. I'm surprised you don't just tell me to go.' Guilt was etched all over Jasmine's face.

'Look, Jasmine. You didn't steal Matt, he chose you. He wanted you more than he wanted me, and you fell in love with him. Matt and I weren't right together and it took a while for me to see that, so I'm grateful to you.' Jasmine looked up with tears glistening in her eyes. 'Jasmine, you have the guts and spirit which I didn't have back then. Do not let Matt take that from you. If you want to abort your child then that is your decision to make, however, if you want to go ahead with the pregnancy then I can promise you that you'll cope, with or without Matt.'

'I thought he would be pleased, Sam. I mean, he goes on and on about missing Lucy. I thought he would be pleased.' Jasmine burst into tears, so Sam leant over and held her while she wept and stroked her hair. When she had calmed down a little, Sam tried a different approach.

'Listen, Jasmine. You've said yourself how good Matt is with Lucy, which he is. But Matt needs to pull his head out of his backside and take a good look at himself. Matt didn't treat me very well, but I believe that you can nip this in the bud right now.'

'But how?' Jasmine murmured.

'Well this won't be easy listening to, but… Matt takes the bits of a relationship he likes and then pretends the other parts don't exist. If you do decide to keep this baby, then you need to believe you can do it with or without Matt by your side. You need to convince him that whilst your dream is for him to be a part of it, if necessary, you will go it alone. He needs to know that if he stands beside you then he will do just that and share the child's life. You must be able to continue with your career and not put it on hold.'

'Matt would never go for that,' Jasmine replied, shaking her head. Sam couldn't resist a dig.

'Well then, he should have thought of that before spreading his seed, shouldn't he?'

'I know, but we were both drunk, Sam. I had to come off the pill a while ago; it had been giving me headaches.'

'Exactly! Matt was aware of the situation and still had unprotected sex with you, so please don't try to justify his behaviour by insisting he was drunk. Sorry Jasmine, but Matt is a spoilt little boy who needs to grow up and take responsibility for his actions, and I think you're the woman to make him do it.'

Sam observed Jasmine's reaction as she mulled it all over. She poured two more cups of tea and continued.

'Do you remember that time at the music conference, when Matt was trying to get you to agree a figure for the German contract? Well, I do. You were hard as nails and wouldn't back down for a second. Matt, on the other hand, was willing to sign a crazy percent away just to seal the deal. You ended up with a much better deal with a stronger company because you stuck to your guns.'

Poor Jasmine looked so confused.

'Jasmine, I lived with Matt for a long time and I know how he thinks. I'm sure he has convinced you that your career will die if you continue with the pregnancy, but that is only true if you allow it to die.'

Jasmine sipped her tea and looked directly at Sam. 'He said that you lost everything and he said people stopped calling him. Blaming him that you were pregnant.'

'I bet he did,' Sam remarked with a grimace. 'He told me the same story, told me none of the big wigs would give me the time of day anymore and do you know what? I believed him! Don't get me wrong, some doors were slammed in my face, but that was only initially. However, further down the line it materialised that Matt had been the only one who was negative about my pregnancy. My own publishers had been pretty off at that time but when I looked into it, Matt was the one who had put them off.'

'Oh no, Sam, that's awful. Matt's a bully.' Jasmine appeared even more worried and Sam felt awful for telling her a few home truths.

'The last thing I wanted was to burden you with my rubbish, Jasmine, please don't worry. That was then, and I have noticed quite a change in Matt since we moved here. I know that he is aware of the mistakes he makes, even if he is not willing to admit to them most of the time. That gutsy, sexy temptress who came to my door a few years ago needs to come to the fore. You knew exactly what you wanted and how you were going to go about getting it. Matt burst blood vessels over you that day. The man fancies you rotten, but he's a fool. He's just managed to momentarily crush you so please, for your sake and the baby, get back up and get angry with him. You have every right to.'

'But he just won't budge on it, Sam,' Jasmine argued.

'Matt's a control freak. He has treated you despicably and you can either lie there and take it like I did, or you can stop it now. Let him know you don't need him. Let him know that your decision is final,' Sam said.

'But how?' Jasmine asked. The poor woman looked exhausted still.

'Tell him you will go it alone. Tell him you can afford a live-in nanny if he leaves you, which you can. Tell him you will not compromise your career and that with or without him, you will make sure that you have excellent childcare in place and you will pursue your career. Even tell him you'll move to the States to live with your parents for a bit, but please my angel, please make him aware that he is either one hundred percent in or out and I swear it will work out for you all. Matt knew I would stay and put up with things because he had tested me so many times, but he hasn't tested you until recently. He doesn't know how much you are willing to put up with, so tell him.'

Jasmine's tears welled up again, but this time she was laughing with relief. She grabbed Sam and virtually pulled her off the sofa.

'You're right you know, Sam. I'm going to go home and kick his lazy butt into shape.'

'Oh please, not in front of Lucy,' Sam said, laughing.

When Lucy saw Jasmine, she ran into her arms. Sam realised that for Lucy's sake, too, she had to help Jasmine deal with this.

As she waved them off, she felt exhausted by the encounter with Jasmine. However, she knew it had been crucial for all their sakes. She decided to have a long soak in the bath before starting work.

Chapter 18

Saturday afternoon, and the town was busy with shoppers milling around. Amongst them was Liz, who bumped into Dominic on the way into Waitrose and decided to hang onto him.

'Ah, Dom, what a stroke of luck. Paul dropped me off to get my hair done, but the salon double booked me, the idiots. Anyway, I need to get home; Paul's taken the kids to the cinema and was coming back for me in a couple of hours. I was going to kill time shopping, but now I won't need to, will I?'

Dominic looked pretty thunderous, but said it was okay. Once Liz got comfortable in the passenger seat of his truck he started up, and so did Liz.

'Right, we have approximately ten to fifteen minutes, traffic permitting, before we get home, so that gives me just enough time to hear why you have been absolutely awful to my new best friend.'

Dominic gave Liz a puzzled look and then tried changing the subject. Unfortunately for him, Liz was as stubborn and as determined as he was.

When he pulled up outside the house, Liz folded her arms and announced that until he agreed to tell her what had happened, she would not get out of the truck. He would have to carry her out, but if he did so, she would scream and kick and say he was abducting her.

Dominic knew that Liz wasn't bluffing and had no shame when it came to embarrassing him. He smiled briefly when he recalled a time he watched Liz in full flow...

Paul and Dominic had been in the pub watching football. Paul was meant to go home for lunch. Suddenly Liz walked in with a tray of food, and Paul and the rest of their table found it all hysterical. Liz looked so beautiful and smiled sweetly at Paul. Then she said, 'Hey sweetie pie, I thought you must be getting hungry.' She then placed the meal and a pot of gravy in front of him and started pouring it over Paul's lunch. Then, she slowly trickled it over his lap and head. Paul had stopped laughing now and learnt never to take his wife for granted again.

'Look, Liz,' Dominic hollered, grasping the steering wheel. 'For one, it's none of your damn business, and second, it's no big deal, okay? Let it go.'

'No big deal?' exclaimed Liz. 'That poor woman managed to salvage enough guts and spirit to leave that no-good idiot of an ex to allow herself to fall for a guy who, may I add, I foolishly encouraged her to fall for. Quite frankly, Dom, you've been a complete and utter poo bag and let me down, and I say poor show! Now then, unless you have had a personality transplant, then I believe something has happened, as I do know that you are one of the good guys with integrity, albeit a tortured soul with a skip-load of issues. You would not lead a poor damsel up the garden path only to slam the door in her face – so pray tell.'

Dominic gave up. He loved his best mate's wife, but she was a pain in the backside.

'A skip load? Okay, how about we go inside and talk?' he suggested.

'Only if you promise you won't drive off the second I get out?' Liz replied.

'Promise,' he agreed.

'Pinky promise.' Dominic stared at Liz, alarmed at the little finger she poked out to him waiting for him to oblige.

'Promise,' he snapped, ignoring the finger and moving over to open his door.

'Oh no we don't, delectable Dom. Pinky promise or we do it here.'

'Oh for… this is stupid, Liz. Okay, I promise.' He linked little fingers briefly, but it was enough to satisfy Liz. Job done.

Once inside, Liz made coffee and opened some chocolate digestives. They sat facing each other on the window seat.

'So,' Liz said expectantly.

'So,' repeated Dom. 'We went out, it was a good night, but then I decided I didn't want to take things further.'

'Why?'

'Why not? It's a free country.'

'Indeed it is, my darling, but I know you. You said you would call her when you got back from your trip but then you didn't, and I know you wouldn't normally do that. Has she got halitosis or something that I haven't noticed?'

'No.'

'Then what? Smelly feet?'

'No.'

'B.O.?'

'No. Liz, ENOUGH,' he shouted.

'Was she obsessive and declared her undying love to you?' asked Liz as she reached for another biscuit.

'You clearly don't know Sam,' Dominic said, laughing.

'Ah see, that's the problem, Dominic,' replied Liz, pointing with her biscuit and spreading the crumbs everywhere. 'I think I know her pretty well, albeit not for very long time. Anyway, I think she has to be one of the nicest, sexiest and creative women I know, and she so rang your ding-a-ling, didn't she?'

Dominic looked to the ceiling and burst out laughing. 'Well I've heard it called a lot, but never that.'

'You're just trying to distract me. Jolly well answer the question, Dominic, before I strike you from our Christmas card list for being a phoney.'

'I like the fact that I'm taking the rap for this, Liz. How do you know I'm in the wrong here?'

'Because you said you would call her, but you didn't. Anyway, you made her feel a fool and you made her question her instincts, which are already an issue with her after the last numpty. Also, you have so many issues.'

'RUBBISH,' Dominic shouted.

'Well, you do. Abandonment issues. You're also scared to have a relationship in case she leaves you, and you're scared you'll become that poor little abandoned boy who was dumped at boarding school and deserted by his own parents at the age of nine, was it?'

'You have no idea what you are talking about. Sorry Liz, but I'm out of here.' He got up and started heading towards the door.

'Oh, stop being a baby!' she shouted. 'See, look at you, rather than have a conversation you're going to storm off and go and drink yourself to sleep. Baby.'

'I am NOT a baby,' he shouted as his hand reached the door handle.

'Dom, Dom's a baby, in the tree top. When the bough breaks, his cradle will rock…'

Liz started singing the "rockabye baby" rhyme so out of tune that it was making him flinch.

'Now who's the baby?' he asked, desperately trying not to laugh.

'Babies leave, babies sulk.'

'I am not a baby.' He was laughing now.

'So, man up, stop behaving like one, and justify your atrocious behaviour.' Liz knew she had won and crossed her arms across her chest. Dominic came and sat back down.

'Look, I didn't call her when I got back that Friday night.'

'Exactly, and do you know…'

'Liz! do you want me to explain or not?' he shouted. 'I drove round and saw some bloke kissing her, so next time get your facts straight.'

Liz was speechless, which was a novelty, thought Dominic, as she was seldom lost for words.

'See, not so cocky now, are you? Now who's the baby!' He was really exhausted by the whole scenario, but it felt good to get it off his chest, and he had to admit that Liz had hit a couple of nerves about his childhood which he had buried so long ago.

'Oh Dominic, I'm so sorry,' she finally spluttered. 'There must be some mistake, are you sure it wasn't her dad?'

Dominic almost choked on his coffee at the idea.

'Not unless John wears his jeans round his knees and is covered in piercings and tattoos!'

Liz burst into hysterics and started shouting *'No!'* over and over again and spluttering on her biscuit. Dominic was at a loss as to what to say and decided to wait until she had calmed down.

'No, you dingbat, that's Ace,' Liz giggled.

'Well, who the hell is Ace?' he asked, frowning.

'He's a singer in a band; he is one of the guys she writes for. Anyway, she only told me because I found her in tears the next day. She was devastated and was worried that she had somehow led him on and hurt him. Anyway, now I reckon she was crying over you really, for being so horrid. Sam told me he had turned up the night before, declaring his undying love or something like that. Well, he was over the limit, so she had got a taxi to take him home, anyway she was seeing him out when he grabbed her, like one of those grabber lorries – ooh, you need a grabber lorry, Dom, don't you, to remove your skip load of issues! Anyway, then he kissed her, like full on, tongue thrust down her throat. Poor little lamb, it nearly choked her, apparently. Anyway, oh gosh, I hope you don't kiss like that, Dom. I mean a subtle and gentle build up is nice, then again, I guess he felt it was his only chance and he was drunk, so wham bam he went for it man.' She finished the last part with an awful attempt at an American accent.

Dominic shook his head fiercely, desperately trying not to laugh.

'Liz, anyway, anyway, anyway. Will you please slow down and stick to the story?'

'Oh, sorry. I do get side tracked, don't I? Right, so, where was I? Ah yes, he snogged her and she shoved him away, but I guess you didn't see that bit did you? I bet you got all hot and bothered and went home to sulk like a baby. Anyway, had you have not been such a baby, you would have seen what really happened, but oh no, poor little abandoned Dom, Dom had to stomp off home. Anyway, she was devastated as she loves him to bits, but not in that way.'

Dominic raked his fingers through his hair in frustration.

'Oh Dom, Dom,' said Liz, sadly. 'You first prize plonker, you absolute numpty, what have you done?'

Dominic stared out of the window, trying to clear his head. *Poor Sam must think him I'm a right sod*, he thought solemnly.

'So you didn't think to share this with me before then, Liz?'

'Don't you dare pass the buck. You messed up. Now go fix it before she moves on to someone more worthy, who incidentally is beginning to look a lot like Jason Tadstock, and don't you dare let her down again.'

Dominic shoulders shook with laughter now.

'Jason Tadstock? Who the hell is Jason Tadstock?'

'He is a landscape gardener, if you must know. He fenced her garden and did stuff outdoors for her. Anyway, I went round there and he was all bulging biceps, drinking coffee with her and making her laugh. She was doing that hair swishing thingy and trust me, when women swish their hair it can only mean one thing.' Liz was on a roll now and Dominic had to admit the woman was hilarious. 'Jason has beautiful blue eyes and he has that Reverend

Gibson floppy hair that he keeps raking off his face, and us girls like that so you better pull your socks up, delectable Dom, before "way hay Jay" steals the heroine.'

Dominic ruffled her hair.

'Man you're weird, Liz. You do know that, don't you? I do love you but how my best mate copes with you, I will never know.'

As he turned to leave, Liz called out.

'Hey Dom, what's the name for a baby cow again?'

'A calf,' he answered, looking irritable and somewhat confused.

'No, a baby.' With that, Liz burst into hysterics all over again.

Dominic decided to go for a quick pint to clear his head. He was angry with himself for misjudging his instincts. He knew Sam was a good person, and yet he had been willing to write her off way too quick, making himself look like a fool in the process. He decided to go over and face her tonight, as Liz had told him that Lucy was staying with her dad. Unfortunately, he should have gone straight round, as Sam was going out.

As his hand went to knock the door, Sam had already started opening it. She took his breath away; she looked stunning. She had a floor length fitted dress in shimmering shades of pink, her glossy red, blond hair was loosely tied up, and her eyes were bewitching. Her stare, however, told a different story, and she looked at him with indifference.

'Dominic, hi,' she said.

'I need to talk, can I come in?'

'I'm going out, sorry.' Then, looking over his shoulder, she nodded, 'There's my taxi now.'

Sam locked the door, then pulled a huge coat over her and wrapped her scarf around, all the time saying nothing. Dominic felt a fool, but he knew he deserved it.

'Can we meet up tomorrow, Sam? I really need to talk to you.'

'I have my friend staying tonight, but I will give you a call tomorrow, Dominic. Right, I don't mean to be rude, but I need to go, see you later.' With that, she got into the taxi and didn't spare him a glance.

Inside, Sam's tummy was all messed up with nerves. Liz had just called her to tell her all about the misunderstanding and whilst Sam could understand it, it had given her a reality check... Dominic had hurt her and she wasn't sure she wanted to give another man that power over her again, power to hurt her or, God forbid, hurt Lucy again. Sam adored Dominic and was more attracted to him than she had ever been to Matt, but maybe Liz was right, maybe the issues Dominic had were just too much for him to be able to commit to a relationship. She realised that the combination of that and her own insecurities could be potentially toxic.

Chapter 19

She met Suzy at the train station and then headed to the restaurant. The two women had a wonderful evening. They talked nonstop and laughed until their sides split. It had been debatable all week as to whether or not Suzy would be able to travel so it was a double celebration this evening.

When they got home, Sam lit the fire, opened a bottle of wine and put some music on. Suzy appeared downstairs in her onesie: a particularly cute one with Winnie The Pooh all over it. Suzy loved Winnie The Pooh. Then she flopped onto the sofa with a great big grin on her face.

'Ok, Sam, so I bet you're wondering what I'm getting you for Christmas this year, aren't you?'

'Well, not as much I hope,' said Sam, handing her a glass of wine. 'You always go mad at Christmas and it really isn't necessary, especially for Lucy, she gets plenty.'

Suzy rummaged around in her bag and handed Sam a piece of folded up paper. Sam opened it and saw that it was an estate agent's sale sheet for Primrose Cottage. Primrose Cottage was two doors up and it, too, overlooked the village green. It was a beautiful property and not too dissimilar to Wisteria Cottage, although the garden was a tiny courtyard garden, unlike Sam's enormous garden.

'Er, you're buying me a cottage, Suzy?' Sam asked curiously.

'No silly, I'm buying ME that cottage.'

Sam was speechless, then when she realised what this meant for their friendship, she felt a lump the size of an apple appear in her throat and the tears stream down her face.

'Oh charming, I must say,' Suzy smiled.

Sam put her hands to her mouth in shock, then grabbed her friend and hugged her.

'Oh Suzy, do you have any idea how happy you've just made me? What made you decide to do this? When do you move in?'

'I always wanted to live near you, Sam, you know that. I always wanted to settle in the country, well within easy reach of London, and I've yet to find anywhere that is as beautiful as here. I managed to save quite a lot and Mum and Dad decided they were going to downsize and help me out with a deposit, so... ta dah!'

Sam couldn't quite believe it. She had known Suzy her whole life and they had always planned to settle down one day within stone-throwing distance, and now it was actually happening. Sam had wanted to help Suzy get on the property ladder herself, but Suzy had given a very adamant no. Suzy had saved since she was nineteen and it was finally paying off.

'Oh Suzy, I'm going to cry again. When is all this going to happen?'

'The current owners can't face moving before Christmas, so I suggested the end of January and they agreed. Sound good to you?' Suzy said brightly.

'Oh, sod this wine!' Sam leapt up from the sofa. 'Let's stick a cork in it and open the champagne I've been saving.'

The two of them never made it to bed. They ate chocolate and drank champagne before going onto camomile tea and watching

The Bodyguard.

The following morning, Liz popped over for a cup of coffee and found the two women camped out amongst all the debris of their celebratory sleepover.

Sam was relieved at how well Liz got on with Suzy. She couldn't imagine Liz, or anyone else for that matter, having a problem with Suzy. She was just perfect. When Liz mentioned Red, Suzy looked puzzled.

'Oh wow, Suzy, I forgot to tell you, I've bought a dog and she's coming a week Friday. That means all hell will be breaking lose, what with end of term and a puppy. I didn't think that through, did I?' Sam said. Suzy sat with her mouth open, catching flies.

'I don't know why on earth they are breaking up so early this year, it's beyond me,' Liz said. 'They will have driven me mad by the time Christmas arrives.'

'Yeah, it is pretty early this year, but never mind. I'm sure we'll all manage. Let's arrange lots of play days to keep them amused. I bought some Christmas cracker making kits and we can make Christmas cards with them, what do you say?' Sam asked.

'Defo. Now, back to you and Dom. He feels awful, by the way. What will you do about him? Will you forgive him?' Liz wanted to know.

'Oh no we don't, back up. He is yesterday's news,' interrupted Suzy. 'I want to hear about the puppy. I can't believe I've been here for hours and you haven't bothered to tell me that you're getting a puppy. Unbelievable.' Suzy was in full drama queen mode now.

'I tell you what, Suzy, my head is in bits right now. I just forgot. I guess I was preoccupied about the Dominic thing. Poor Suzy had to hear about him all evening,' she added to Liz. 'Right, Suzy, we need to get ready to get to Mum's for lunch, and I will show you the photos of Red, she's utterly beautiful.'

Liz left them to it. The women got ready and headed across the common, after gazing back at Primrose Cottage excitedly.

The Sunday roast was delicious, the homemade cherry pie equally so, and Suzy filled them all in with her plans for Primrose Cottage. Mary and John had known a couple of weeks ago, but been sworn to secrecy so she could tell Sam herself. John had been on the lookout for the right place for Suzy, so when Primrose Cottage came up, he'd contacted her, knowing it was her dream location.

By the time the two of them got back to Wisteria Cottage, they were full to the brim.

'I so love your mum's cooking. I can see I'm going to pile on the weight once I move here.'

'Oh Suzy, I still can't believe you're going to be living in Willow Green. How on earth did Mum and Dad keep all this from me?'

'To be fair to them, I made them promise to stay quiet until we were sure it wasn't likely to fall through. Your dad's missed his vocation; he should have been an estate agent.' Suzy yawned and stretched contentedly. 'So, what time is Luce back?'

'Matt said they were leaving at five, so hopefully in about half an hour. Are you going to stick around and see her, or do you need to get home?'

'I think I'll stay put tonight and head back first thing, that ok?'

'Of course you can.' Sam gave her a hug and kissed her cheek. 'I love you, Suzy.'

'Yeah I know, and I love you too. We are going to have the best summer next year, Sam. I like Liz, by the way.'

'I know, she's lovely. I can't wait for you to meet all the others, they're a scream. I think I should organise a welcome party for you.'

Sam was shocked, Suzy seldom travelled in daylight. They'd always joked about her being a vampire, when the reality was that her agoraphobia made it difficult for her to travel in the day, preferring the darkness. Sam wondered if Willow Green would help to heal her best friend, just as it seemed to be healing her.

Matt and Jasmine dropped Lucy back at six thirty and Sam was delighted to see that they all looked happy. Lucy was fit to burst when she found out that Suzy was having a sleepover and demanded that she sleep with her.

'No way, baby cakes, I snore worse than anyone and I'll keep you awake all night. I'm going to crash in mama's new studio with the blinds back, under the stars.'

Sam noticed how awkward Matt was, but at least Jasmine looked a great deal more confident. She asked Sam if she could see the new studio, leaving Matt and Suzy downstairs with Lucy. It was clear that she needed to talk.

'Oh Sam, I don't know how to thank you. You were so right. I waited for Lucy to go to bed and then I packed my bag. I went down to the studio and told him that I would be leaving him after running Lucy back today.'

'Oh wow, what did he do?' Sam asked, surprised.

'He asked why, and he looked so shocked it was actually funny. Anyway, he begged me to stay and promised he would change.

He even took up your suggestion of going to therapy with me. He spent all last night emailing local councillors.'

Sam hugged her tight. 'Jasmine, that's wonderful news. I had a feeling that if anyone could get through to Matt it would be you.'

'Well it's early days, but fortunately I like a challenge. He told me some home truths, too, so I'm not squeaky clean. We are going to get a cleaner and someone to do the washing and ironing. Apparently my cooking sucks, too, so I told him he can cook from now on.'

'Jazz, that's incredible, good for you. He can cook, by the way,' Sam added.

'Oh, I know, he used to make an effort.' Jasmine quickly gave the studio the once over. She liked what she saw. 'Sam, I know it's a lot to ask and I know you already said no, but is there any chance you could reconsider writing something for me? I keep getting sent rubbish and I just can't connect with any of it.'

A week ago Sam would have said no outright, but things felt different now. This week Sam felt she had connected with Jasmine and had grown particularly fond of her.

'Let me have a think. I will see what I have and email it to you. I don't have a lot of spare time to write something new, but I have written a few songs recently and I know one is right up your street.'

The two of them agreed on the plan of action and descended the stairs back to the others. Sam was pleased to see that the air wasn't quite as frosty as it had been before she left.

Lucy was entertaining the adults. She had already taken Suzy's bag from the studio and carried it into her own room, placing a pillow at the bottom of her bed and putting a teddy on it. She informed Suzy that she was to sleep top-to-tail with her as she was so big and wouldn't fit beside her.

'Don't worry,' Sam whispered, 'she will crash tonight, and it takes a lot to wake her, so we can sneak your things up to the studio later.' Suzy gave a relieved sigh.

'Do you mind me sleeping in the studio, or would you rather I stayed in the spare room? It's just that the studio is stunning, and I love the disco ball.'

'Suzy, you can sleep in the beach hut if it makes you feel comfortable, you know that,' Sam replied.

'Trust me, I'm going to sleep out there in the summer,' Suzy said, smiling.

'I'll hold you to that, we can have a camp set up.' Sam said.

'Deal.'

By the time Matt and Jasmine headed home, Lucy and Suzy had both changed into their onesies. Sam looked at them both sitting side by side on the sofa, sharing a bowl of popcorn. She smiled. Suzy was so childlike and at times she seemed no older than Lucy.

Sam had said no to popcorn, but Suzy had persuaded her, and the truth was Sam was so excited that her best friend was moving here that she could deny her nothing this evening.

Lucy went to bed later than usual; she was excited but sleepy, at least. A few pages from her story book were all it took to send her on her way. Sam tiptoed downstairs to Suzy and they played cards and opened a bottle of wine.

'I thought I'd give my liver a rest here. When did you turn to the bottle, Sam?'

'The day I moved in,' Sam joked. 'Seriously though, I need to cut back. In London I guess I got in the habit of pouring a glass of wine once Lucy was in bed, but I made sure it was just the one. Living here, it stretches to at least two glasses a day and weekends, well let's just say that they blur into a drunken haze.'

'Quite honestly, Sam, after all you've gone through, I think you deserve a bit of a holiday from the stress.'

'I know that, but the last thing I need to develop is a drink problem. Do you fancy a camomile tea to take to bed, Suzy?'

Suzy sniggered. 'Yes please, I quite like them.' *No time like the present,* she thought.

When Suzy woke the following morning, she knew that she wasn't alone. When she opened her heavy eyes, she saw a dear little girl lying beside her, sucking her thumb with a big beaming smile on her face.

'Morning, Auntie Suzy, shall we have a cuddle?'

Suzy smiled and pulled the little girl into her arms. 'Oh Lucy, I love you, my sweetheart. I can't wait to move here so that I'll be able to see you and Mummy a lot more.'

'I'm going to see you every single day, Auntie Suzy, and so will Mummy because you are her favourite friend in the whole wide world, she told me that. Who is your favourite friend?' Lucy asked.

'Mummy, of course. She always has been and always will be forever and ever and ever.'

They both got the giggles and wandered downstairs to find Sam scrambling eggs in the kitchen.

'I take it you had an early morning visitor, Suzy?'

The friends gave each other a knowing look and smiled. The three of them sat down and ate breakfast together then, school bag packed and warm hats and coats pulled on, Sam and Suzy walked Lucy to school.

Sam was surprised by how laid back and relaxed Suzy was. She usually avoided daylight and people. She seldom ate breakfast and yet yesterday and today Sam had seen a completely different side to Suzy.

'Suzy, is everything okay? Only I've never known you to be like this, well not since we were eleven.'

'Like what?'

'Relaxed. You know, calm.'

'That's because I'm moving here with you.'

By the time Sam dropped Suzy to the train station, it was almost lunchtime. She had time to go shopping but wasn't able to write. She was too excited about all of Suzy's news. She made a to do list and added 'song for Jazz'. She had to remember to take a listen tonight and see if there was something suitable; it was crucial to give Jasmine something to focus on outside of Matt and the pregnancy. In all the excitement she had also forgotten to call Dominic, so she sent him a quick text.

'Sorry I didn't get back, had a friend stay. I will call you later.'

'Cool. Dx' He replied.

She picked Lucy up from school and almost had to restrain her while walking home. The little girl was beside herself and talked obsessively about Suzy moving to Willow Green and the puppy, asking if they could go and see her again at the weekend, asking when they could go and buy the little dog's bed and crate and bowls, wondering what colour lead and collar would suit her and what type of bed and food to buy. Sam was struggling to keep up, Lucy was rambling almost as much as Liz did.

'Lucy, darling, now listen. We still have eleven more sleeps until we bring her home, so you need to try your best to be calm or else you will wear yourself out. By the time we get her you will be too tired to enjoy her. Now what we can do is make a kind of countdown, a bit like your advent calendar. We can even hang it in the kitchen beside the advent calendar, if you like.'

'How are we going to make it, Mummy?'

Lucy looked up to Sam for the answer. Sam took a deep breath.

'Well, we could make eleven little doors and inside each one we will have a number, counting down to the day we get Red. If we say tomorrow is day one, then we might write on the calendar 'buy a book on caring for your puppy'. Day two might say 'get a lead and a collar', then…'

'Day three the bed, day four her food!' shouted Lucy.

'That's right, darling, then finally on day eleven it will say 'collect our little Red'. Does that sound good?'

'Yes, yes. Oh Mummy, thank you. Can we make it when we get home?'

Poor little Lucy was jumping up and down on the spot again.

'Why not, my sweetheart? We could have our after-school snack and then get to making it, okay?'

By bedtime the new puppy calendar hung proudly in the kitchen beside the advent calendar. There were eleven little doors ready to be opened, although Sam was doubtful the doors would open, as Lucy had stuck so much glitter and tinsel onto them. Behind each door were things to do or buy for the puppy.

It had been a magical evening together, planning for their new arrival. Lucy fell fast asleep on the sofa, exhausted by all the excitement. Sam gathered her up and carried her to bed.

Sam felt ready for work, so went up to the studio and ran through five songs. She decided that a track called "Cry For Help" would suit Jasmine's voice perfectly and that the subject matter of the song would connect with her. She emailed the track to Jasmine with a brief message. She then put a little piano down on Abigail's track and then went downstairs.

She was about to pour herself a glass of wine but decided that a chamomile tea would be healthier. Unfortunately, the chamomile tea didn't quite do the job of aiding relaxation.

Chapter 20

Sam woke the following morning with a start. She had a headache from hell and was uncharacteristically grumpy with Lucy. Breakfast was eaten quickly, and Sam hoped the walk to school would help lift her head.

By midday her headache was still not shifting, so she took a couple of pain killers and lay down. John had called in for coffee earlier and had obviously told Mary that Sam wasn't feeling so good, because Mary turned up with a flask of soup and a crusty roll. She ate lunch with Sam and reassured her that she would get Lucy from school and take her back home for tea. Sam agreed to pop over later. She was about to go up to bed when the doorbell rang.

She opened the door to Dominic, who looked concerned.

'Whoa, is this from the night out on Saturday?' He asked. She must clearly look awful, thought Sam.

'Hi Dominic. No, I didn't sleep so well last night and I've got a headache from hell. How are you? I missed a call from you last night, sorry I didn't get back.'

'No worries, I just need to talk to you. Look, can I get you anything?'

'Thanks, but Mum just came round with some soup so I'm pretty stuffed, unless you fancy making a cup of tea?'

'Sure, can do.'

Sam flopped back on the sofa and when Dominic placed the mug beside her, he crouched down, looking at her.

'Do you get migraines?' he asked, looking concerned.

'Not to my knowledge I don't, no. To be honest I think I'm dehydrated.'

'Your eyes look pretty bloodshot.'

He reached across and massaged her temples, then slowly moved around to the back of her neck, pressing points on her neck and scalp that she never knew existed. The relief was sensational and disturbingly erotic, she thought.

When he stopped, she found that although she was lightheaded, there was only the faintest hint of pain.

'Wow, what are you, some kind of witchdoctor or something?'

Dominic grinned. 'It was part of some training I did in case of injuries or difficulties with the guys. It is meant to relieve tension, seeing as a lot of headaches are linked to stress.'

Sam smiled at Dominic. She knew he was about to talk to her, as he looked a little awkward.

'Right, so here goes… Sam, I got the wrong end of the stick.'

'So I believe,' Sam said slowly.

'I'm not into playing games, Sam. If I don't want to be with someone, then I let them know. If it's for one night, just casual sex, then I make that perfectly clear.'

'Now I'm lost,' Sam said.

'If I'd wanted a one night stand, I would have made that perfectly clear.'

'Well, you wouldn't have got one.' Sam folded her arms and tried to sound as matter of fact as she could. 'I've never had a one night stand and I'm not about to start now, even for you, delectable Dom.'

They both laughed. Sam had used Liz's pet name for him.

'Can you believe it? She shouted that out in the post office the other day. If she wasn't married to my best mate, I'd give her a wide birth. She's trouble, that one!'

They laughed again and Dominic took hold of Sam's hand.

'I came round that night because I couldn't wait to see you again, Sam. I had told the guys about you and well, let's just say I hadn't been prepared to find you tickling the tonsils with some other guy, I can tell you.'

Sam laughed hysterically.

'Tickling the tonsils! I've never heard that one. You and Liz have such bizarre sayings, you sure you two aren't related?'

'No, thank heavens. Anyway, I got it wrong. I felt a bit bruised, so I backed off. You must have thought me a right sod.'

'Oh, indeed I did,' Sam fired back, then she relented and smiled. 'Under the circs, Dom, I would have done exactly the same as you. Poor Ace was mortified the next day, and I wasn't too happy.'

'So, has he tried it since?' he asked.

'No, fortunately not. I've introduced him to a young singer I know, Abigail. I've been working with her lately and they hit it off big time. She's quite a bit younger than him, but her attitude is great, and I think it will work out, although they've only been out twice so it's early days.'

'Woah, that was quick! Didn't take him long to get over you then, you couldn't have meant that much to him.'

Sam punched him on the arm.

'Cheeky pig. I actually felt responsible for him. A couple of the guys had said he had a soft spot for me and I guess I didn't really believe it. I just thought if I acted maternal towards him then he would see me differently, but it didn't work.'

Dominic lazily scanned her face and licked his lips. 'Mm, can't say I can blame him. You aren't exactly easy to resist. You are just so damn sexy. I keep picturing you wearing nothing but those pink cowboy boots.'

Sam went bright red. 'Oh, I'm surprised you noticed what I was wearing that night, seeing as you barely looked at me.'

'Oh trust me, Sam, I was blatantly aware of you. I was so aware of you that I read the same article about a dozen times, and I still have no idea what it was about.'

'So, delectable Dom isn't quite so cool and collected after all then!' Sam replied.

He laughed but then checked his watch. 'I'm meant to be at an appointment in half an hour. You're a nightmare, Ms Tate. I'm usually pretty unshakable, but you, lady, have got right under my skin. What are you up to tonight?'

'I have some work to do after Lucy's in bed, why?'

'Why don't I bring a bottle of wine round and a takeaway, save you cooking? Or do you eat with Lucy?'

'Save me cooking! Do you know, since moving here I have hardly cooked at all? I actually miss messing about in the kitchen. Problem is my mum's cooking is better than mine, thanks for the offer though. I'm eating at Mum's, but a bottle of wine sounds good, if you don't mind it being a little later, say ten?'

'Cool, I'll get my quotes out the way and see you then.'

He pecked Sam on the forehead like some dotty old aunt, not like the sexy vixen he had just made her feel, and then he was gone. Dominic's truck screeched off up the road.

Sam was in shock. What had just happened? She had just spent the last half an hour with a man she had only known for a couple of months, and yet she had felt more relaxed with him than any other man she had ever met.

Mary had cooked a delicious Beef Wellington. Lucy was telling them all about Red and enjoying looking through the pictures of the Border Terrier book Sam had bought over.

'I'm surprised you made it out to get that book, love,' Mary said affectionately.

'I didn't, Liz got it for me,' Sam admitted. 'Oh, by the way, she has invited us all there for drinks Christmas Eve, but I said I would check with you first. She is going to call you.'

'Oh, that sounds lovely, darling. I was going to suggest that you and Lucy sleep here Christmas Eve so that you and your father can pop next door for a drink; you know how he loves that. Anne wants me to go to midnight mass, you could come too, if you fancy it.'

'Oh I'd love to, Mum, but that means that Dad can't go.'

'That will be fine. I'm sure he only ever suffers it for me. Mind you, we will need to get there early, as last year there were people standing, it was full to the brim. He really has worked wonders for this village, Reverend Gibson has,' Mary said.

'Mm, think lots have a crush on the Reverend, don't you?' Sam asked with a twinkle in her eye.

'Well, yes, he is rather dashing,' Mary said, blushing scarlet. Sam was trying not to laugh; she had never seen her mother blush like this before.

'Can you believe that Christmas is only a couple of weeks away? It seems only yesterday we moved in, and yet at the same time I feel as though I have lived here my entire life.'

Mary sat back and thought for a while. 'I know. This village seems to captivate you pretty quick. I still regret not moving here years ago when you were Lucy's age, but hey ho, hindsight is all well and good. Now then, Lucy said she breaks up next Friday, so your father and I were wondering if it would help you to work if we had her in the afternoons?'

'Sounds wonderful, and thanks Mum, but remember – we're going to have a scruffy little pooch that Lucy will find hard to leave, so be warned and don't take offence if it takes a little per-suading to get her out of the house.'

'When will she have her jabs, Sam? Only I was thinking of Sooty and Christmas,' Mary asked, concerned.

'Well she's having her first lot before I get her, so there will be a little protection in place, and she will be crate trained so we can keep her separate from Sooty.'

'Ah good, so all should be okay. What time do you collect her next Friday?'

'Lucy finishes at lunchtime, so I think I will drive straight there after lunch. Do you fancy coming?'

'Oh, I thought you'd never ask,' Mary laughed. 'Of course I would.'

'Matt is having her Sunday, Monday and Tuesday the following week, so at least she will get settled with her for the first couple of days. Lucy will be back Christmas Eve.'

'When else is she seeing her father over Christmas?' Mary asked.

Sam had noticed that Mary seldom used Matt's name these days and referred to him as 'Lucy's father'.

'He is collecting her around three on Boxing Day. He wants to keep her for a couple of days. I think he and Jasmine are having his parents to stay, so they will no doubt have a good time and make a fuss of her.'

'What about Jasmine's parents and family, Sam?'

'They live in the States, so she usually goes over in the New Year. Not sure how close they are, to be honest.'

'I didn't know she was American,' Mary said.

'Her mum is. Her dad's English, and they all lived here for a few years, but they moved when Jasmine was thirteen. She was put in a boarding school over here, and she visited them in holidays.'

Mary was taken aback at this information.

'Poor love.'

'I know what you mean, but Jasmine is made of strong stuff and she needs to be strong, living with Matt.' Sam thought again of poor Dominic being sent to boarding school so young. She could see why he struggled with relationships.

Sam took a freshly-bathed Lucy home to bed and by the time Dominic pulled up, she had finished the work she needed to for the day.

She was pleased that Jasmine had got back to her regarding the track that she had sent. She was most enthusiastic and keen to come and sing, so Sam suggested that she come early on Friday and put a rough guide vocal down before taking Lucy back to London.

Dominic loved Wisteria Cottage. It was much more comfortable and homelier than his own place, The Manor, with its great big imposing rooms. He found Sam's place stunning, just like its owner, who tonight was dressed in yoga pants and a sweat shirt with thick slipper socks. She had not a scratch of makeup on and her hair was up in a knot, but she was beautiful. Magic Radio played softly through her sound system and he noticed most of the tunes were Christmas songs, which she clearly loved. At virtually each and every one of them her face would light up as she announced, 'Oh, I *love* this one.'

Privately, Dominic was already getting fed up with the Christmas tunes which were played tirelessly throughout the day, but he was captivated by this beautiful woman and her childlike passion for music and Christmas. At one point she had walked into the kitchen and, forgetting he was there, had started to sing along with one of the songs. Goose pimples burst onto his skin. Her voice was so effective and beautiful; there was a depth of passion and such raw pain. Dominic hoped she was reconsidering performing again and felt he had to address it over the weekend to see if she had given it any more thought.

Dominic and Sam sat beside one another and yet chatted like two old familiar friends. Every now and then he would reach across and kiss her, but he was also aware that Sam was very protective of Lucy's feelings and wouldn't want the little girl wandering down stairs and finding Mummy in the arms of someone who wasn't her daddy. He liked Sam's principles and her integrity.

By the time they said goodnight and she saw him out, the logs had died down to glowing red embers. Sam had promised Lucy that they were going to buy the Christmas tree tomorrow and put it up, but then realised that she had no decorations whatsoever.

Chapter 21

The following morning Sam grabbed Liz at the school gates and asked if she fancied going shopping for a Christmas tree and decorations. Liz said she knew just the place and took Sam to an enormous garden centre which held more Christmas decorations than Lapland.

Liz had decided that she would get their tree too, so they had the time of their lives choosing just the right ones, and they stayed on to have a delicious vegetable soup for lunch. Fortunately, they had taken Liz's estate car which had a roof rack. So, although laden down with not one but two Christmas trees, they just made it back to school on time.

Liz helped Sam get the six-foot tree indoors and then carefully placed it its stand. Then she left them to decorate it.

Sam and Lucy opened the boxes of decorations and Lucy's little face lit up.

Sam had decided on just two colours, pale pink and gold. They unpacked glass balls and beads and clear lights that you could set to flicker or still and as promised, she got Lucy some pink and gold tinsel for her bedroom. Lucy was enchanted with it all.

When the pair had finished the tree, it looked absolutely breath-taking. Sam had put it in the orangery so that the lights flickered and reflected on the glass roof and windows.

She ran a garland along the mantle shelf, with more pink and gold ball balls dangling from it, and threaded fairy lights through it.

Lucy didn't get to bed until nine because Mary and John had wandered over with Sooty to see the tree.

John went up to marvel over the studio again.

'He really is extraordinary is Dominic, isn't he?'

Mm, thought Sam, *he most definitely is.*

Sam retired to bed with her Mac and Horlicks. She had a couple more verses to work on, but it was difficult trying to concentrate, as she and Dominic exchanged texts which got her all hot and bothered. By the time she switched off her lamp, it was past midnight and only half a verse was written.

Jasmine arrived at five o'clock Friday afternoon to record her guide vocal. Sam was pleased with her performance, and Jasmine said it was the loveliest song she had ever heard. Sam knew it would hit a nerve.

Mary and Lucy walked in just as they had finished. Sam was glad to see how excited her little girl was to be going home to her father's. Matt and Jasmine were taking Lucy to a Christmas pantomime tomorrow evening and Sunday they were going to visit the Winter Wonderland at Hyde Park. They were also planning on taking Lucy to Hamley's toy store tomorrow to visit Santa Claus, of course.

Jasmine reassured Sam that Matt was making an enormous effort and had even booked himself out for the entire weekend to spend it with Lucy and Jasmine.

After the pair had said their goodbyes and set off for London, Sam locked the door and climbed the stairs. She tuned into Magic Radio, placed a glass of wine within reaching distance and had a long soak in the bath. She sang along with the songs and let her mind wander, only realising too late that by the time she got out she'd only have half an hour to get ready.

Dominic picked her up at eight and took her to a lovely Italian restaurant. He sensed that there was something preoccupying her and told her so. Sam found she was relieved to unburden herself.

'I can't honestly say that there is anything wrong, I just feel odd.'

Sam tried to explain her mood but then felt self-conscious and blushed. Dominic sat quietly, waiting for her to continue. She loved this about him: he always gave her time and space to find out what it was she was thinking or feeling. Sam tried again.

'Would you think me odd if I said that I feel as though I don't know myself? When I moved to the village, I was so miserable. I believed I was still in love with Matt. I kept hoping we would get back together and yet, within days of being here, I was finding myself growing further away from him. I kept finding fault, too, and now it's like I can't recognise myself anymore or how I felt about him either.'

'Yeah, you've had quite a journey I guess, these last couple of months.'

'Thing is, Dominic, when I lived in London, I was so lonely and private and yet here, well there's Liz, for example.'

'Oh yes, there's always Liz,' he said, smiling.

'I mean, I hardly know her and yet know her better than friends I had for years in London, with the exception of Suzy, of course.'

'You know, Sam, personally I don't believe that you need to know someone years to connect with them. I know I joke about Liz, but I can promise you that she's sound. She has a huge heart and she loves you and Lucy to bits. Paul's lucky to have her as she's kind of got it all going on, really. Mind you, she's not my type, she's just like my mum and she would do my head in. As they say, horses for courses and all that.'

Their waiter was hovering in the background, so Sam and Dominic ordered from the menu and got a carafe of red wine.

'So, why do you think you're so unsettled?'

'I just don't recognise anything. I was so down and miserable that I honestly can't believe I've finally got away from that house. You know, I had no idea that things were quite so bad until recently, I mean, I knew Matt treated me badly, but it's like I didn't get it until moving here and talking about it.'

'Yeah, but sometimes we need to distance ourselves from certain people or situations before we're able to process it all,' Dominic added wisely.

'I think the lies were the worst part. He told so many and he was good at it, so when someone is that convincing, it is hard to believe anything that comes out of their mouth. I mean, I morphed into this woman I didn't know, let alone like. I went through his phone, his pockets. How sad am I?'

'That's just it. You're not. He caused this, Sam, not you. I have a mate called Ed. He told his wife so many lies. Then one day, he comes to me and calls her a bunny boiler 'cuz she'd been through his phone and stuff and found out he was having an affair. He made it her problem, not his. Laura had been such a sound woman, really confident, and he managed to knock the stuffing out of her. I hated him for what he did to that woman, and all because of his own insecurities which eventually became hers.'

'Oh, poor thing. Did she stay with him?'

'No, he did it once too often and she got strong and left. She's married to a really cool guy now who treats her like a princess, something Ed should have done.'

'What about Ed?'

'Ed's on his third marriage and is currently cheating on his new wife. I avoid him these days.'

'I wish I could just get over it all, Dominic, I really do. I mean, it's like I'm ill or something. I keep getting light headed.'

'Yeah, that's probably the effect I'm having on you,' he teased, realising that she needed a change of subject as she was getting quite anxious.

Sam giggled. 'Hey, big head! Although I won't deny that I'm a little smitten with you.'

'A little! You go scarlet every time I see you. You're as nuts about me as I am you.' To prove the point, Sam blushed scarlet again.

'You're actually, really, quite arrogant, aren't you?' She said still blushing.

'Am I actually, really? Or am I actually, really, being quite honest?'

Dominic was playing with her now and they both giggled.

'Look, Sam, I'm not about to diminish how you feel or patronise you by telling you that all is perfect. I can't imagine what it must have been like living all those years with a man who, by the sounds of it, didn't treat you as he should, and with a little girl as well. What I can tell you, though, is that you are safe. You have bought yourself one of the most beautiful cottages in the village. You have a lot of new friends who have welcomed you because you deserve them. You're a good person, Sam, and it seems you are finally getting what you deserve.'

Sam looked away for a moment. Was she hearing the truth from Dominic, or was it all make believe?

'I wish I could see myself that way.'

'Try not to focus on the uncertainty of it all and try to enjoy the here and now. I know what it's like to look back or look forward, and it was only once I learnt to focus on the here and now that I felt at peace. I'm here for you, Sam, so are Liz and Paul 'n Sue and Tom, and you've got terrific parents. I'm not as sure about your other friends, I don't know them nor do I have any desire to get to know them any better, no offence.'

'Oh, Dominic, that's awful. They're lovely once you get to know them,' laughed Sam.

Sam smiled. She realised that Dominic was a man who knew himself inside out. She couldn't imagine that he would ever feel intimidated or uncomfortable. The days he had spent working on her studio had proved that he was comfortable in his own skin. She wondered if he had always been this way or if it was the military that had created this incredible man.

Sam was deep in thought as he looked at her.

'What's up?'

'Mm, I was just wondering whether you've always been this way or was it being in the military.'

'Meaning?' he asked, giving Sam a sideways glance. His eyes lit up with mischief; she knew he was teasing.

'Well, you're hardly shy or nervous, are you?'

'Definitely never been accused of being shy.'

He drank his wine and gave her a really sexy smile and a wink. Sam went scarlet. He had a really annoying habit of making her blush, which he thoroughly enjoyed.

'I mean that you seem to be comfortable with who you are, and I bet that you never struggle with self-doubt, do you?'

'Yeah, being serious for a moment, I guess I do pretty much know myself. The military obviously conditions you a particular way, but I was always a loner. Boarding school kind of did it for me. The day I got dropped off, I kind of split myself in two, left the kid back here, and guess I pretended to be an adult pretty quick. Yeah, I am a loner, but I kind of like it that way... present company excepted, of course.'

Sam looked so sorry for him, making him laugh.

'Hey, it's not that bad, Sam. I like company, I enjoy spending time with my mates, but I guess you could say that I don't really need others to be happy. Besides, I find I'm a pretty cool guy and like my own company more than most other people,' he said, winding Sam up again.

'God, you really are big headed. Liz told me that you haven't had a full-on relationship for a few years.'

'Yeah, Liz has been trying to set me up for a while now, but apart from the occasional casual thing, I guess I would rather be alone than in the wrong relationship.'

'Liz told me about your fiancé. I guess that must have put you off women for a while.'

Dominic gave a rueful laugh.

'Ah, good old Liz. I'm not put off at all. In fact, I was relieved when that whole thing was over. I would have tried to get out eventually anyway. Back then I wasn't as direct as I am now and I had this misplaced loyalty thing going on. Now that's something the military did condition me for.'

Sam wanted to know more. 'But Liz said that you adored her and that you were devastated.'

Dominic roared with laughter this time. 'Oh man, that woman is so funny. Embarrassed, yes, a few holes in my ego, absolutely, but devastated? Definitely not.'

'Liz said she was beautiful, a model.'

'Well if Liz said so then it must be right, eh?'

'Why, wasn't she beautiful?'

'Oh, she was, you could not take that title from her. Physically she was beautiful, but inside she was emotionally barren. Weird stuff happens when you go off to war. I would not do that again, to myself or anyone else for that matter. I decided I wouldn't put myself through it and it taught me to be brutally honest.'

'So what are we about, Dom?' pondered Sam. 'Are we mates or what? I think we have established that it's not going to be a quick frolic under the duvet.'

'Frolic! Now there's a word I haven't heard for a while, I like frolic.' Dominic laughed and then relented. 'Sam, I have all the mates I need. I don't get enough time with them as it is, so I do not require anymore, thank you. As for casual sex, I think that by the time we do get to have sex we'll have already gone way beyond casual, don't you?'

He gave her that special look again and she blushed madly. Sam was staring at the tablecloth, shaking her head.

'Well, I don't know, it's just freaking me out. It all seems to be racing ahead and to be honest, I'm uncomfortable.' There, it was out. She had said it at last.

'Uncomfortable with what?' Dom looked genuinely surprised.

'That's just it, I don't know. I was trying to tell you earlier, but I don't understand what's going on in my head.'

He reached across and took hold of her hand.

'Oh, lady, you really do think too much, don't you? I can't guarantee that we will make each other happy forever, but right now I am going nowhere. I can't think of anything else I would rather be doing than hanging out with you. So does that help?'

'But you seem so calm about everything, Dominic.'

'I can't apologise for the way I am, Sam. It would be a lie, and I can't pretend that I'm uncomfortable with this because I'm not. I fancy you something rotten.'

Sam was so shocked by his directness that she flew her hand across the table to silence him. In the process she managed to knock over the bottle of water, sending it cascading over his shirt and trousers. Dominic laughed his head off, while the poor waitress frantically tried to mop up the water and Sam apologised profusely.

She excused herself and went to the toilet to calm down. The woman who stared back at her in the mirror could have been an identical twin, removed at birth. Her eyes were those of someone else. They glowed and shone with an inner light. Her lips appeared glossy and pouting and seemed to be stuck in a permanent smile, which made her look incredibly sexy. Sam was shaking like a leaf. She could not control her racing heart. Dominic had obviously found the whole episode hilarious.

When she finally returned to the table, he had his hands cupped on the back of his head, looking as though he had just won gold at the Olympics.

'You are *so* not funny, do you know that, Dominic?'

'I think I'm hilarious and I love making you squirm.'

'Right that's it, I've had enough, you can jolly well take me home.'

When they got into his car, he kissed her hard on the lips. Sam tried feigning a temper all the way home, but he was so irritatingly chatty and had a knack of tricking her into answering him. He pulled up outside the cottage and went to get out.

'Do you know what, Dominic, after the way you behaved tonight you can jolly well go home. I shall see you tomorrow, perhaps.'

He kissed her passionately on the lips. 'You sure you want to leave it here?' he asked, in such a deep and husky voice it was so damn sexy.

'Oh just go, you've annoyed me now.'

She jumped out of the car and was opening the door when he caught up with her. He started kissing her and gently pulled her head closer to him to deepen the kiss. The sensations flooding her body were unlike any she had felt before. He stopped kissing her and looked deep into her eyes.

'Sure you don't want me to come in, Sam?'

'I hate you, Dominic, you are so damned annoying. Just go.'

He laughed, said goodnight, got back in the car and drove off.

Sam didn't know whether to laugh or cry. Her body was on fire and it didn't help a bit later when her phone pinged, alerting her to a text massage. He had sent a photo of himself smiling that sexy smile, raising a glass of what looked like whiskey and winking, with the words "cheers Sam x" written underneath.

'Ugh, big headed man,' she raged before switching her phone off and flinging it across the island.

Chapter 22

Dominic had hardly slept a wink and his hormones were rife.

To make matters worse, his mate Al had called at 3am in a right state, needing someone to talk to and somewhere to crash. He was due at the train station midday. Dominic tried calling Sam but her phone was switched off, which made him chuckle.

Eventually he managed to get a hold of her.

'Oh, if it isn't my hilarious friend,' she said, the sarcasm dripping from her voice.

'Have you forgiven me?' he asked.

'I would find you easier to forgive if you weren't so sure of yourself.'

Dominic roared with laughter and Sam could picture his beautiful face. 'Shot myself in the foot though, didn't I?' he said, making her laugh at last.

'Because?' Sam asked, already knowing the answer.

'I couldn't sleep, Sam. I wound myself up. I kept picturing you.'

'Huh. Well picture away, my friend, because that's as close as you're going to get for now.'

He really found this hysterical.

'Now you've laid down the gauntlet, I shall have even more pleasure proving you wrong, Ms Tate. Anyway, you might as well give in, because it will help you with the headaches and stress.'

'Oh, you really are the most frustrating man, Dominic. For two pins I would refuse to come to the cinema with you tonight.'

'Ah yes, the cinema. Look Sam, I'm so sorry, but I have a mate coming. He's in a bit of trouble and I don't know how long it's going to take me to sort him out. I don't want to let you down about the cinema, but if he's not gone by then, can we postpone till tomorrow night?'

'No, I have Lucy tomorrow, Dom. Look, it really doesn't matter. Your friend is more important, and I have so much work I need to get done, so just let's see later, shall we?'

'He's a pain in the backside is Al, always has been. We'll catch up later. Listen Sam, thanks for last night, I had a blast.'

'Yes, didn't you just!' she fired back.

Sam was actually relieved that they'd postponed the cinema; she was so tied up in knots about Dominic that she was grateful to have a little respite. She knew she was falling in love and it scared the hell out of her.

Dominic kept in touch with Sam via texts all day and then at nine o'clock, he rang.

'Hello, you.'

'Hey Sam, how's it going?'

'Well apart from being over full up on Mum's cooking, all's good. How about you? How's your friend?'

'He's shaping up,' Dominic replied. 'Looks like he's going home tomorrow, so I could come round tomorrow night after Lucy's gone to bed?'

'I'd like that, yes.'

'Cool, shout when it's convenient.'

Sam had managed to get quite a lot of work done in the peaceful hours before Lucy returned in the afternoon.

Lucy had enjoyed the most amazing weekend; Matt was being particularly attentive to Jasmine and Lucy when they arrived at the cottage. Sam invited him up to the studio to listen to Jasmine's vocal and she chose this opportunity to have a brief word with her ex.

'I beg of you, Matt, please don't blow this with Jazz. She loves you, but something tells me she won't stick around if you don't treat her fair, and besides, Lucy loves her.'

Sam was expecting him to get angry and start shouting. She had made sure she closed the studio door just in case he did, but instead he just smiled.

'Yeah, thanks for talking to her, Sam. She said if it wasn't for you, she would have gone.'

Sam was gobsmacked. Was this actually Matt, thanking her? She couldn't quite believe what she had just heard and he didn't elaborate, he even complimented her on her studio.

After listening to the song, they went back downstairs. Matt made a huge fuss of Jasmine and Sam, announcing that 'Cry For Help' would be a hit. He didn't seem in a hurry to leave and accepted the tea and cake Sam offered. Lucy asked Jasmine to show her mum the photos of Winter Wonderland and by the time the little girl had described in minute detail the sheer magic of 'Wonderland', it was late. Matt and Jasmine said their goodbyes, kissed Lucy for the last time and made their escape.

Dominic turned up at nine thirty that evening, looking unshaven and exhausted. Sam noticed purple shadows developing below his weary eyes.

'Gosh! You do look tired. Rough night?'

'You have no idea! Now I know why I don't like to keep whiskey in the house, and why I only visit Al at home when Janey is there. The man's an animal. Fortunately I'd polished the brandy off before, else we would have no doubt got stuck into that too.'

'Oh dear, shall I get you a coffee?'

'No thanks, Sam, what I need is a hair of the dog,' said Dominic with a sideways glance as he wandered into the lounge.

'Well I don't have whiskey, only wine or lager.'

'I'd love a glass of wine, thanks.'

'So what was wrong with your friend? That's if you want to tell me,' Sam asked. She placed the bottle and two glasses in front of Dom. She was curious to know more about his friend.

'His wife has kicked him out,' Dominic said at last.

'Oh gosh, poor thing.'

'Idiot, more like.'

'Oh! Right,' Sam said.

'He is a good mate, but an idiot. He's married to a cracking woman and has a newborn baby, and then he goes and sleeps with someone else who just so happens to be one of his mate's wives, and so the whole thing kicked off.' Sam could see Dominic was still furious with his friend. 'I just don't get it. If you don't want to be with someone, let them go, but don't go playing away with a mate's wife, of all people. The man is an idiot.'

'Maybe his marriage has hit a rough patch,' Sam wondered, but Dominic frowned at that.

'Oh right, so that makes it okay does it? To go sleep with someone else?'

'Well no, I wasn't saying that, I just remember how low I felt after having Lucy. I didn't want Matt to come anywhere near me.'

'I'm not surprised, you'd just had a baby, like Janey. She's given him the ultimate gift and he repays her by sleeping with someone else.' He could see Sam was shocked by his outburst. 'Sorry Sam, but I'm sick of cowards, I really am. If your marriage isn't working then try to fix it, and if it doesn't work out then end it. Why put yourself and them through that pain just because you can't be bothered to make an effort?'

Sam was shocked and didn't quite know what to say. Dominic, the light-hearted joker who confessed to having casual sex at times, was actually quite moralistic when it came to marriage.

'I wish more men were like you,' Sam replied.

'Don't kid yourself that it's all men, Sam, there are plenty of women out there who do the same. I don't like to judge anyone's life choices, but when it comes to hurting others and dragging them down with you, then that really sucks.'

Dominic stopped talking and stared at her. Was he looking for a reaction? Sam was unsure, but then he relaxed his shoulders a little and his eyes softened.

'Sorry, Sam. I've walked in here banging on about my mate and haven't even asked how you're doing. Sorry, come here you.' He pulled her towards him and kissed her, but gently this evening. His gentle manner was equally erotic to Sam and she was grateful, seeing as he hadn't shaved and the stubble was already prickling her.

'Please don't apologise, it's fine,' whispered Sam. 'To be honest, it's good to hear you have integrity, gives me a good feeling.'

'Rest assured, Sam, I would never disrespect you. If, for whatever reason, I choose not to be with you, then you would be the first to know, and I hope you would return the favour. Now, enough of the negative. Come and tell me about your day.'

They spent the next couple of hours talking about the music scene. Dominic had gently raised the subject of Sam getting back into performing again. She had burst into life at the thought of getting back out there again. It made him sad to see she was weighed down with so many insecurities.

'Do you think it was Matt who did this to you?' he asked after a while. Sam breathed deeply and tried to articulate her feelings on the matter.

'Much as I would love to be able to offload the responsibility onto someone else, it would be a lie,' she sighed. 'I have always struggled with this, Dom. It isn't just the fear of rejection; I find it all rather embarrassing. I'm absolutely fine being up on stage, but struggle with the aftermath of it all.'

'Aftermath?'

'You know, after the music stops. The mingling with people, having them praise you or criticise you. It just doesn't sit right with me. It's more than that, though. The comedown is hard as well. I've never taken drugs, but I get why people do.'

'Why not try something local to begin with?' suggested Dominic. 'Keep it intimate with friends and family, and see how it goes?'

Sam jumped up from the sofa, dragging her fingers through her hair. She strode about then turned back to Dominic. She looked like a cornered cat.

'Oh, let's change the subject please, just talking about it really stresses me out.'

Dominic looked at Sam for a moment. He wanted to push the subject a little further but he could see her breath was becoming panicky, so he didn't.

The following week flew by. Along with the usual juggling of hours, Sam was trying to get everything organised for the little dog's arrival. Who knew a puppy needed so much stuff?! As for Lucy, she was all over the place and couldn't sleep with the excitement. Sam questioned herself as to whether or not she had made the right decision. What on earth had she been thinking of? Buying a dog at Christmas! Poor Lucy was losing enough sleep as it was.

Fortunately, Dominic was a tower of strength. He called in for coffee most days, or a glass of wine in the evening. Sam found his company calming and reassuring. Their relationship had become very deep, both of them sharing stories of their past, coming to terms with some pretty unpleasant feelings but helping one another through them.

By Thursday, she was as exhausted and emotional as Lucy. When she crawled into bed that night, she asked herself once again if she had made the right decision about sharing their home with a puppy.

Too late, she's coming home tomorrow, she thought, and switched off the light.

Sam and Mary pulled up to school gates around noon. Sam had packed Lucy a sandwich and some fruit in the hope that nutrition would keep the excitement at bay. They then headed off for Trisha's place.

Red was ready to go with her little puppy pack and all her papers when the three of them arrived. Sam, Mary and Lucy couldn't get over how much she had grown in just a couple of weeks.

Trisha had written out lots of helpful tips for Sam to take away, and she gave them a comfort blanket for the pup which had the scent of Mildred, Red's mother, on it.

Trisha urged Sam not to break the training under any circumstances. She promised her that persevering with the crate training would eventually make a happy dog; the crate would be seen as Red's sanctuary.

Lucy cradled Red all the way home and the three of them spent the next few hours taking her into the garden every few minutes and showing her around the utility room, which was to be her domain for the foreseeable future. Sam decided to keep the door to the utility room open so that the little dog could hear them.

Sam told Lucy that they needed strict rules for Red in order to help her get used to them, and said that the little dog needed lots of play time and attention but would also need to sleep, as she was only a baby.

Liz turned up with Marcus and Faye and then Sue called round with Daniel, all eager to meet the new arrival.

By the time everyone left them, the puppy was fast asleep and Mary was, too. Sam smiled and gently woke her mother as John came through the kitchen door, keen to greet the little dog. Sam suggested they stay for tea and cooked pasta for them all. It was way past Lucy's usual tea time when they sat at down to eat, but the little girl was ravenous and finished her plate.

Sam tucked Lucy into bed at nine and although the little girl had been reluctant to leave her puppy, she didn't take long to fall fast asleep.

Mary and John had loaded the dishwasher and were just leaving when Dominic turned up. His arms were full with flowers and champagne. He looked a little uncomfortable, but genuinely pleased to see her parents.

'Dominic, good to see you. How are you?' John asked.

Dominic placed the flowers and champagne on the island and shook the older man's hand.

'Good to see you too, John. Why don't you and Mary stick around for a glass of this? I bought it to welcome the new arrival.'

'Oh no, we couldn't possibly, we've taken up enough of Sam's time today as it is,' Mary said, pulling on her coat.

'Don't be silly, Mum, please stay,' called out Sam from the utility room.

'So where is she?' Dominic asked.

Sam popped her head around the door and nodded to the crate in the corner of the room. As if on cue, Red stood up somewhat shakily and wobbled her way to the front of what seemed like an enormous crate, although apparently the perfect size for a Border Terrier.

Dominic dropped to his knees and burst out laughing.

'Man, that's cute. What a funny little thing. Can I get her out, Sam?'

'You can, but you need to carry her straight outside and say "busy".'

Dominic burst out laughing again.

'"*Busy?*"'

'Yes, "busy" for a number two and "twinkles" for a number one. Apparently it helps them to understand that you want them to go to the toilet. "It" needs its own name and the book suggested "busy", Sam declared, almost keeping a straight face.

Dominic couldn't stop laughing as he lifted up the tiny little puppy to eye level and looked at her closely.

'Wow, little Red, you really are one funny little pooch, and man do you stink.'

Red wagged her tail like mad and kept trying to lick him.

Dominic carried her outside, and while he didn't use the words twinkles or busy, he waited patiently until she had performed both. He then thoughtfully asked for a poo bag and picked up after her. Sam's thought's turned to Matt who, if he came anywhere near an animal, treated them as though they were contaminated toxic waste or something equally as sinister.

Sam found four champagne flutes in the cupboard as Dominic popped the cork. Mary was looking for a vase to put Sam's flowers in and John was checking on Red. So when he thought they weren't looking, Dominic stole a brief kiss and Sam felt her insides go all jittery, nearly dropping one of the glasses.

This man is quite a hazard to have around, Sam thought. He interfered with her writing, too. She spent too much of her time fantasising about him. *Maybe he's just an occupational hazard,* she mused.

The four of them polished off the bottle and then started on a second that Sam had in the fridge. Mary and John were pleasantly pickled by the time they walked home. Sam and Dominic stood at the front door together and watched them cross the green, arm in arm. The evening was so peaceful that they heard Sooty howl with delight when Mary and John opened their front door.

'Oh poor Sooty is not going to be impressed tonight, especially once he smells Red on them,' Sam giggled.

Dominic put his arm around her and pulled her indoors before planting a kiss on her lips. He had the most delicious kiss, which always started gentle but seemed to get more passionate and deeper as it continued, taking her breath away.

'I wondered if you fancy coming round for dinner tomorrow night?' Dominic asked.

'I would love to, Dom, but I have Lucy and I don't want to leave the puppy too long for the first few nights. Do you think I'm being overly cautious?'

'Not at all, it's understandable. They're both welcome too, y'know, but you may be right Sam. It might be best to let her get used to her new home first couple of nights.'

'Why don't you come here? You and Lucy can watch Red and I'll cook.'

'Yeah, sounds good, what time?'

'Seven? I can feed Lucy early and then get a couple of fillet steaks for us, if that sounds okay.'

'Yeah, sounds good. Right, you better let me scoot now. Sweet dreams.'

He kissed her again so passionately that she thought her legs would collapse.

Chapter 23

Sam had anticipated a lie in, at least until about eight o'clock, but Lucy had other ideas. At six she came bounding in to Sam's bedroom and got in with her mummy.

'Oh Lucy, sweetheart, you need to go back to sleep darling.'

'But Mummy, I have tried and tried and tried. I've counted sheep, I've sung songs, but I just keep getting more and more awake and I think I heard Red cry.'

'Sweetheart, she will cry to begin with, but do you remember what Trisha said about leaving her to cry?'

'I know that, Mummy, but it's making me feel so sad and you never leave me to cry.'

Sam smiled at her daughter's logic and kissed the little treasure on the forehead. She knew there was no way that Lucy was going to go back to sleep, so she reluctantly got up and put her dressing gown on. Fortunately, the central heating had kicked in, as it was bitterly cold outside.

They crept down to the kitchen and peered through to the utility room, where little Red was curled up fast asleep. On the puppy pads beside her in the crate were a couple of deposits, but Sam noticed the little dog had made sure that she had gone as far away from her bed as was possible in the confined space. They lifted her out and removed the soiled puppy pads before replacing them with fresh. They took the little dog out onto the patio for "twinkles" and "busy", but it was frosty and Red slipped a couple of times.

'Mummy… Is she meant to be this small?' Lucy asked, clearly anxious after watching the poor little dog slip.

'Yes darling, they are particularly tiny to begin with, but she will get as big as her mummy.'

It's going to be a long morning, thought Sam.

Lucy gave the poor pup hardly any peace. Sam gave up on the idea of getting work done and so decided to bring on the domestic goddess and spring clean.

Lucy sat glued to the utility room, watching Red's every move. Sam was relieved when Mary wandered over mid-morning and suggested Lucy come for a walk with her and John to get some fresh air. As soon as they were off, Sam put the little dog back in her crate where she curled up, relieved to be left to sleep. Then Sam finally went up to the studio to work.

The weekend was long, with Lucy waking up in the night to see Red as well as at the crack of dawn, but it passed by quite readily for Sam and the pup. She was amazed at how easy the little dog was fitting into Wisteria Cottage's comings and goings. Lucy, on the other hand, was the exhausting one, as she had to be constantly reminded that Red was very young, got tired easily and did not want to be dressed up and pushed around in the doll's pram. Sam actually found herself relieved to see her off when Matt and Jasmine collected her after tea on Sunday.

She had half expected Lucy to refuse or play up because of the puppy, but it seemed that Matt had planned another action-packed couple of days for her.

Jasmine hung back when they were leaving, letting Matt settle Lucy into the car. She squeezed Sam around the waist as she left and whispered, 'Thank you,' before kissing her cheek.

Dominic had invited Sam round for dinner again. She called Trisha to ask if it was a good idea so soon. Trisha had reassured her that she really must start as she meant to go on. If she did decide to get back into performing, then the dog would need to stay away sometimes and with others, too, so Sam packed up her food and her little toys with confidence and loaded it all into the car.

As Sam pulled up onto Dominic's gravel drive, she actually found herself feeling nervous. He had a knack of calming her down, but this evening she could only think of how sexually aware of him she was, and it sent her nerves into orbit.

Liz had described his house as stunning. Sam had driven past it lots of times and was aware of its imposing size. So now, as she looked up at The Manor, she steadied her nerves and reminded herself that she knew the owner, well one of them at least, and she couldn't wait to see him.

Dominic appeared. He waited for her to step out, then he pulled her into his arms. Sam looked absolutely stunning this evening and Dominic did not want to let her go.

There was the small matter of a scruffy pup to attend to first. Dominic lifted out the crate while she carefully carried Red around to the back of the property and through the doors into an enormous yet beautiful kitchen. Dominic seemed to know exactly where to place the crate, and he positioned it near a radiator but on full view to whoever was in there.

A huge black Aga had something delicious bubbling away in the corner and Sam felt in awe. He had exquisite taste.

The cupboards were black and the work surfaces and island were made from a gleaming black marble. There were beautiful pale grey floor tiles and the walls completed the look with the subtlest hint of grey.

The lighting set the mood; it was modern and tasteful. Dominic handed her a glass of wine.

'Oh Dominic, this place is stunning. Can I look around?'

'Sure, let's just sort Red, then I'll walk you through.'

Red was so excited that she didn't quite manage to hold her bladder until they got outside, but Dominic just laughed and wiped it up. Sam adored him. She constantly found new and remarkable things about him to love, but that made her petrified as she had never felt like this before in her life.

Dominic gave Sam the guided tour. The kitchen, all hand built, led onto an enormous hall which had a huge dining table and twelve chairs. Two candelabra decorated the table; they each carried four red candles, but were unused, noticed Sam.

The lounge was equally huge, with a high ceiling. There were a number of art prints on the walls which Sam could inspect later. Dominic seemed to like dark earthy tones, as the room was a harmonious mix of heathers and russets, leafy greens and rich dark browns. He too had a log burner, and worn, comfortable sofas. Sam noted a utility room, an office and a cloakroom before Dominic whisked her upstairs to the first floor. Here there were three bedrooms, all with en suites and the usual necessities, but the top floor was staggering. Sam slowly turned to take it all in.

She judged it to be the same size as the other floors, but this was all open plan. The pillars had been left for obvious reasons and he had tastefully placed spectacular lighting in each one. The attic had been converted and the beams were exposed in the extremely high ceilings.

At one end, Sam spied a double bed with en suite bathroom. There was a beautiful jacuzzi surrounded by Moroccan mosaic tiles and piles of fluffy white towels just waiting to be used. The other end of the room had a lounge area with a couple of sofas and a wide screen TV, but in the middle, dividing two areas, there was a large desk, nestling by an enormous window which overlooked the green. Sam glanced at the photo frames arranged on the desk. There seemed to be family portraits and quite a few featured military personnel, comrades in arms, thought Sam. She stood for a while and took it all in; she felt speechless for a few moments.

'Dominic, this place is something else.'

'Thanks,' he said, smiling.

She was aware that he was uncomfortable being praised in spite of all the cocky bravado that he liked to put across.

'Liz said you designed it all and did all the work yourself.'

'It was in pretty good shape to begin with, so it was just cosmetics really,' Dominic said modestly.

'Mm, doesn't tie in with what those guys told me,' she said with mischief. 'Paul said you rewired the whole house and re-plastered it. Oh, and you even had to fix the roof and plumbing.'

'Ah, my secrets aren't safe with those two, then. To be honest, it was initially for commercial reasons. I was getting it done up to sell. Initially we were going to convert it into six luxury apartments but then I followed Tom's advice and decided to sell it as a whole house rather than pour loads more into it, but then the recession hit and Luke and I decided to take it off the market.'

'Is that because of the promise you made to your dad, of not selling it?'

Dominic stared directly at Sam. 'Wow, so my secrets really aren't safe with those two, are they? I didn't promise my father that I wouldn't sell. I promised him that I would try not to sell it, but maybe rent it out instead. Then, as time passed, I wanted to find a buyer. It's way too big for my taste, which is why I wanted to convert it into apartments. Me 'n Luke could then sell a couple, rent a couple out and keep one each, but as I said, the recession came along, so...'

The log fire was blazing by the time they returned downstairs, its cheery glow lighting up the room, making it feel cosy and intimate. Sam was starting to feel hungry after the tour and whatever was cooking smelt delicious.

'Mm, what have we got to eat this evening then?' Sam asked.

'I cooked a Thai curry seeing as you said you loved Thai food,' he said, reaching to top up her glass. She put her hand out to stop him.

'Dom, no more, I'm driving.'

'So leave the car and get it in the morning,' Dominic suggested.

'Oh right, and carry Red home in her crate, worse the wear?'

'Then stay over, Sam.'

'I don't think that's a good idea.'

She spoke in what she hoped was her most assertive voice, letting him know that under no circumstances would she be sharing a bed with him tonight.

'Sam, look, I know you're not ready for taking things any further right now and you need to understand that if you were to stay, you have my room. I will sleep in one of the spare rooms. This is way too special to blow by rushing things and as attracted to you as I am, I know you would regret rushing things, and so would I.'

Sam was stunned, she could not believe how amazing it felt to hear Dominic say that.

'I'm sorry, Dom. Apart from Matt, there's been no one else and I, I… I guess that for Lucy's sake, too, well I need to make sure, and oh look, I've never been into stuff. Matt said I'm frigid…' She hung her head, embarrassed. Dominic cupped her chin.

'Sam, look at me. In my opinion, frigid is a derogatory word that is usually used to hurt people or to bully them into giving more than they are comfortable with, so please take no notice. You are not frigid, Sam, you just have boundaries.'

'But that makes me sound like I'm judgemental and I'm not. I don't judge others who have one night stands, you know,' she interrupted, embarrassed.

'I can't imagine you would judge anyone. Now how about you stop worrying, and we enjoy our evening. I have a spare toothbrush and you can borrow one of my t-shirts to sleep in. Rest assured, you will be left alone to sleep here tonight, and I never break a promise.'

The evening was quite possibly the most romantic evening that either of them had ever had.

They listened to music while sitting beside the log fire. St Mary's Church's annual carol singers came round on Santa's sleigh, which was a tractor wearing huge reindeer antlers and a trailer decorated in fairy lights, holly and tinsel. This made the evening particularly magical. Dominic carried out sherry to warm them all as they all stood on the "sleigh" in the bitter cold, trying to keep their balance as they had apparently just enjoyed Mulled wine and mince pies at The Fox.

Sam thought back to the Christmas cards she would gaze at as a teenager. She would dream of finding a future depicted by the picture on the cards. A beautiful home, beautiful family, a little dog. Living in the perfect village. No, Lucy wasn't here right now, but tingling sensations hinted at the possibility of years to come.

Red was so overexcited to be exploring a new space and when they let her out for her final toilet break, the little dog refused to go back into her crate, resulting in a hilarious game of chase around Dominic's enormous kitchen.

True to his word, Dominic put no pressure on Sam whatsoever. He carried up a hot water bottle, a glass of water, found her a t-shirt and toothbrush and kissed her goodnight. It did cross both their minds how easy it would be to snuggle in together, but they knew it was the magic of the evening and the wine talking and that Sam was not ready.

Waking up in that stunning room, Sam felt like a princess in a beautiful castle. *When had her life gone from living in a nightmare to such a beautiful fairy tale?*

She luxuriated in the warmth of his bed for a moment. She stretched, and was about to get up, when he sauntered in with a tray laden with a full English breakfast, mugs of coffee and a glass of orange juice. Sam sat up and pulled the bed sheets up around her chin. She suddenly felt a little shy.

'Oh wow, this just gets better and better, thank you,' she announced, looking at the tray and all its delicious offerings.

Dominic noticed that Sam was really shy this morning and so managed to keep any jovial comments to himself. Sam was special and he wanted her to know that. He kissed her on the forehead and placed the tray down.

'Red, I've forgotten about Red! What time is it?' she shouted, appalled that she could forget the little dog and not even set her alarm.

'It's fine, Sam. Red is fine, she's been out and been very busy. She's had her breakfast and I let her play for a bit, but she's now safely back in her crate.'

Dominic sat on the edge of the bed and smiled to himself.

'Did she make you chase her again?' Sam asked.

'Yeah, but I've sussed out how to get her back. I managed to bribe her with a sock rolled into a ball.'

'Thank you so much for making last night so special. No one has ever done anything like this for me before.' Sam started tucking into her breakfast.

Dominic was saddened by Sam's lack of confidence: she really did not see herself as beautiful and he couldn't wait until the day she did.

He really didn't want to have to go to work that morning, but he had promised his client he would finish her loft extension. He had a couple more full-on days before Christmas, but at this moment he just wanted to stay with Sam.

'Sam, I need to do a couple of hour's work, so did you wanna stick around here for a bit and I can sort some lunch when I get back?'

'That would be lovely, but I need to get back and finish up a song.'

'Right. No hurry, but I'll load the crate in your car – if you put Red in, I will scoot round to yours now and take them both in for you, okay?'

'It's fine Dom, honest, I can lift it fine,' Sam argued.

'I know, but it gives me longer with you,' Dominic replied, smiling.

Sam was relieved to hear this.

'So last night, it was okay?' she whispered.

Dominic stared at her and felt a blow to the chest. She looked so unsure and so vulnerable. He cursed himself for being so insensitive. Of course someone like Sam would feel vulnerable and in need of reassurance. He cupped her face in his hands.

'Sam, last night was one of the best nights I have ever spent in my life. You are so beautiful and I'm falling for you big time. I told you, we can take as much time as you need, okay?'

Sam dropped her head and shrugged her shoulders. 'I'm just no good at that sort of thing, especially so soon after Matt.'

Dom placed his lips on hers.

'Shh. Please stop putting pressure on yourself and putting yourself down. I'm in no hurry and I'm going nowhere, okay? Now, I have to get that loft extension finished, but can I scoot by tonight?'

'Yes. I'll cook for you, if you like?'

'I thought you said you had work you needed done this side of Christmas?'

'Yes, you're right I do actually,' Sam laughed.

'Well in that case, a takeaway will do. I was thinking that we could shoot over to The Fox with your parents later for a drink. I know that they're having carols and mulled wine tonight and I've learnt how much you love Christmas.'

Her face lit up, making him smile, too.

'Oh Dom, that sounds perfect. Thank you so, so much, and thank you for a wonderful night last night.'

The rest of the day panned out perfectly. Sam managed to get two songs to a finished state and when she emailed them to the record company, they received the type of approval she was looking for. In fact, you could say she blew them away with the songs. She smiled across at The Fox, the ultimate village pub. The owners had a marquee erected for tonights carols and mulled wine. Dominic had said it had been pretty run down before they had taken it over and she was already falling in love with her new "local".

Wisteria Cottage was so Christmassy and cosy; she could not believe how much she had grown to love this place. She decided to have a soak in the bath and prepare for tonight.

Chapter 24

Dominic arrived at seven thirty. He had already called her from the Indian takeaway to find out what she wanted and now the lovely aroma of tarka dhal, rogan josh with pilau rice wafted around the kitchen. They sat at the island, eating and chatting.

Dominic seemed pleased with how much work he had managed to get done and Sam told him about the terrific reaction she'd gotten for her songs. Outside, houses twinkled their fairy lights back at them. Sam never closed the curtains at night here, it was like a kaleidoscope of colours at Christmas.

She reflected now that all those years she had lived with Matt she had never felt this at ease with him. She had known Dominic only a few weeks but felt so comfortable in his company that they could almost pass as an old married couple. She also realised that she had spent more time in Dominic's company than she had for the last four years with Matt.

Red had wriggled with delight when Dominic arrived and was now fast asleep in her crate. The little dog hadn't slept once today, so Sam didn't feel too guilty about going out as she would need to rest. They were meeting Liz and Paul at The Fox, and Mary and John had said they would call in a little later as well.

Sam face timed Lucy so that the little girl could see her puppy again. Sam was relieved that Lucy was having a wonderful time with her dad and Jasmine. She'd visited a studio in East London with Matt and helped him set up a recording session with a band. The little girl was full of charming self-importance.

By the time Dominic and Sam got to the pub, it was heaving. The atmosphere was absolutely magical. Fires crackled either side of the room, they ordered their drinks and went out into the marquee to find the others. Carol singers were singing beautifully, encouraging all to join in. Sam was delighted to see that Sue was there with Tom, who had everyone in stitches joining in with the choir.

'Oh li"le tan of beff'lee'em 'ow still we see thee lie...'

Mulled wine was being ladled into glasses and handed round. Liz sat in the centre of things with a glazed expression that could only mean she was really tipsy and even more mischievous than usual. Paul and Dominic were so matey and relaxed with each other that Sam simply sat and observed them.

Matt had never really been relaxed around other men; he had always tried to outdo them somehow and came across as inferior and a bit of an idiot.

Sam and Liz joined in the Christmas carols. 'Hark The Herald Angels Sing' was Sam's all-time favourite carol and, judging by the sound of Liz singing tunelessly at the top of her voice beside her, it was her favourite, too. Dominic caught Sam's eye every now and again and they were both reduced to hysterics.

'I know you two are making fun at my singing, but you're just jealous because you can't harmonise like me,' Liz slurred. 'I want to say, Sam, if you ever need me to sing one of your songs for you, then you only have to ask.'

Sam hugged her tightly. 'Thank you, my angel. I most certainly will keep it in mind.'

They stayed on until closing time with what seemed like most of the village, including Reverend Gibson, who Sam noticed was as handsome and as friendly as everyone said he was, she also reminded Liz on several occasions that he had a very beautiful wife too.

Dominic and Sam finally said their goodbyes to neighbours and friends around midnight and swayed happily across the green to Wisteria Cottage. The little puppy, as ever, was pleased to see them. Dominic made some strong coffee and let Red out to perform while Sam put her pyjamas on and came back downstairs. Dominic lit the log burner and they cuddled up on the sofa, it was so cosy.

'I was thinking, let's be teenagers and make a camp by the fire, what do you say?' Sam asked playfully.

'Mm, sounds good,' Dominic replied.

They went up to her bedroom and hauled Sam's king size duvet and pillows into the lounge. Sam placed a throw down on the rug and they set up camp. With the Christmas lights twinkling on the tree and on the garland, it really was a magical scene, like Santa's grotto.

It was almost four in the morning when Dominic walked home. They'd had a wonderful carpet picnic with the remains of their takeaway and had snuggled down to watch a film.

The following morning, Sam gave Red her breakfast and played with her for an hour. She hugged herself over and over, thinking of how romantic last night had been, and decided to go back to bed. This surprised her, as she never normally did this during the day, but knew she had a busy few days ahead.

She managed to sleep for an hour, but her racing mind woke her up and wouldn't let her relax.

She had arranged to go Christmas shopping with Sue and Liz that afternoon. She didn't like shopping, but she had nothing for Lucy yet and couldn't decide what to buy Dominic either.

Tomorrow was Christmas Eve and Matt had said he would drop Lucy off about three. Sam called her mum to arrange details.

'Hi Mum, are you and Dad coming to Liz and Paul's tomorrow night?'

'Yes, but we won't stay long, my love, as I like to get organised Christmas Eve. Suzy called, she said she will be coming Christmas morning. I did invite Dominic, by the way, but he said that he can't, as Luke's coming home.'

'Yes, apparently they spend it just the two of them. They try to be together Christmas Day when they can,' Sam explained.

'Well, I don't like to think of them being alone, Sam.'

'They'll be fine, Mum, I promise.'

Dominic had told Sam that Luke needed time out whenever he got home; he always struggled being around people and just wanted his brother. Sam understood that the last thing he would probably want is to be thrust into the throes of a family party.

'Right, so, about tomorrow. Matt's dropping Lucy back at three. I will bring our things round tomorrow morning and then I'll wrap presents and leave them locked in the studio. I can come back and collect them after dinner. Liz and Paul have said to come after six, so should we drop off Red at about five thirty then go there for a drink?'

'Lovely,' Mary said.

'Why don't you forget cooking tomorrow night, Mum? Liz has spent a fortune at Waitrose, and I know she's collecting a load of canapés tomorrow afternoon.'

Mary chuckled at the thought.

'Oh, what a wonderful idea. I had made my Beef Wellington but I could freeze it. Oh, Sam, what about Lucy? She'll need to eat when she gets back.'

'I'll cook her something about five, just before we come over. She will be fine.'

'Okay, darling. Y'know, I still can't believe you and Lucy live here in the village, it's wonderful. This year is so special.'

'I know. I still can't believe it either.'

'How do you think Lucy will cope without Matt?' Mary asked.

'Well, apart from Christmas morning, Lucy never really got to see him that much! See, that's the good thing now, Lucy is finally getting to spend some quality time with her dad, all thanks to Jasmine.'

'Well good, it's about time.'

'I'm about to go Christmas shopping, Mum. I'm obviously going to bring wine and champagne, but is there anything else you can think of?'

'Just yourselves and that dear little dog, darling. That reminds me, do you want me to pop over and check her later?'

'Oh yes please, good idea. Listen, is it okay if I bring the bottles of plonk over later? It'll save me unloading it here only to bring over to you tomorrow.'

'That's fine, darling. Oh, and if you see some thick walking socks, I know your father would love some, size ten.'

'Will do, Mum. Okay, see you later.'

Sue, Liz and Sam had an absolute scream Christmas shopping. They called into The White Horse for lunch. Sam was driving, so while she drank elderflower cordial, the others had two large glasses of wine each with their meal. This was a huge mistake, as for Sam it was like taking around two badly behaved teenagers.

Liz and Sue decided to try on some 'Wonderbras' and basques in a lovely little underwear boutique in town. Selfies were taken and sent to anyone and everyone they knew. They then decided to visit Santa in his grotto but were asked to leave when they both sat on either knee and were being most inappropriate, bouncing up and down and singing "this is the way the ladies ride" over and over. Poor Santa looked shattered by the whole experience.

Fortunately, Sam managed to shake them for an hour. While they poured over the perfume counters, she was able to finish her Christmas shopping with presents for Lucy and aftershave and a jumper for Dominic.

Sam decided to stop at the garden centre on the way home to look for walking socks and mistletoe. This too was a huge mistake: she tried to distract them both from the mulled wine being offered to shoppers but alas, Sue smelt the delicious aroma and it didn't take long to track down where it was coming from. The pair spotted some rather vulgar garden gnomes which they each bought for their in-laws. One gnome was spending a penny and the other was pulling a moon. Sam eventually coaxed them back to the car before any more embarrassing purchases could be made.

'Oh, mine will hate them,' roared Sue as she fell into the back-seat.

'Mine will love theirs, they have a great sense of humour,' Liz squealed, then shouted, 'ooh, turn this one up Sam, I love this song. So here it is, Merry Christmas! Everybody's having fun...' Sue joined in singing.

Sam shook her head; she could not believe that her two new friends sang as atrociously as one another.

When they got louder and louder, Sam wanted to switch the radio off, but instead joined in and had tears of laughter pouring down her face within seconds. She could hardly keep herself in tune with the two of them screaming out their own melody like some bizarre harmony. It was an absolute hoot.

They pulled up at traffic lights. Sue spotted something to amuse her and loudly announced, 'Ugh! That man is picking his nose. Ugh he going to eat it! No, no, NO, NO.'

Then Liz joined in. 'NO, NO! Oi, pick us a winner!' screamed Liz.

'Mind your head doesn't cave in,' shouted Sue.

Sam wanted to duck down and hide; it was like being back at school. The poor man heard the screams and looked to see the three of them staring at him. He went bright red and shot off when the lights changed.

'It's amazing how many people like to recycle themselves, isn't it?' Sue said calmly.

'I know, I once had a boyfriend who ate his toe nails,' Liz replied. Sam had heard enough.

'Guys, please, that's enough now,' Sam begged. 'You're being disgusting, and my sides are killing me. You're making me feel sick.'

'Well, how do you think I feel Sam? He used to kiss me after he'd eaten them.'

All three screamed now.

Sam was glad to drive into the village and drop the pair and their wacky purchases off at Liz's. They were more trouble than Lucy and her three, little friends who had come to tea the other day.

Paul had wandered out to the car to greet them. Sam apologised for the state of his wife, but he just laughed.

'Ooh lucky you, I love to bump the uglies when I'm drunk, it's the only time I enjoy it,' Sue shouted.

'BUMP THE UGLIES!' Liz screamed. 'Where the hell did you hear that?'

Sam was squealing with laughter and Paul just shook his head and gently steered Liz into the house.

'Wait for me,' shouted Sue, stumbling after them both. Paul reached for her arm to help her as well.

Oh, poor Paul, thought Sam, but at least Sue was his problem now, until Tom collected her.

Sam drove to her parents, where Mary was waiting to help her unload the car. Sam gave her mum all the grisly details about the shopping expedition.

'Oh Mum, I'm so pleased I gave Sue a second chance, I really am. I can't believe I disliked her so much at first. Honestly, those two could have their own reality TV show; they are so funny, but totally inappropriate.'

'I know, and just imagine once you add Suzy to the mix!' Mary said, smiling.

'Oh no, can you imagine? Poor Sheila really will call the Reverend, won't she?'

'Either that or leave the village,' quipped Mary as she gathered up Sam's shopping and took it indoors. 'Would you like to come and stay tonight, darling?'

Sam played with her coat buttons and blushed. 'Thanks Mum, but Dominic is coming round and I'm going to cook. He's going to help me wrap all Lucy's presents, and trust me, it will take an evening.'

Mary smiled thoughtfully. 'He's a good man, Sam, I hope you know that. He isn't Matt, you know?'

'I know, Mum. He's wonderful, but I'm scared. I'm kind of falling for him and to be honest, I could do without it.'

'Oh, my darling, don't you think you've been lonely for long enough? Don't you think you deserve a little happiness? And to be honest, so does Dominic. His life has been hard, too.'

'I know. It's just all going so fast, Mum, I keep expecting it to all go wrong.'

'Then stop worrying about the future and try not to hold the past as a benchmark. Dominic is a good man.'

'You must admit it is all rather a bit too good to be true, don't you think, Mum?'

'But it is true, Sam. If there weren't incredible, genuine men out there, then thousands of chick flicks and romantic novels wouldn't be sold each year, would they? It has to come from somewhere.'

Mary squeezed her daughter's hand and Sam could no longer keep her feelings to herself.

'Oh Mum, he's just gorgeous.'

'Yes, he is, but he too has his issues. His childhood was quite abusive by all accounts. No wonder the poor love couldn't wait to join the army.'

'I'm just not used to it, Mum. He does things for me. He takes me places, he helps with Red. He is nice to me and he is lovely to Lucy.'

'If you ask me, Sam, it's long overdue. Besides, it will be a good example to set for Lucy. It must be nice for her to see a man being kind to her mummy. No one could ever accuse Matt of that, could they? By all accounts he was a pig to you.' Mary put her head down, saddened by the thought of all her daughter had been through, and the guilt and shame were etched in her face for abandoning her and leaving her to deal with it. Sensing her sadness, Sam decided to change the subject.

'What's his brother like, Mum?'

'Stunning. Handsome. Alpha, like Dominic, but a lot more serious. Your father thinks it's because he has been in the military a lot longer. He's been in Afghanistan, and by all accounts has seen more than enough. It will be good to see Luke again.'

Sam's curiosity in all things Dom was growing again. 'What was their mother like?'

Mother and daughter sat at the kitchen table with their tea, surrounded by shopping bags.

'Obviously I wasn't here when she lived in the village, but she was Jenny's closest friend. Jenny has told me the whole sorry tale. From what I have seen and heard, she was full of life, but the old admiral drained her spirit until she could stand it no longer and decided to get away.'

'Liz said she was beautiful,' Sam interrupted.

'She was, and apparently she had the most beautiful voice. She sang in the choir. People often praised her voice, but the old admiral would put her down and tell her to be quiet, said it was like living with a canary and that she twittered irritably all day. The day she left the village, Jenny said that a dark cloud descended over The Manor, and it wasn't until Dominic took it over that it finally went.'

Sam was struck by this last comment. She recalled a story she had told Dominic about how she'd learnt to stop singing around the house as Matt always said it gave him a headache. She remembered now that Dominic became quite angry and said how frustrated he got with people trying to break the spirit of others. She got it now: it seemed as though his own father had tried to do that to his mother. But at least their mother had managed to escape. Although she had been taken from the boy's life too early, Dominic had said that she wouldn't have wanted to go any other way.

'Dom said his mum died in a boating accident. He said it was an accident that was unavoidable, but Liz had heard that his mother and her friends had gone sailing and ended up drunk and it all went horribly wrong.'

'Yes, sadly it did. She was a live wire,' Mary said with a smile on her face, remembering all the many stories Jenny had told her.

'I wish I could be more of a live wire. I mean, look at Liz and Sue, they are an absolute hoot. I just sometimes wish I wasn't so afraid of everything, Mum. I wish I could stop thinking too hard or worry so much.'

'Darling, I honestly believe that if you weren't the way you are, then all those beautiful songs you have written would not exist.

Now, how sad would that be? Look how many lives your music touches.'

Sam shifted uncomfortably in her seat and stared into her empty tea cup.

"Cut Raw' is a stunning song,' Mary continued. 'Can you honestly imagine if you hadn't written it? Think about it, Sam. Do you remember the Radio Four interview with the three school girls who had been self-harming? It was 'Cut Raw' that had reached them, urging them to stop. They said that they believed the song saved their lives. How does that make you feel?'

Sam hadn't forgotten that moment, she hadn't forgotten all the letters the publishers had forwarded to her from others, writing to thank her. Charities had written asking her to become an ambassador.

Mary mistook the look of angst on Sam's face and took hold of her hand.

'Darling, I'm sorry. I didn't mean to upset you, I just wish you saw what the rest of us see: a beautiful, talented woman.'

'Oh Mum, honestly it's good you reminded me, but I was just thinking about Suzy.'

'I know, my love, but she's coming home. Suzy is so different these days. She will have us all here for her, on her doorstep.' Mary soothed.

Sam glanced at her watch.

'Right, well I'm going to head home. Thanks for checking in on Red today, Mum, and for everything else. I'll see you in the morning for coffee.'

The women hugged. Sam was so excited; she loved Christmas and she couldn't believe that tomorrow would be Christmas Eve, her favourite day of the year.

Chapter 25

Dominic, on the other hand, could not believe how many presents Sam had for him to help wrap.

'Woah, Sam, Lucy must be the world's most spoilt child. Look at all these bags.'

'No, they're not all for Lucy, some are for my parents and some for Suzy. We all spend Christmas together. Oh, by the way, is your brother coming to Liz and Paul's tomorrow evening? Only I can't wait to meet him.'

'He should be here by lunch time, so I'm sure he will put in an appearance if he's up to people. By all accounts he is dying to meet you as well. Don't think he can believe his big brother has finally found someone who he wants to spend time with.'

'Oh dear, I do hope he's not disappointed.' Sam bit her lip nervously and started messing with the gift wrap. Dominic walked over to her and cupped her face in his hands; she loved it when he did this.

'How could anyone be disappointed with you, Sam?' he murmured and then kissed her.

'Right, enough of that, else we will be in trouble. Besides, I need to cook and you need to start wrapping up the presents, if you're sure you don't mind. Oh gosh, I bought a Christmas CD today which has all the favourites on it. Shall I put it on now, really loud?' giggled Sam.

'Great,' lied Dom. 'I can't wait.'

Despite Dominic's initial reservations about the music, he was actually having the time of his life. Wisteria Cottage had to be the cosiest home he had been in since his childhood, evoking thoughts of the last Christmas his mother had been with them and his father had been away. Sam was just like his mum in that she had a knack of making you feel comfortable and at home. He remembered that his mum too had an obsession with Christmas, candles and fairy lights.

The Christmas tree was beautiful, the log fire crackled and the music was magical. They drank mulled wine, which was warming and aromatic. They decided to eat off trays in the lounge as they didn't want to leave the fire. Red was happily snoring in her crate after running off several times with the wrapping paper and ribbons.

Dominic couldn't actually remember the last time he felt this relaxed or happy.

Lucy called at bedtime and insisted on Face-timing so that she could see Red. She told her mummy all about the wonderful time she was having. They had gone to see the Christmas tree in Trafalgar Square and all the pretty lights in Oxford Street. Lucy got Jasmine to forward Sam all the photos of their trip. They were lovely and showed Lucy clearly having the time of her life. Dominic was so touched because he heard Lucy tell her mother that she had bought him a gift, which was totally unexpected. He was pleased, as he enjoyed spending time with the little girl and had grown quite fond of her.

After the presents were wrapped and labels attached, they carried them up to the studio. Sam squeezed his hand.

'Honestly, Dom, I love this room. I never ever tire of being up here you know. Thank you so so much.'

'It's what you asked for, Sam. It's your design.'

'But I love it so much. I should have bought you a gift to say thank you.'

'Okay then, can I ask for a thank you present?' Dominic said eagerly.

'Sure...' *Uh oh, will it be inappropriate?* Sam thought, but was surprised by his request.

'Can I listen to some of your songs through the system, some of the new songs you said you've kept in your 'best kept secrets' file?'

'Gosh, you've got a good memory. You can, but I won't be able to stay in here with you. I can't listen to my voice with someone else in the room, and I should warn you they're nothing like the album. They're pretty scratchy demos with just piano and my voice,' she said humbly.

'Cool, just how I want to hear them. Oh, and one other request, would you bring me a glass of mulled wine, please? Think that's enough of the 'thank yous' now, don't you?' Dominic said grinning.

Sam brought him up a glass of mulled wine before setting the computer to play the five chosen songs and then, true to her word, closed the door and went downstairs.

She loaded the dishwasher, called Suzy and then let Red out and carried her in for a play.

A little while later, Dominic emerged from the studio and sat beside Sam. She turned to look at him as he gently stroked her face and saw his eyes looked so sad.

'Sam, please, you need to do this. You need to perform again. Your voice, the songs… they are so perfect. Please don't blow this opportunity, Sam. I promise I will support you all the way…'

Sam was taken aback by Dominic's reaction to her work.

'Oh, don't do this to me Dom, please. I already decided to just write for others and I feel that's what I must do.'

'Must do, or want to do?' he asked directly. He could see Sam was panicking. 'Sam, give me one good reason why you feel you shouldn't and I swear I'll get off your case.'

'I don't think that's fair. All my reasons are valid, Dom.'

'Oh, Sam. I'm not being unkind, it just breaks my heart. You are so talented, and I don't believe there is another artist alive that could do those songs justice. Please reconsider, Sam. I promise you, no one will reject you. No one is going to turn their back on those songs and your voice; it's just something to be shared. Chris was talking to your dad about asking you to do a couple of songs New Year's Eve. They have a band to see the new year in, but he said it would mean a lot to the locals if you were to perform a couple of your songs.'

'The Fox?! Sing at *The Fox*? You have to be joking,' Sam squealed, terrified.

'But think about it, you'd have so many of your friends there, even Lucy – she would be made up to hear you perform, I bet.'

'Dad never mentioned it.'

'No, he asked me to speak to you. Please, Sam, think about it. Just a few locals and friends, that's all.'

'Look, if you promise to stop talking about it now then I promise I will give it some serious thought, okay?'

'Guess I will have to accept that,' smiled Dominic.

Dominic pulled her to him and kissed her for what felt like an eternity. She was in heaven. It was only when the little dog tried jumping onto the sofa and landed on her back that reality brought them both back down.

Waking up in Willow Green on Christmas Eve was so special. When Sam noticed the alarm clock again and saw it was past ten, she panicked.

'Oh gosh, I have so much to do before Lucy gets back,' she said out loud. Her phone started ringing, it was Dominic.

'Hey, Sam. I'm meeting Luke for lunch, but I wondered if you fancied scooting out for a quick coffee now?' he asked.

'Oh, I'd love that, but I have way too much to do. Are you excited about seeing him?' she asked, pulling on her jeans.

'It's always great to see him, but it's hard work too. It seems each time he goes out there, it's like a little bit more of him gets lost. It usually takes a couple of days for him to get reacquainted at home and then it's time for him to go again. Think he struggles a bit – it wasn't exactly 'Walt Disney' growing up in that house.'

'I wish I had known your mum, she sounded wonderful,' Sam said.

'I wish you'd known her, too, she would have loved you. Mind you, I think you would find her a bit over the top. She would have dragged you back on stage kicking and screaming.'

'Yeah? Mum said that Jenny told her she had a wonderful voice.'

'She did. She was funny, too.'

'Do you miss her?' Sam asked.

'Yeah, every day, but I think Luke misses her more. He really struggles on her birthday.'

'Oh Dom, I'm sorry. She was taken so young and it's awful.'

'Like I told you the other day, she would have rather gone out that way. She went when she was at her peak. If you had known her, you definitely would get why that was a good time for her to go.'

'Dom?'

'Sam?'

'Look, tell me to mind my own business, but why do you think she married your father? He sounds so, well, different.'

'She got pregnant with me and, as you can imagine back then, it was not cool. Anyway, my father married her before he went away on his next tour, and then Luke came along. I guess back then he wasn't around long enough to bully her so she coped, although I don't know how, we were a nightmare!'

'Do you think your father missed her when she'd gone?'

'More 'cuz he had no one to bully any longer. He couldn't bully Luke or me – we were away at school, and by the time we both had returned to him we'd already signed up.'

'I'm sorry I keep asking questions. I guess I want to know more about you.'

'At this rate we could've had two cups of coffee,' he said, laughing.

'I will see you at Liz's later?' Sam asked again.

'Yep, see you there.'

Sam went to the supermarket to buy some last-minute goodies. It was chaos in there, but she managed to lay her hands on a case of decent champagne and a mixed case of wine. She made a mental note to take a bottle to tonight's drinks party. Sam was actually nervous about meeting Luke.

She went along the high street to a boutique and saw the most beautiful long dress. She tried it on and was pleasantly surprised by how good it looked. It was quite fitted, with long sleeves and it flared once it reached below the knees. It slightly swept the floor so she would need to lift it up outside but apart from that it was perfect. It was a dark charcoal grey colour so shouldn't show if the bottom did get slightly scuffed.

'If you wear heels it should just be about right,' the kind assistant reassured Sam.

Sam smiled, knowing that would never happen. She never wore heels, as she couldn't walk in them and never felt relaxed. The highest heels she owned were her cowboy boots, but most of the time she chose her converse trainers. She had bought herself a black pair recently which would work fine with this dress, she thought.

Sam made the purchase, wished the assistant a Merry Christmas and headed home.

Matt was on his own when he turned up with Lucy. Jasmine was doing a little last-minute shopping in Knightsbridge, apparently. He attempted to feign interest in Red, but Sam could see not even the cutest, most beautiful puppy in the world could win him over. He complained about how much the dog smelt. Sam explained how it was too soon to wash the mother's scent off the pup. Matt was hilarious; anybody would think she had served him up horse manure to eat.

Sam couldn't quite work him out. He was acting out of character. He kept going to say something to her but couldn't seem to get the words out and avoided eye contact. She was relieved when he went home, as she needed to feed Lucy and they both needed to get ready for the party. She wanted to have a little time chatting to Lucy, but Lucy only had eyes for Red. Sam gave up, went to get ready, leaving the little girl playing with Red in the kitchen.

Mary called at six thirty.

'Darling, are you coming over soon? Only we are late already, and your father and I wanted to help you in with the crate. What are you doing about Lucy's presents? Are you bringing them now?'

'Sorry Mum, we are on our way now. I just loaded the crate. I'm going to come straight back and get the you-know-whats and put them in your dining room, if that's okay?'

'Of course. See you in a minute.'

Chapter 26

They unloaded the dog and the crate into her parents' house. Sooty was shut in the kitchen, so they carried Red through to the utility room, then Mary and John took Lucy to Liz's so that Sam could settle the puppy and bring the presents over.

She climbed the stairs three times to load the car and cursed herself for buying so many bulky things and wearing such a long dress. She wished she'd taken up Dominic's offer to take the presents over but she had said not to worry. She couldn't wait to see him, especially as Liz had just text saying:

'Wow you're gonna burst a blood vessel when you see delectable Dom and finger-licking Luke!'

Sam giggled at Liz's unusual sayings and pet names for people and she was relieved that Luke had made it to the party. She was satisfied that she had hidden the presents securely in the dining room and she knew Lucy wouldn't go in there, as she couldn't actually lift the heavy latch on the dining room door.

She drove to Liz's and all of a sudden got the worst nerves, worse than any stage fright she had ever known. She walked in through the front door and thought she would faint, for there, smiling back at her and looking unbelievably handsome, was Dominic. Standing beside him was another equally stunning man that she recognised must be Luke. They both made their way over and Dominic introduced him. They were so alike in build and colour, yet where Dominic's eyes were dark brown and mischievous, Luke's were a piercing blue and had a depth of sadness in them which seemed to belong to some other place. Luke's gaze was penetrating. Sam found him intimidating on first sight, but he couldn't have been more polite and she realised that he was making a huge effort with her.

Dominic went to get them all a drink and left her with Luke. For a moment, she couldn't think of what to say. She watched him gaze around the room at all the different people.

'This must be really weird for you,' she said.

'Yeah, I should be fit for communicating by midnight. I just dread getting caught by Liz or Sue, only they're hell bent on marrying me off.'

Sam laughed.

'No! Not you too! Funnily enough, that's what Dominic said Liz always tried with him.'

Luke looked into her eyes and smiled. 'Seems she did him proud with you.'

Sam felt herself blush, but she was pleased to have his brother's seal of approval. At that moment, Dominic returned with a glass of wine for them both.

'Thanks. I don't suppose you've seen Lucy yet, have you?' Asked Sam.

'Yeah, she and Faye are tracking Santa on Paul's iPad. Last I checked he was over India.'

'Oh, poor Santa,' laughed Sam. 'Bet he's tired. I'll go and find her, see you in a bit.'

Dominic looked at Luke. The two just stared for a few seconds.

'Well?' Dominic asked his brother, shocked by how eager he was for his brother's opinion.

'Gorgeous. What the hell is she doing with you? Man, you are so punching above your weight.'

Dominic swore at his brother profusely but smiled at his approval.

Liz and Sue were on a roll in one corner and Sheila was as poisonous as ever, spreading her gossip in the hallway. Sue had admitted a few weeks ago that she wasn't spending time with Sheila these days, as she felt that she had nothing particularly kind to say about anyone. Sue had also told Sam and Liz that she had made a promise to herself that she was not going to gossip or be unkind to anyone anymore; she said it was an early New Year's resolution.

Liz had been rather ungenerous at the time and said, 'Hell will freeze over before that happens.' Sam, however, felt that Sue would succeed, if nothing else than just to prove Liz wrong.

Sam found Lucy sat with her parents on the sofa, happily tucking into a bowl of crisps and nibbles. The atmosphere at Liz's was magical and Paul was the perfect host, making sure everyone was welcome. Suddenly, Sam felt her phone buzzing. It was Suzy.

'Hey Suzy, how's it going?'

'I'm here,' Suzy said.

'Where?' Sam said, looking around, her heart racing in excitement.

'I'm at your mum and dad's, but there's no one here.'

'Oh Suzy, I thought you weren't coming till the morning.'

'I know but I was too excited and couldn't face the daylight, so thought I would drive up tonight. Besides, your mum asked me to try to come early.'

'Look, we are at Liz's, I'll come over and get you,' Sam said, making her way around people.

'No, it's okay. If I can just get into the house, I will wait for you there.'

Sam could hardly hear Suzy over the din of the party so she just hollered, 'Wait there, Suzy.'

Liz was now in the kitchen, heating up yet more canapés. Sam explained that Suzy had turned up and asked if she could bring her back.

'Of course you can! I love her, she's even funnier than Sue and she's not a bitch,' Liz said, blowing a noisy raspberry at Sue.

'All I said, Elizabeth, is that I preferred the dress you wore the other night, that's all,' Sue said in her poshest voice.

'So, what happened to you being nicer?' Liz demanded.

'I am nicer. I am not being unkind, I am merely giving you my opinion, seeing as you did ask if I liked your dress.'

'Well then, add the art of lying to your New Year's resolution please,' Liz announced.

Sam started laughing and went to find Dominic to explain where she was going.

'Let me come with you,' he said.

'No, honestly, I've only drunk half a glass of wine so I'll drive.'

When she got to her parents, Suzy was waiting in her car, singing along beautifully to a Christmas love song. They hugged for ages.

'Oh Sam, I couldn't wait, I had to see you. Can you believe I'm going to move here?!'

'I know, I keep pinching myself.'

'I keep staring at it, look at it it's so pretty.' They both looked across at Primrose Cottage and the Christmas lights twinkling through the window.

'Grab the bin liner, would you? Only it's got presents in.'

They carried Suzy's bags up to the spare room that the two of them would share. She bounced down on the bed and then noticed Sam's party dress.

'You look stunning, by the way.'

'Most of the village has been invited to Liz and Paul's, we're all round there. I said I'd take you back with me. The food is absolutely delicious, Suzy.'

'Oh Sam, I'm not dressed for a party.'

Sam looked at her incredulously, for she was dressed in a pair of fabulous black jeans and a black fitted sweater, her hair was in a knot and she only had a hint of makeup on. Sam knew her friend would stand out at any party.

'Suzy, you look wonderful. Don't do this, please come over. I really want you to meet Dominic.'

'Sam, don't do this, you know I don't do parties.'

'Neither did I 'til I moved here but Suzy please, it would mean so much to me and Lucy.'

'Okay. Oh, but first things first, where's that little puppy? I am desperate to see her.'

'She's downstairs in the utility room, but leave her, else she'll get over excited.'

'No, I need to see her, and I want to see Sooty, too.'

'But then he'll get over excited and set Red off,' worried Sam.

'Look, it's Christmas Eve and besides, I need a drink, I can't possibly face a party sober.' Suzy looked over to Sam appealingly. 'I'm trying to decide whether or not to get a Border Terrier or a Lab, what do you reckon?' Suzy asked.

'Definitely a border,' Sam said.

'Yeah but a lab would be needier, think I'd like that,' Suzy argued.

The two then debated what dog would suit Suzy and decided in the end to get Red out and also make a fuss of Sooty. Suzy had demanded a second glass of wine to calm her nerves – Suzy never attended parties – so Sam poured them both a glass of wine and decided to leave the car.

Mary's kitchen was quite possibly the second, most cosiest place this Christmas time. The only lights on in the room were the fairy lights Mary had threaded through the shelves and dresser. They twinkled and shone, illuminating family photos and Mary and John's treasured nic-nacs, collected over a lifetime together. Sam drank her wine and looked across to her own home, Wisteria Cottage. The little Christmas tree on the porch was shining out in the darkness.

'Suzy, I never dreamt I could be as happy as I am living here and now you're moving here, it's just the icing on the cake.'

Suzy squeezed her hand; there was nothing more to be said.

They arrived at Liz's frozen to the core. Sam regretted not driving. She introduced Suzy to the few people she knew and was about to take her over to meet Dominic and Luke when a very excited Lucy burst in.

'Auntie Suzy, Domnic said you were here.'

The little girl seemed to fly through the air and into Suzy's arms. Suzy spun her round and kissed her, then blew fuffles on her neck, making Lucy squeal with delight.

Dominic came over and Sam introduced him to Suzy, then introduced his brother. In all the years Sam had known Suzy, not once had she seen her become so coy… but tonight was the exception. Suzy had always seemed to switch her emotions and attraction off completely but not tonight. Luke shook her hand and the look exchanged between the two of them was quite something. Sam tingled and noticed that Dominic had a hint of a smile, too.

Unfortunately, the perfect moment was soon to be crushed… Sheila chose that moment to walk over. Sheila couldn't stand to see the way Luke was looking at this woman. Several years ago, Luke had briefly dated Sheila but soon established that when it came to Sheila, beauty really only was skin deep. He'd found Sheila self-absorbed and negative about almost everyone, so he left her pretty quick. Sheila had been spoilt growing up and had been given everything she asked for; she wasn't accustomed to not getting her way and had become quite the poisonous woman scorned, badmouthing Luke and trying to destroy any other relationship he tried to have.

Martin, her husband, although handsome and successful was everything Luke wasn't and not a day went by without Sheila being bitterly reminded of this.

Sam felt obliged to introduce Suzy to Sheila. Sheila gave Suzy a strange look.

'I've met you before, haven't I?' she asked pointedly.

Suzy said she didn't think so, but Sheila was beginning to piece it all together.

'Ah, yes I do remember now,' Sheila said triumphantly. 'The last time I saw you, you were dressed in just your underwear and bracelets.'

Suzy tried to laugh it off. 'Doesn't sound like me, does it, Sam?'

Sam needed to rescue her friend as Sheila was really enjoying herself.

'I think Sheila is referring to the night I moved in, when we drank all that champagne. Do you remember you went out to dance in the rain? Right, how about you and I go and find Mum and Dad?' Sam tried moving away with Suzy. However, Sheila, like a dog with a bone, wouldn't let go. She blocked the kitchen door.

'Yes, I do remember. Well, it was most inappropriate, and my poor children were quite distressed.'

Sam could see that Suzy was getting nervous, because she did what she always did when she was nervous, she started scratching the scars on her arms. Unfortunately, the sleeve rolled up on Suzy's arm, revealing her scars for all the people gathered around to see. Sheila, eagle-eyed, honed in. Sam felt awful. Suzy had mentioned she had forgot to put her bangles on, which she always described as her second line of defence, but they had been halfway to Liz's and were cold, so Sam persuaded her not to go back to John and Mary's to get them.

'Oh my goodness, look at your arm! Urgh! Are they drug marks?'

'N-no, I don't do drugs,' Suzy said.

'Well, I've seen it all now. Now it makes sense, honestly, how disgusting.'

Dominic caught hold of Suzy's hand and moved Sheila aside.

'So, Suzy, how about we go and see where Santa's got to?'

Suzy was grateful. As she turned to Dominic, she had tears in her eyes.

Luke was glaring at Sheila. He had clearly grasped the death stare; it shook Sam to the core. She would never, ever wish to be on the receiving end of that.

'You just can't help yourself, can you?' he said, glaring at Sheila.

'Did you see her arms? Disgusting! She's a drug addict, isn't she?' Sheila said loudly to Sam. She had an appalled expression on her face.

'No, she is not a drug addict, and I think you've said enough,' Sam said. Tears were rolling down her face. She could not stand to see the woman she loved being so humiliated.

Liz, who had caught the end of it, walked up to Sheila and removed the glass from her hand.

'How dare you insult my guest in my home? Get your coat, Martin and your children and leave, Sheila. I also recommend you attend midnight mass this evening and pray that you can find some goodwill.'

Sheila tried appealing to Sue.

'You saw them, didn't you? I know you saw them, Sue.'

Sue, who had moved on from her once spiteful friend, always liked the last word, so she said, 'Guess who's just bought Primrose Cottage Sheila? Suzy!' Sue linked arms with Sam, winked and said, 'Sorry, Sam. I guess once a bitch, always a bitch.'

'Well, as long as you're our bitch we don't mind, do we, Sam?' Liz said gleefully, putting her arms around them both.

Luke followed a sobbing Sheila out to the car and helped her load the children. She was desperate to justify herself, but Luke just stared with indifference now. He then went to find Martin who, as usual, was flirting with someone else's wife. Martin was furious and told Luke where to get off, before Paul intervened and told him to get out and take his family with him. Sadly, the evening was ruined. Paul was absolutely furious with Sheila and John suggested that they get Lucy home. Lucy, fortunately, was blissfully unaware of the latest upset.

Chapter 27

Dominic and Luke walked back with them and then John suggested that the three men pop into The Fox and Hounds for a nightcap. Tom, on hearing his best mate had returned, came bursting into the Fox looking for him.

'I just got to Liz's 'n Sue told me what 'appened. She alright, is she? Sam's mate?' Luke was so pleased to see him, and they had a brief man hug.

'Yeah, she's gonna be ok,' Luke said. The four men enjoyed a pint in front of the fire. It was blissfully quiet, as most of the locals had been invited to Liz and Paul's.

Mary ran a lovely warm bubble bath for Suzy whilst Sam got Lucy ready for bed. By the time the men got back, Lucy was fast asleep and Suzy had relaxed and had her onesie on.

The fire was crackling and the events of the evening melted away. It was most welcoming. Dominic, Luke and John had a glass of port and some Stilton while the women poured themselves a liqueur. They didn't make it to midnight mass; it didn't seem to matter. They all seemed to need the comfort of Lavender Cottage this evening, with Sooty and the fire.

The fire had died down and everyone was sleepy when Dominic turned to his brother and said, 'Right Lukey boy, we'd best scoot, else Santa might forget to come like last year.'

Luke laughed. 'Oh man, that was grim, wasn't it? We forgot to get each other anything so we got up and had breakfast and then went back to bed, didn't we?'

Luke smiled at the memory and Sam noticed how much more relaxed he seemed compared to earlier. She was also aware that he and Suzy couldn't keep their eyes off one another.

'Sam, can I have a quick word?' Dominic asked as he walked out to the kitchen. She followed.

'Look at you.'

He gazed at Sam and then kissed her. The kiss grew more passionate by the second and they were both shocked by how intense it was. Sam felt brave in the knowledge that there was nothing they could do with the room full of people next door, so she flirted outrageously.

'I think your brother quite likes Suzy,' Sam whispered.

'Yeah, tell me about it. I must admit he is behaving out of character, most unlike Luke. Think she's pretty hot for him as well. I'm so sorry about Sheila. I think Suzy seems to have put it behind her, don't you?'

'To be honest, Dom, that's nothing compared to what she is used to, but thank you. You were amazing, so were Luke and Paul.'

'From what Luke told me, your two mates handled it pretty well.'

'I know, I love those two. Never, ever thought I would say that about Sue when I first met her. Right, do you fancy spending a few minutes with Red in the garden?'

When Sam and Suzy got into bed, they chatted like the old days. Suzy asked all about Dominic and Luke.

'Do you know, Sam, neither of them asked what the scars were. Didn't even mention them.'

'Think they're a couple of special men, those two. Besides, poor Luke seems to have enough of his own scars, albeit psychological, don't you think?'

There came no answer, Suzy was sleeping.

Christmas Day dawned and was the most magical one yet. Sam and Suzy got up early and cooked everyone a full English breakfast. They all sat round the tree in their dressing gowns exchanging gifts. Lucy disappeared under a mound of wrapping paper, the only sounds were her squeals of delight as she received all the presents she hoped for.

The two friends, dressed in new scarves and gloves, took Lucy and Sooty out for a long walk in the glorious frosty countryside around Willow Green, leaving John and Mary to cook the lunch. As ever, it was delicious and very traditional. By the time the Christmas pudding was cheered to the table, it was five thirty.

Lucy played contentedly with her new presents, entertaining Mary and Suzy, while John had a doze in his chair, so Sam decided to go and have a long soak in the bath. She thought she'd start reading the raunchy book that Suzy had given her for Christmas. By the time she came downstairs, Dominic and Luke had turned up and Mary was fussing over them, making tea and offering mince pies.

Luke was sat on the sofa next to Lucy and looked a lot more relaxed than he did yesterday. Sam noticed Suzy was acting coy again and most out of character.

Dominic had bought Lucy a beautiful music box which, when you wound it up, had ice skaters moving around on the ice. It also had twinkling lights around the lid and it played a delightful tune that kept Lucy entranced. She was so grateful.

He had on the black cashmere jumper that Sam had given him, and he looked delicious in it. Dominic handed Sam a small box tucked inside a midnight blue, velvet pouch. She was intrigued, and slowly opened the box. Inside was the most beautiful diamond bracelet. Sam was overwhelmed by the intimate gift Dom had given her and felt embarrassed that her gift to him was nothing like this.

Mary had wrapped the two men up a bottle of port each and some chocolates, which they gladly received. Then Lucy insisted they all played on the Wii. Watching Dominic and Luke play 'Just Dance' was hilarious, and Lucy did not stop laughing at their efforts.

By the end of the night, everyone was full to the brim and ready to sleep. Luke and Suzy said they would walk Sooty around the common to save John the task and while they were wrapping up warm and putting on Sooty's lead, Sam whispered to Dominic to come into the conservatory as there was something she needed to say.

'Dominic, I called Richard and my publishers yesterday to wish them a happy Christmas and I have decided to do the awards ceremony. I think Chris's request would be a good warm up, don't you? I should warn you, though, I am a nightmare to be around when I'm nervous.'

Sam couldn't stop grinning; she had finally made the decision. Dominic was genuinely surprised at the news. He pulled her into his arms.

'Oh man, this is something else. It's the best Christmas present you could give yourself, let alone me. You are going to be fine, you know, and you'll blow them away, I promise you. Luke's gonna still be around, too.' He held her for what seemed like forever, praising her for her brave decision. Eventually he pulled away slightly.

'So, what are you up to Boxing Day? Any rituals?' he asked.

'No, none. Mum and Dad are off to my aunt's for the day and Matt is collecting Lucy after lunch, so I guess Suzy and I will be eating too much chocolate and relaxing at home. What about you?'

'Not a lot, we usually play squash and go to The Fox for lunch.'

'Maybe you two can come for dinner?' she asked.

'Mm. Sam?' Dominic said softly.

'Yes?' Sam replied, looking up at him.

He stared at her for what felt like an eternity.

'You do know I'm falling in love with you, don't you?' He didn't wait for her to say anything, he just turned around and went to say goodnight to Mary and John.

Sam sorted Red out and then settled Lucy into bed and decided to turn in herself, but she couldn't sleep. Just thinking about what Dom had said made her tingle. Fortunately, Suzy was full of beans once she got back and provided a welcome distraction. Luke had invited her to The Manor for dinner tomorrow night. Sam was pleased for them both, but it also meant she could have Dom all to herself.

When Matt and Jasmine came to collect Lucy the following afternoon, they looked happy and united. Lucy was fit to burst as

Matt showed her a picture on his phone of all the gifts under the Christmas tree waiting for her at home in London. He asked Sam if he could have a quick private word while Lucy took Jasmine to play with Red. Fortunately, Suzy was soaking in the bath.

Matt stood silent for a couple of minutes with his hands in his pocket. He took a deep breath.

'Sam, I dealt you a marked card and I'm sorry. It's weird, I've only been to counselling twice, but it's really got to me and I'm sorry.'

Sam could tell Matt was being sincere.

'Wow. Twice already, that's brilliant. I thought it would take a while,' she said, nervous.

'Yeah, we managed to get someone urgent, which I guess it was. Sam, I don't know where to start.' He raked his fingers through his hair and paced.

'Make it up to me by being there for Jasmine and Lucy, okay?' she bargained.

'I can't forgive myself, Sam. It's honestly tearing me apart what I did to you.' Tears were welling up in his eyes and Sam knew that this time they weren't crocodile tears. She knew that she needed to let him talk.

'Matt, look, come and sit down. I'm just going to get Jasmine to distract Lucy with Red, okay?'

Sam closed the utility room door so that Lucy wouldn't hear them as she squealed her delight, playing with Red. Sam returned with a small glass of mulled wine for them both and sat beside him. Taking comfort from the warmed wine, Matt took a deep breath.

'Do you hate me?' he asked.

'Matt, how could I hate the man who gave me Lucy? I loved you so much and a part of me always will.'

'But I treated you so bad, Sam.'

'Yes. Yes, you did. I won't deny what you did to me, and I guess it's only right that you should know that I am still struggling to come to terms with it all. However, knowing you are going to therapy and knowing that you are treating Jasmine and Lucy better is a good start for my own recovery.'

'Can you ever forgive me, Sam?'

'I already have. Now come on, it's Christmas. Cheers.' She gently touched his glass with her own.

'B-but Jazz said it was abuse, coservice control or something!' He kept raking his fingers through his hair. Sam actually felt sorry for him.

'Coercive control, yes it was. Look, Matt, now really isn't the time to talk about this. Suzy's in the bath and Lucy wants to get to your house and open her presents.'

'But I can't deal with it. The book Jazz gave me is hideous, makes me look like a monster, and the counsellor doesn't help, keeps agreeing with me every time I tell her how bad I've been.'

Sam smiled sweetly.

'Matt, the councillor is doing her job. She is helping you take responsibility for your actions, whilst trying to help you understand them. Don't underestimate the power in therapy, it saved Suzy's life.'

'Would you be willing to come with me, to talk it through?' he asked.

'Look, let's see what your councillor says, okay? But this is your therapy, Matt. One thing I do need you to know is that I really appreciate the apology. I believe you have it in you to change, I really do. And I hope you can take time out from the guilt trip and enjoy your time with Lucy and Jasmine. This will be a very long process, and you are brave and strong to go through it, but there isn't any quick fix with therapy, Matt. You will need to buckle in for a long ride, you just need to trust yourself and your councillor.' Sam got up and he did too. He pulled her into his arms.

When Jasmine and Lucy came into the lounge, they were shocked to see Sam and Matt in an embrace. Jasmine hugged Sam, before turning to wrap her arms around Matt. Matt called Lucy over and the four of them had an unusual 'family' moment, where they all held one another until Lucy broke away and told them to hurry up.

With them all gone, the house felt quiet for a second, then familiar sounds gently soothed Sam's soul. Little Red was scratching around in the kitchen after her tea. Suzy was singing upstairs, getting herself ready for dinner with Luke, and Sam went over what had just happened between herself and Matt. She knew he could do it and knew that his councillor was clearly working wonders with him already.

Sam turned the main lights off, leaving the fairy lights on, poured a couple of glasses of wine and carried one up to her friend.

Suzy looked so beautiful and happy. Sam told her about the conversation with Matt.

'Wow, can't believe I missed that. Haven't watched Jackanory for years, I love a good story.'

Sam smiled but gently said, 'No, it wasn't a story Suzy. It was genuine.'

'Yeah right, and I'm the tooth fairy,' Suzy joked.

'Well, I believe he has it in him to change. I know that therapy will help.'

'Yeah, but how long will it last? I mean, this is Matt we're talking about,' Suzy said, whilst trying to apply her mascara and take a sip of wine.

'Good thing is that Jasmine won't stand for it, unlike me.' Sam hung her head. She hated the way she had put up with Matt for so long. She squeezed Suzy's shoulder and then went downstairs.

She lit the candles on the mantelpiece. They flickered into life, casting their friendly glow around the room. The lounge looked spectacular and the orangery reflected the lights from the tree like a star-spangled sky.

Wisteria Cottage really had become Sam's very own fairyland. She had even put a tree and lights outside the beach hut on the little veranda. Dominic was coming round later, they were going to light the fire pit, wrap up warm and sit outside the beach hut, drinking champagne and eating canapés and nibbles.

Sam thought back now to her time in London and how lonely she had felt there. All those years she'd been too anxious to leave the house. Yet in just a few short months, she had finally felt as though she had come home, at last. She sat on the sofa and stared into the fire. She sipped her wine and contemplated the future, a future that included Matt, Jasmine and their new baby, who would hopefully be born sometime in July. Lucy would have a baby step brother or step sister by the summer, who would have thought it? She shook her head in disbelief, but something told Sam that Lucy would embrace her role as big sister, and that Matt would give Jasmine all the support she needed, something he hadn't been able to muster up for Sam.

She thought of all her wonderful new friends being rather like the pick 'n' mix at the cinema, with all their many flavours and colours. What a selection of remarkable women!

She thought of Liz, her lovely new friend, and of Suzy, her good old faithful best friend, whom Sam knew would fit perfectly into life at Willow Green.

She smiled in anticipation. She and Dominic were meeting Suzy and Luke for lunch tomorrow and she couldn't wait to hear how tonight would go. Sam knew it was early days for Luke and Suzy. Luke was due to go overseas again shortly. However, she knew that the two of them shared a link. Somehow, she knew that Luke would not care about Suzy's scars. In fact, she was certain that it would make him love her friend all the more.

She gazed across at her parents' cottage with their fairy lights twinkling across the porch, which Lucy had insisted Grandpa put up. Last but not least, she thought of Dominic. Sam found herself falling deeper and deeper in love with him every day. She looked back to her most prized Christmas present from Dominic. At some point yesterday, he had borrowed her keys and come into the house and hung her most precious gift. The painting they had seen at St Katharine's Dock. The beautiful woman seemed to be staring at Sam now, as if to invite her over for further inspection, something Sam had been doing on and off all day.

Chapter 28

Sam had set the perfect scene for her evening with Dominic. She had put all the lights on leading up to and around the beach hut. The heater was on, and when she had checked it half an hour ago, it was warm and cosy.

The fire pit was stocked up and ready to go. It had been Dominic's request that they spend the evening at the beach hut. That was another thing she loved about him, his sense of adventure. Matt would never sit outside in the middle of winter, but Dominic had convinced her that they would be warm enough and if not, they had agreed to sit inside the hut.

Suzy came down looking beautiful and yet vulnerable. She topped up her glass and stared up the garden.

'Oh Sam, have you ever seen anything as magical as that,' she said, nodding to the garden.

'I know, I can't wait. You're nervous, aren't you?' Sam said, getting up.

'How can you tell?' Suzy asked, smiling.

'You keep scratching your arms.'

'To be honest, I'm thinking of crying off sick.' Suzy turned and revealed the fear written all over her face.

'I think you'll be in safe hands, Suzy. My angel, don't let that idiot spoil this for you. It was years ago, and with a silly little boy disguised as a man. Luke would never do that.'

'But we don't know him really, do we?'

'No, but I know his brother, and if Dom says Luke's a good guy then I believe him. Look, he's due in half an hour, why don't we have a camomile tea and I will give your shoulders a massage?' Sam suggested.

By the time Luke arrived, Suzy was a lot calmer. Sam gave Suzy the spare key and hugged her.

Dominic came with two bottles of champagne. He pulled Sam into his arms and kissed her.

'Oh Dom, poor Suzy was terrified, did you see her?'

'Yeah, never seen Luke so nervous either. He made her his signature dish, so she should be impressed.'

'What's his signature dish?'

'Coq au vin. Mum taught him years ago.'

Squeals were coming from the utility room. Dominic laughed and headed there.

'I'm sorry little Red, am I neglecting you?' He lifted the little puppy out, who was frantically trying to lick him. Sam smiled, she loved the way that Dominic was so at home here. He carried Red outside for the toilet and then back into the lounge and the two of them sat in front of the fire, snuggling the wriggling creature. It didn't take much to wear her out, so they put her back in her crate.

'Right, let's do this Sam.' Dominic put his jacket back on. Sam was taking no chances and put on several layers and her hat and gloves.

'Do you need me to carry anything?' he asked.

'Just the champagne, Suzy helped me set it up earlier.'

They wandered along the fairy lit path between the fruit trees. By the time they reached the beach hut, Sam was already wondering if they had made a mistake, it was so freezing, but as soon as she saw it all she changed her mind. The trees were ablaze with fairy lights. The reflection on the water was mesmerising. The beach hut was so warm, and Dominic praised the effort they had gone to. She had filled the little fridge with olives, cherry tomatoes and avocados. The cheese board seemed to hold every type of cheese and pickle.

'Oh man, this is something else Sam, thanks for this.'

'Well, it was your idea.'

'Yeah but this is just perfect. Look, sit in here whilst I light the fire pit. It won't take long to get going. Did you want me to carry up the free-standing heater from the patio, too?'

'Let's see how we get on, shall we?'

Dominic left her and lit the fire. The little pink bistro set looked so welcoming and by the time she joined him, the whole scene was like something out of the movies. Dominic poured the champagne and they sat in silence for some time, just enjoying their food and drink and listening to the little river and all the wildlife going about their business. When Dominic noticed Sam shivering, he collected one of the blankets warming in the beach hut.

'I need to use the loo, so I'm gonna carry the other heater up.'

'Yes, I must say, that is the only negative thing I can think of to say about my haven, there's no toilet,' Sam said, sipping her champagne.

'It wouldn't take much, you know, we could put a saniflo toilet next to the hut, paint it the same colour and run some electric in it. I put something similar in another garden.'

'Oh Dom, can we do that? It would save me so much time when I'm working.'

'Yep, I'll get a couple of choices for you.'

He wandered back to the house and Sam sat staring into the distance. Tears pooled and then tumbled from her eyes. Never in her life had she felt as safe and as happy as she did right now. By the time the patio burner was lit too, Sam was so warm and snug that she could lose the gloves and blanket. They played cards until the early hours. They carried everything back to the house and Dominic went back to make sure all was safe and locked up.

Sam noticed Suzy's boots by the door and also a couple of little deposits left by Red. Suzy forgot to lock the crate, every time. Fortunately, Red was curled up, clearly exhausted and fast asleep, and judging by the teeth marks on the island and the chewed-up box strewn all over the kitchen floor, it was clear the little pup had had quite an evening.

Dominic kissed her endlessly before he left, and yet again Sam was gripped by the fear of losing all of this. She took a Horlicks up to bed with her but was so exhausted that she hardly touched it.

New Year's Eve at The Fox and Hounds was magical. Chris and Danny, his wife, and their staff had turned the little pub into a 1970's disco. The tribute band had already sound checked and set up and were all a little in awe of Sam, which she found a bit embarrassing, but sweet all the same.

Delicious smells were wafting from the kitchen doors. Tickets had all been sold out and Sam was relieved that she would know some friendly faces. The empty little pub seemed to be ablaze in colour and warmth in its anticipation of all its guests.

John and Mary were designated babysitters and it was arranged that after Sam's performance they would take Faye and Lucy back to their house for a sleepover, so the little girls were fit to burst with excitement. Marcus was staying at Sue's with Daniel and Sue's sister.

Sam placed her guitar on its stand and walked home across the common. Her nerves were getting the better of her and she needed to get out. Red wagged her tail half-heartedly. The poor little dog was exhausted, she'd had a long afternoon playing with Faye and Lucy.

Sam went to the fridge and got out a bottle of champagne. She wanted to mark the occasion by herself… she smiled. *Sam Tate, singer songwriter, finally putting on a performance again.* Funny, she reflected, she really was more nervous about tonight's gig than she was about the award show.

She gazed at the painting again. The beautiful woman stared back as though silently urging Sam to believe she could do it. Again, she got lost for several minutes gazing at her beautiful new companion hanging on the wall. It was as though they were both trying to figure one another out. Her phone pinged. It was a text from Liz:

'Hey maestro, we are all here, where are you? Btw, do you want Sue and I to be your backing singers?'

Sam smiled and went back to the painting; she would never tire of gazing at it. Her phone rang. It was Dominic.

'Hey,' she said, smiling.

'Hey you, how are you holding up?'

'I'm terrified, Dom.'

'Shall I come over?'

'No, I need to be by myself for a few minutes, that okay?' she asked, worried she had offended him.

'Course it's okay. Sam, you will be wonderful, I promise. Oh, hang on a minute, Sam. What's that sweetheart? Oh, hold on, Lucy needs to speak to you.'

'Mummy! Come on, hurry up, else you won't get in, it's so busy. Are you wearing your lucky necklace?' Lucy asked.

Sam touched the homemade, multicoloured necklace around her neck. Lucy had made it especially for her for Christmas with enormous beads and dried pasta.

'I'm wearing it, darling,' she said, smiling.

'Oh good, I told Domnic that it will keep you safe. He is worried about you but tomorrow Domnic said you and me and him and Red are going to have lunch at his house to celebrate, with Auntie Suzy and his bruvver, and Faye is coming too.'

'I know darling, I think he has invited quite a lot of people. Now sweetheart, Mummy loves you with all my heart and I will be over in about half an hour, okay?'

'Okay Mummy, I love you, and Domnic needs to say something.'

'Hey Sam, man, she's so sweet. You should see her strutting around, telling everyone that her mama's going to sing.'

'Ah, thanks Dom. Could you ask Suzy to come over please?'

'Course, see you in a bit.'

Suzy arrived, looking absolutely stunning as always. Sam handed her a glass of champagne. The two of them stood gazing out across at the pub. Suzy put her arm around Sam's shoulders and pecked her on the cheek.

'You're going to be amazing, Sam. I know you're scared.'

'Oh Suzy, do you remember that first gig I ever did? No-one showed up except you.'

'Well, it's rammed over there tonight. Oh wow, Sue and Liz are hilarious, what a double act. Oh no, and guess who turned up like five minutes ago.'

'No idea.'

'Matt and Jasmine!'

'What?! Lucy must have told them. Oh Suzy, why did I agree to do this?'

'Because you need to do this. It's in your soul Sam, let it out.'

The two women walked across to the pub. Sam squeezed Suzy's hand and refused to let it go, even once they were inside. Lucy rushed over and threw her arms around her mummy, then peeled herself away, as someone had picked up Sam's guitar and was looking at it.

'That is my mummy's guitar, please be careful,' the little girl said earnestly. The young man smiled at her.

'Oh sorry, I just always wanted one of these,' he said, embarrassed by being told off by this dear little girl with her hands on her hips and a very serious expression.

'They are very expensive, aren't they, Mummy?' Sam smiled apologetically at the young man, who smiled back.

Sam took her seat to check everything was set up and for a moment thought she was going to back out. She gazed around the room at so many faces, all of them urging her on, even Matt, who was clearly making an effort with Sam's parents. She was touched that Liz, Sue and all their gang had 'Sam Tate' t-shirts on. They had all dragged their husbands and partners along, who had also been forced to wear the t-shirts. Sam realised that Liz must have got them all made somewhere.

Dominic took her breath away as usual. She knew he was nervous for her and tonight she realised that she had fallen helplessly in love with him.

He brought her over a glass of wine and a bottle of water, he checked Lucy was distracted and then gently kissed her lips before walking back to his brother, who saluted her with his glass. She noticed that Suzy and Luke were still so shy together. They both insisted on remaining "just friends", but no-one could deny the attraction simmering between them.

Everyone started staring at her expectantly. Sam knew she could not let these people down and picked up her guitar to do a quick line check before a last-minute dash to the loo. Just at the moment, the door opened and in walked Richard, with the five guys from Tremor and Abigail. Richard and Ace came straight up and kissed Sam, wishing her luck. Matt came over and offered to deal with the little PA system and Sam was relieved, knowing that in his capable hands her songs would sound perfect.

After popping to the toilet, she took a huge breath, took a sip of her wine and finally her nerves evaporated, instead pouring all their power into her voice and playing which was so, so beautiful. 'Leave me Gently' was hard to get through, as Liz had decided to join in in a full pelt, tuneless volume. Sam missed several lines due to being in hysterics. Fortunately, Paul eventually persuaded his wife to pipe down so that Sam could finish the song.

'Cut Raw' was even harder to sing. Sam watched nervously as Suzy excused herself immediately to Dom and Luke and went to the toilet. She noticed that she didn't return until the song had finished.

She chose to close with a song she had written recently about Matt. The song held so much pain. However, Sam needed to sing this new song more than any other. An exorcism, closure to their relationship...

MASTER OF DISGUISE

Fooled once again by the master of disguise
Truth spoken contradicts the lies in your eyes
Do you get a kick watching me crying out in pain?
Does it get you off knowing you fooled me again?

Who are you now?
Which one are you my love?
Who's coming home tonight?
Who are you now my love?
Who are you now?
Who are you now?

She continued singing the song, weaving in and out of the chords. Ace stood with his mouth open. He had never heard such a heart-breaking vocal performance and his long-standing crush on Sam was reignited with such intensity that he knew he needed to get his head together to spare Abigail's feelings.

Matt hung his head, knowing what this song was about. Suzy knew this one was equally as hard as 'Cut Raw', but for different reasons. Suzy looked down now and quickly pulled at her sleeves, which had started creeping up. Luke noticed, took her hand and squeezed it for a second before letting it go again. The scars were still on show but for the first time ever, she left her sleeves where they were, her scars exposed.

Everyone in the pub whistled, cheered, clapped for more. Sam was overwhelmed by how much she had enjoyed herself. After she had finished, Richard came over and hugged her. Her friends and family left them alone, knowing that this was a huge moment for them both. Richard's constant patience and support, combined with his and Sam's hard work, meant her career as a performer was finally finding its wings.

Sam packed her guitar up and Dominic bought her over a drink. Everyone rallied around her, complimenting her, and she was astounded by their generosity. She needed to see Lucy, who was bursting with pride.

'Mummy, Daddy cried, and so did Auntie Suzy!'

Matt smiled. 'It was hayfever, Sam, I'm not used to the country air,' he lied, smiling.

Sam put her arms around him, before reaching down and lifting Lucy into her arms. For a moment Lucy was embraced by her mummy and daddy and Sam reflected how special this moment was for the three of them. Matt needed her forgiveness in order to move on with his new life.

'I love you to the moon and back, my little poppet. Shall you, Dom and I go see little Red?' Sam asked, kissing the little girl's forehead.

'Can Faye come, Mummy?'

'Of course.'

Dominic held her hand as they walked across the common. Faye and Lucy were singing at the top of their voices. Sam was touched that Faye had already learnt some of the words to her songs. Dominic had hardly said a word, and it wasn't until they closed the door and the little girls let Red out, closing the utility room door, that he spoke.

His voice got caught in his throat and Sam was momentarily concerned by the sadness she saw in his eyes.

'Is everything okay, Dominic?' she asked.

'Sam, man I don't know what to say. Your voice, those songs, I, I… I don't know what to say.'

'Then don't. Just kiss me, but quick before the girls come back in.'

Fortunately, the girls took a long time, seeing as Red was refusing to be caught, so Sam and Dominic had a beautiful tender moment together whilst listening to the girls screaming and squealing at their failed attempts at catching the naughty little puppy.

As the four of them made their way back to the pub, Lucy asked Faye if she had a new year's resolution. Faye said that she would eat less chocolate and clean her teeth more, but it was when Faye reciprocated the question that made Sam and Dominic stop abruptly:

'Are you gonna make one Lucy?' Faye asked.

'Yes, I am wishing that Domnic marries my mummy so I can have a baby sister.'

'But what if it's a boy?' Faye asked concerned.

'Then he can live with my daddy and Jasmine.'

Sam and Dominic roared with laughter and were delighted to have Lucy's seal of approval.

Sam thought back to the Christmas cards again and momentarily pictured being married to Dominic, with a baby brother or sister for Lucy, and the four of them walking across the common together with little Red. She stopped for a second again. Dominic asked if she was okay. She looked back to Wisteria Cottage, before gazing across at her parents' house, then back across to Primrose Cottage, where Suzy would soon be living. She smiled up at him.

'Dom, you do know I have fallen in love with you, don't you?'

END

Acknowledgements

I would like to thank The Romantic Novelist's Association, particularly Katie Ffords, Melanie Hilton, Immi Howsen, Liz Harris & Anita Burgh. Their encouragement and support has been a blessing. Thanks to Woman's Aid for making me a 'Campaign Champion'. To Mandy Thomas & Luke & Ryan Hart for their incredible bravery. Martin McCorry (Senior) & Jane Pickering-Lings for their support. Judy Stoppe, the wonderful paramedic who came to my rescue, whilst holidaying at Centre Parcs. Thanks to Laura Bill, Kady Braine & Denise Parsons for their help in promoting 'Beach Hut'. Thanks to my friends and family who have encouraged me to follow my heart and to keep writing. Mum, Dad, Leila, Fabian, Alice, Joanne, Oli, Stephen, Dawn, Pete, Fran, Alan, Rev Will, Barbara, Liz, Vince, Mel, Gary, Ali, Lynne, Paul, Ruby, Jenny, Kate, Nicola, Nyk, Jane, Carley, Finn, Jackie, Steve, Tracey, Mark, Hannah B, Lorna S, Emma C, Dolly, Jo V, Julia and to all mine and Hannah's lovely friends, old and new who mean so much to us both.

With Special Thanks To:
Sarah Grace & Malcolm Down for publishing Beach Hut. My talented brother Barry, for designing the cover. Catherine Jones, for her inspiration and guidance. Carly Robson & all the staff at Sopwell House, for providing me with a wonderful safe space to

work. Thank you to Lib Gorton & Ruth Berkowitz for finding my voice. Liz, Sara & Ruth SAHWR for showing me a different path to take and their continual support whilst I travel along it. Thank you Nitin, Karen, Dean McLoughlin, Claire, Andrew, Katy, Sam & Sara West for accepting me for who I am.

Last But No Means Least, My Soulmates:
Rudy, Murphy, Travis, Nibbles & Scarlet O'Hara